SOLAR
BONES

Also by Mike McCormack

Notes from a Coma
Forensic Songs

SOLAR BONES

Mike McCormack

First published in 2016 by Tramp Press
An extract of an earlier form of this novel appeared
in *Shine On: Irish Writers for Shine*, edited by Pat Boran.
Published by Dedalus Press, 2011.

Published in the Unired States of America in 2017 by
Soho Press, Inc.
853 Broadway
New York, NY 10003

Library of Congress Cataloging in Publication Data
McCormack, Mike, 1965–
Solar bones / Mike McCormack.

ISBN 978-1-61695-853-4
eISBN 978-1-61695-854-1

I. Title.
PR6063.C363 S65 2017 823'.914–dc23 2017007611

Interior design by Marsha Swan.

Printed in the United States of America

10 9 8 7 6 5 4 3 2 1

for Maeve

the bell
  the bell as
  hearing the bell as
      hearing the bell as standing here
      the bell being heard standing here
      hearing it ring out through the grey light of this
      morning, noon or night
      god knows
      this grey day standing here and
      listening to this bell in the middle of the day, the middle of
the day bell, the Angelus bell in the middle of the day, ringing out
through the grey light to
      here
      standing in the kitchen
      hearing this bell

snag my heart and

draw the whole world into

being here

pale and breathless after coming a long way to stand in this kitchen

confused

no doubt about that

but hearing the bell from the village church a mile away as the crow flies, across the street from the garda station, beneath the giant sycamore trees which tower over it and in which a colony of rooks have made their nests, so many and so noisy that sometimes in spring when they are nesting their clamour fills the church and

exhausted now, so quickly

that sprint to the church and the bell

yes, they are the real thing

the real bells

not a transmission or a broadcast because

there's no mistaking the fuller depth and resonance of the sound carried towards me across the length and breadth of this day and which, even at this distance reverberates in my chest

a systolic thump from the other side of this parish, which lies on the edge of this known world with Sheeffry and Mweelrea to the south and the open expanse of Clew Bay to the north

the Angelus bell

ringing out over its villages and townlands, over the fields and hills and bogs in between, six chimes of three across a minute and a half, a summons struck on the lip of the void which gathers this parish together through all its primary and secondary roads with

all its schools and football pitches

all its bridges and graveyards

all its shops and pubs

the builder's yard and health clinic

the community centre

the water treatment plant and

the handball alley

the made world with

all the focal points around which a parish like this gathers itself
as surely as
the world itself did at the beginning of time, through
mountains, rivers and lakes
when it gathered in these parts around the Bunowen river which
rises in the Lachta hills and flows north towards the sea, carving out
that floodplain to which all roads, primary and secondary, following
the contours of the landscape, make their way and in the middle of
which stands
the village of Louisburgh
from which the Angelus bell is ringing, drawing up the world again
mountains, rivers and lakes
acres, roods and perches
animal, mineral, vegetable
covenant, cross and crown
the given world with
all its history to brace myself while
standing here in the kitchen
of this house
I've lived in for nearly twenty-five years and raised a family, this
house outside the village of Louisburgh in the county of Mayo on
the west coast of Ireland, the village in which I can trace my seed and
breed back to a time when it was nothing more than a ramshackle
river crossing of a few smoky homesteads clustered around a forge
and a log bridge, a sod-and-stone hamlet not yet gathered to a proper
plan nor licensed to hold a fair, my line traceable to the gloomy
prehistory in which a tenacious clan of farmers and fishermen kept
their grip on a small patch of land
through hail and gale
hell and high water
men with bellies and short tempers, half of whom went to their
graves with pains in their chests before they were sixty, good singers
many of them, all
adding to the home place down the generations till it swelled to
twenty acres, grazing and tillage, with access to open commonage on
Carramore hill which overlooks the bay and

this pain, this fucking pain tells me that
to the best of my knowledge
knowledge being the best of me, that
that
there is something strange about all this, some twitchy
energy in the ether which has affected me from the moment
those bells began to toll, something flitting through me, a giddiness drawing me
through the house
door by door
room by room
up and down the hall
like a mad thing
bedrooms, bathroom, sitting room and
back again to the kitchen where
Christ
such a frantic burst
Christ
not so much a frantic burst as a rolling crease in the light, flowing from room to room only to find
this house is empty
not a soul anywhere
because this is a weekday and my family are gone
all gone
the kids all away now and of course Mairead is at work and
won't be back till after four so the house is mine till then, something
that should gladden me as normally I would only be too happy to
potter around on my own here, doing nothing, listening to the radio
or reading the paper, but now the idea makes me uneasy, with four
hours stretching ahead of me till she returns,
alone here for four hours
four hours till she returns so
there must be some way of filling the span of time that now
spreads out ahead of me, something to cut through this gnawing
unease because
the paper

yes

that's what I'll do

the daily paper

get the keys of the car and drive into the village to get the paper, park on the square in front of the chemist and then stand on the street and

this is what I will do

stand there for as long as it takes for someone to come along and speak to me, someone to say

hello

hello

or until someone salutes me in one way or another, waves to me or calls my name, because even though this street is a street like any other it is different in one crucial aspect – this particular street is mine, mine in the sense of having walked it thousands of times

man and boy

winter and summer

hail, rain and shine so that

all its doors and shop-fronts are familiar to me, every pole and kerbstone along its length recognisable to me

this street a given

this street is something to rely on

fount and ground

one of those places where someone will pass who can say of me

yes, I know this man

or more specifically

yes, I know this man and I know his sister Eithne and I knew his mother and father before him and all belonging to him

or more intimately

of course I know him – Marcus Conway – he lives across the fields from me, I can see his house from the back door

or more adamantly

why wouldn't I know him, Marcus Conway the engineer, I went to school with him and played football with him – we wore the black and gold together

or more impatiently

I should know him, his son and daughter went to school with my own – we were on the school council together

or more irritably

of course I know him – I lent him a chainsaw to cut back that hawthorn hedge at the end of his road and

so on and so on

to infinity

amen

the basic creed in all its moods and declensions, the articles of faith which verify me and upon which I have built a life in this parish with all its work and rituals for the best part of five decades and

this short history of the world to brace myself with

standing here in this kitchen, in this grey light and wondering

why this sudden need to rehearse these self-evident truths should press so heavily upon me today, why this feeling that there are

thresholds to cross

things to be settled

checks to be run

as if I had stepped into a narrow circumstance bordered around by oblivion while

looking for my keys now

frisking my pockets and glancing around, only to see that

Mairead has beaten me to the job, she has been out early and bought the papers – not one but two of them, local and national, both lying in the middle of the table neatly folded into each other, the light glossing unbroken across their surface, making it clear she has not read them herself that I might have the small pleasure of opening up a fresh newspaper, hearing it rattle and creak as it discloses itself, one of those experiences which properly begin the day or the afternoon as is the case now, turning it over and leafing through it

starting at the back, the sports pages, to read the headline

Hard Lessons in Latest Defeat

as if this were the time and the place for a sermon

which prompts me to close it again quickly, not wanting any homily at this hour of the day with the paper showing the date as

November 2nd, the month of the Holy Souls already upon us, the year nearly gone so

what happened to October

come and gone in a flash, the clocks gone back for winter time only last week and

the front-page stories telling that the world is going about its relentless business of rising up in splendour and falling down in ruins with wars still ongoing in foreign parts – Afghanistan and Iraq among others – as peace settlements are being attempted elsewhere – Israel and Palestine – while closer to home, the drama is in a lower key but real nonetheless – bed shortages in hospitals and public sector wage agreements under pressure – all good human stories no matter how they will pan out, you can feel that, the flesh and blood element twitching in them, while at the same time

in the over-realm of international finance other, more abstract indices are rising and falling to their own havoc – share prices, interest rates, profit margins, solvency ratios – money upholding the necessary imbalances so that everything continues to move ever forward while on one of the inside pages there is

one year on

a long article with an illustrative graph and quotes outlining the causes and consequences of our recent economic collapse, a brief résumé of events that culminated on the night of September 29th, feast of the archangel Michael – the night the whole banking system almost collapsed and the country came within a hair's breadth of waking the following morning to empty bank accounts and

for clarity's sake

this article is illustrated by a sidebar which gives some indication of just how outsized the nation's financial folly was in the years leading up to the collapse, debt piling up till it ran to tens of billions, incredible figures for a small island economy, awe-inspiring magnitudes which shifted forever the horizons of what we thought ourselves liable for and which now, stacked on top of each other like this – all those zeroes, glossy and hard, so given to viral increase – appear like

the indices and magnitudes of a new cosmology, the forces and velocities of some barren, inverse world – a negative realm that, over time, will suck the life out of us, that collapse which happened without offering any forewarning of itself, none that any of our prophets picked up on anyway as they were

all apparently struck dumb and blind, robbed of all foresight when surely this was the kind of catastrophe prophets should have an eye for or some foreknowledge of but didn't since it is now evident in hindsight that our seers' gifts were of a lesser order, their warnings lowered to a tremulous bleating, the voices of men hedging their bets and without the proper pitch of hysterical accusation as they settled instead for fault-finding and analysis, that cautionary note which in the end proved wholly inadequate to the coming disaster because pointing out flaws was never going to be enough and figures and projections, no matter how dire, were never likely to map out the real contours of the calamity or prove to be an adequate spell against it when, without that shrill tone of indictment, theirs was never a song to hold our attention and no point whatsoever meeting catastrophe with reason when what was needed was

our prophets deranged

and coming towards us wild-eyed and smeared with shit, ringing a bell, seer and sinner at once while speaking some language from the edge of reason whose message would translate into plain words as

we're fucked

well and truly fucked because

with the signs stacking up like this there will only be one outcome and

here's more of it

the eyes on that woman

a local story featuring in both the national and local newspaper, the story of

an environmental campaigner who has begun a hunger strike against the energy consortium planning to run a pressurised gas pipeline through her particular part of North Mayo and which has already commenced work on the seabed of Broadhaven Bay, the articles in both papers illustrated with the same picture of a haggard-looking woman in her late fifties wrapped in a blanket and staring bug-eyed from the back of a car as her hunger strike now enters its second week, by which time she has reportedly lost ten pounds from a body that weighed less than seven stone before she began her fast so that, day by day, she is approaching that dangerous weight threshold, the critical loss of body mass at which point her health could be irreparably damaged as she begins to fade from the world entirely, the sight leaving her eyes first, followed by muscle mass and bone density, so that now – both articles make this clear – there is a special urgency to all those pleas and petitions and representations which have been made to the relevant public and private bodies on her behalf but which as yet – eight days into her fast – have elicited no official response from either the government or the energy consortium and while

this woman weakens day by day

she vows to continue her strike till the largest pipe-laying ship in the world, registered in Switzerland, the *Solitare* – all three hundred metres of it, with its ninety-six thousand tons and four hundred crew – leaves Broadhaven bay and Irish territorial waters beyond so that

two images coming together

this small woman against this ship

recalls that photograph of the lone protester standing in front of the column of tanks in Tiananmen Square, way back in 1989, similar in that it's equally unlikely the *Solitare* will run aground on the slight body of this woman who, wrapped in a blanket, peers out from the back of the car, another drama that has the weighted, irrefutable sense of the real about it, that dangerous confluence of the private and political converging on this frail woman's body to make it the arena of the dispute and, not for the first time, stories like this always strike me as

peculiar to Mayo

Mayo God help us

Mayo abú

a county with a unique history of people starving and mortifying themselves for higher causes and principles, a political reflex that has twitched steadily down the years and seems rooted in some aggravated sense of sinfulness because, like no other county it is blistered with shrines and grottoes and prayer houses and hermitages just as it is crossed with pilgrim paths and penitential ways, the whole county such a bordered realm of penance and atonement that no one should be surprised that self-starvation becomes a political weapon when, to the best of my knowledge, no other county in the Republic has called up three of its sons to starve to death for flag and country so late in the twentieth century

McNeela, Gaughan, Stagg

Arbour Hill, Parkhurst, Wakefield

valiant souls who took their inspiration from our martyred land and saw a world beyond themselves as did

my own favourite

a young hermit who, towards the end of the last millennium, took up residence in a ruined bothán on the side of a hill not ten miles from here, a young woman who, by way of some ancient rite, was professed a hermit by the Vatican with licence to beg and preach among these rainy hills, claiming that God had called her to go deeper into the desert so that she could be more aware of his presence in greater silence and solitude but who, after a few years living the full sacramental life on the mountains of West Mayo with nothing to distract the eye or hand save damp sheep and stone walls, came forth with her message to the world, telling us that

hell is real and it's not empty

simple and blunt as that

hell is real and it's not empty

she said, the sum total of everything she had gleaned from all her years of prayer and penance, her savage epistle with no mention in it anywhere of the redeemer having passed this way on his mission of mercy or forgiveness and

this is how you get carried away

sitting here in this kitchen

carried away on an old theme, swept up on a rush of words and associations strewn out across the length and breadth of this county, a hail of images surging through me while at the bottom of the page another story of how

a large, abandoned industrial facility in the north of the county is being assessed as a possible site for an asbestos conversion plant which will form part of a massive toxic dump to process industrial and medical waste from the rest of the province in a state-of-the-art incineration process which, if economic studies and environmental assessments prove favourable, could come online in a few years' time with the promise of jobs and subsidiary investment across the county and

something out of the past

a psychic link which dates back to my childhood when

my father worked on its construction

he fucking did

worked on it at a time when, with a similar promise of prosperity, it was spoken of as if it were a cathedral or a temple that was being built on that raised site above the small town of Killala, such a beacon of industrial progress that for the two years of its construction I would watch my father pack his bags every Sunday evening for the week ahead and when seven o'clock came he would kiss my mother and sister goodbye and walk up to the top of the road where he would be picked up by a minibus full of other men from around the parish, tradesmen and labourers, men who would spend a full two years concreting and block-laying and steel-fixing this massive facility into existence which, when fully operational, would employ three hundred and fifty men and women in the manufacture of acrylic yarn and fibre, an end purpose which initially disappointed me as it seemed such a puny thing considering all the hope and effort invested in it, unworthy in every way, until I learned that the manufacturing process would utilise a highly toxic compound called acrylonitrile, a chemical that would have to be transported overland in the middle of the night under security escort, shipped in double-hulled, crash-proof containers, a vivid circumstance suffused with enough danger to recast the whole project in a more credible apocalyptic glow so that it now appeared, to my refired imagination, a pioneering enterprise which called for fearless, heroic men like my father whom

I would accompany every Sunday evening to the top of the road to watch him head off in that minibus and every time feel his leaving so keenly it was as if a part of myself was going off to work on that distant project so that in this way, my own father working on this facility, it was readily established in my young mind that I too was heroic and courageous and possibly cut out for some notable destiny, all this just twenty years before the facility would cease production entirely, the last of the dirty industries in this part of the world, the whole enterprise succumbing to a convergence of adverse factors – oil rising through fifty dollars a barrel and the world's turn to natural fabrics principal among them – till the day came when it stood empty and dilapidated on a shallow plateau above the town of Killala – the last shipment of yarn gone through the gates, the workers paid off and the lights turned out – a monumental example of industrial gothic corroding in the winds which blew in from the Atlantic, an empty facility fully serviced with state-of-the-art utilities – road, rail, water and electricity – but which no one would touch because the whole thing was sheathed in asbestos, walls, roofs and ceilings, acres of it and with a projected cost of dismantling it in accordance with EU environmental code calculated to run close to ten million euro, it was decided that its owners, the county council, would leave it there to fuck and not disturb it in any way lest it shed its lung-corroding fibre over the whole of North Mayo

Crossmolina, Ballina, Attymass and

west into the badlands of Ballycroy and Mulranny

the terra damnata of Shanamanragh

the land that time forgot but

well known to us as it's

near Mairead's home place and we have driven there many times, particularly so in the early years of our marriage when Agnes and Darragh were young and we would take them to visit their grandparents for their summer holidays, pack them into the car and drive north, the journey itself about sixty miles but one which crossed into terrain so different to this part of the world a few miles north of the small village of Mulranny at precisely that point where the N59 twists its way under a single-arch stone bridge set among blazing rhododendrons, the bridge always marked for me that complete change of terrain from the hills and drumlins of South Mayo to the open and more desolate expanses of the north, this bridge always affected something deep in me because every time I passed beneath it, with Mairead beside me and the kids in the back, I would experience that subtle shift within me which I always imagined was my soul flinching in the landscape that opened up beyond that bridge, where, within a few miles and with a sudden thinning of the light the mountains withdrew into the clouded distance and the world levelled down to that open bogland through which the road wended its way towards Ballycroy and Bangor and out onto Doohoma Head where Mairead's parents lived on a small farm which had come down on her mother's side and where Darragh and Agnes would run wild through the fields of hay and tillage which stretched in a neat stripe from the gable of the house to the shore for a couple of weeks of every summer and

this is how you get carried away again

in memory of

swept up in that sort of reverie which has only a tangential connection to what you were thinking of, in this case the collapse of our banking system and the economy, a collapse so sudden and comprehensive that one year later it still threatens to have a domino effect across several linked economies, fully capable of undermining banking systems across Germany and France, not to mention crippling our neighbour's export trade to this country, the collapse of a small bank in an island economy becoming the fault line through which the whole universe drains, the whole thing ridiculously improbable, so unlikely in scale and consequence it's as if

something that never was has finally collapsed

or revealed itself to be constructed of air before eventually

falling to ruin in that specific way which proved it never existed even if all around us now there is that feeling of something massive and consequential having come asunder, as when certain pressures exceeded critical thresholds to admit that smidgen of chaos which brings the whole thing down around itself so that even if we believe this collapse is essentially in some adjacent realm there is no denying the gravitational pull we feel in everything around us now, the instability which thrills everywhere like a fever, so tangible you have to wonder

how come we never noticed those tensions building

were we so blind to the world teetering on the edge that we never straightened up from what we were doing to consider things more clearly or

have we lost completely that brute instinct for catastrophe, that sensitivity now buried too deep beneath reason and manners to register but which, once upon a time, was alert to the first whining vibrations radiating from those stress points likely to give way first, that primal faculty which lies in the less evolved, reptilian part of our brain and which we credit to

dogs and vermin and birds as

their ready reflex to flee or take flight en masse just before the ground or the tree or the building beneath them begins to shudder, their primal attunement to danger stampeding them in droves from buildings and structures before they come crashing down around them, a sensitivity we have lost apparently, a faculty which has atrophied through the softening circumstances of our ascent because

collapse is never far from an engineer's mind

and

as ever

and ever again

any image of collapse or things coming apart, always summons up memories of my father – not the ragged shambles he would become at the end of his life, but the quick man with the large hands and ready laugh I knew from childhood, the man who was such a deft touch at dismantling things and putting them back together again – harrows, ploughs and scufflers – not necessarily because of any fault or redundancy in the constructs themselves, but because there was in him that need to know how these things held together so that he could be assured his faith in them was well placed and

one of my first memories dates back to a day in childhood when I stood beside him in the hayshed and he had one of those implements dismantled across the concrete floor

the harrow, the plough or the scuffler

one of those robust constructs that slept standing at the far end of the hayshed, dreaming their iron dreams through the winter months – implements which, even if they had not essentially evolved since the medieval period in which they were perfected, were still in use on our farm as on many others right up to the 1980s

harrows, ploughs and scufflers

implements from a more solid age when the world was measured out in lumpish increments, like pounds and ounces, shillings and pence

standing at the far end of the hayshed during the fallow months of autumn and winter, all tempered blades and forged spikes, held together with iron-banded timber and biding their time as if they were the very embodiment of their own names and were indeed instruments of torment

harrows, ploughs and scufflers

names so clearly evocative of torment that years later, when I attended a conference on bridge construction in Prague or, as months later Mairead would cry in a broken howl

fucking bridge construction

I found myself browsing through the Museum of Torture near the Charles Bridge and was shocked to recognise in scale and material the exact same principles of construction echoed in those instruments of torment standing in the murky light of that dilapidated exhibition, baleful assemblages which were the persuasive tools of various judicial and ecclesial authorities, all dating from a time when the world was ever mindful of its sinfulness but sure of its judgements and had, by way of engineering, gone to some lengths to prise, screw, and pressurise the truth into the light so that they stood now in their shadowed gloom

the maiden, the rack and the wheel

and they too were all banded timber and spikes, blunt constructs held together with bolts and dome-headed rivets which, at that crucial stage of their forging, would have glowed white hot, contraptions so evocative of pain and torment in the tenebrous light of the museum that gradually my mood sifted down within me to an anxious shame as it became clear from their craft and complexity that these machines, with their screws and gearing mechanisms were, at a time when the level of engineering was at its lowest point in the Western world since antiquity, the highest technical expressions of their age, the end to which skilled minds had deployed their gifts, this wretched end such an ignoble instance of the engineer's vocation that I felt sorrowful for although I was young at the time I already had a keen sense that engineering was a high and even noble calling, firmly on the side of human betterment where it stood with a host of other values loosely grouped at the social democratic end of the political spectrum as I understood it then, so that

lost in these thoughts, I wandered through the exhibits, among the shadows and brocade until I realised or, had to admit to myself, that I had been stalking an auburn-haired woman in a quilted anorak whose face was burnished red from the sub-zero temperature which crippled Prague in February of that year, and which was causing her to sniffle into a tissue as she moved past the exhibits, dwelling on each one in turn before ticking them off in a scraggy catalogue and her allure was not merely her looks nor the methodical way she went about the exhibition, but the fact that we were the only two people present on that winter afternoon and in our separate solitude had now come together in a kind of intricate courtship dance with and against each other, a delicate gavotte around the exhibits and down through the golden age of mechanised agony till we finally came together and stood shoulder to shoulder before a Catherine wheel, one of those complex mechanisms which deployed with

clamps and blades and spikes

all those pressures and tensions which sunder flesh and bone, all the ways of engineered anguish which quickly lost me in my attempt to fathom exactly what sort of imagination lay behind such a machine with all its evident ingenuity, most especially that awful alignment by which the body weight of the accused slowly but inevitably overcame the strength needed to uphold it and the gradual downward pressure collapsed it eventually, impaling it slowly, these thoughts going through my mind when I heard the woman standing beside me say in an American accent

it's all about sex isn't it, they were obsessed with it

something I had not noticed but which now, with the idea prompted, seemed obvious enough, the true origin and object of all this pressured penetrating and tearing and now, with these images clear in my head and this woman looking at me from over her tissue, it appeared also that I had assented to something more than the truth of her proposition

fucking bridge construction, Mairead wailed, when she stumbled upon all this and even if

the encounter never quite delivered on all the shameless fucking it promised in those first charged moments among the exhibits, even if it was something genuinely tender over the course of a few days in a small hotel in the workers' suburb of Žižkov, an erotic interlude which at the time I both held dear and was ashamed of in one and the same moment, grateful in many ways but relieved that we took leave of each other with no intention whatsoever of further meetings or keeping in touch so that it was

bridge building, Mairead choked

the story of another man from another age, something remembered

standing here in this kitchen

only because it is woven into that memorial arc which curves from childhood to the present moment, gathering up memories of that time with my father on our farm, a skein of connections I am not likely to unravel at this moment for fear they might banish forever the image of all those agricultural implements and machines which were kept around the barns during my childhood and which my father would take apart on the floor of the hayshed, simple constructs from an age when the world understood itself differently

ploughs, harrows and scufflers

pounds, shillings and pence

rough-hewn, vernacular instruments that were primitively crude compared to the lathed elegance of the one true machine around which all the energy and work on the farm centred – the farm's soul in many ways – the grey Massey Ferguson 35 my father bought at an agricultural show in Westport in the late sixties, paying four hundred and eighty pounds for it, a machine he was forever tinkering with, always scrutinising some part of its engine, peering into it, standing back from it and cleaning his hands on an old rag after having made some adjustment to its workings, a memory so clear to me now here in this kitchen

that I could reach out and touch it with my hand

man and machine

same as they were

the day I came home from school and walked into the hayshed to find him standing over the engine completely broken down and laid out on the concrete floor that was dusted with hayseed, piece by piece along its length

cylinder head, pistons, crankshaft

to where I stood in the doorway in my school trousers and jumper, terrified at the sight because to one side lay the body of the 35, gutted of its most essential parts and forlorn now, its components ordered across the floor in such a way as to make clear not only the sequence of its dismantlement but also the reverse order in which it would be restored to the full working harmonic of itself and my father standing over the whole thing, sighting through a narrow length of fuel line, blowing through it till he was satisfied that it was clean through its length before he laid it on the floor, giving it its proper place in the sequence and explaining to me, saying simply

it was burning oil

as if this were some viral malfunction likely to spread from the machine itself and infect the world's wider mechanism, throwing the universe itself out of kilter to bring it crashing down through the heavens because I knew well that this dismantlement went beyond a fitter's examination of a diesel engine, well beyond stripping out the carburettor to clear the jets – once again my father had succumbed to the temptation to take something apart just to see how it was put together, to know intimately what it was he had put his faith in as

he stood over this altar of disassembly with nothing in his hand but a single, open-end spanner which he waved over the assemblage as if it were a gesture of forgiveness and when he told me that this single tool was capable of breaking down the entire tractor, dismantling the whole thing to its smallest component and that it was then sufficient in itself to put it back together again without need of any other instrument my fear only deepened as I recoiled at the thought that something so complex and highly achieved as this tractor engine could prove so vulnerable, so easily collapsed and taken apart by this single tool and so frightened was I by this fact it would be years afterwards before I could acknowledge the engineering elegance of it all and see it as my father did – something graceful and beautifully conceived, not the instrument of chaos it presented itself as to my childish imagination and

this may have been my first moment of anxious worry about the world, the first instance of my mind spiralling beyond the immediate environs of

hearth, home and parish, towards

the wider world beyond

way beyond

since looking at those engine parts spread across the floor my imagination took fright and soared to some wider, cataclysmic conclusion about how the universe itself was bolted and screwed together, believing I saw here how heaven and earth could come unhinged when some essential cottering pin was tapped out which would undo the whole vast assemblage of stars and galaxies in their wheeling rotations and send them plummeting through the void of space towards some final ruin out on the furthest mearing of the universe and even if my fear at that specific moment did not run to such complete detail, only such cosmic awareness could account for the waves of anxiety that gripped me as I stood over those engine parts on the hayshed floor

soul sick with an anxiety which

was not soothed one bit the following day when my father drove the tractor out of the hayshed with a clear spout of smoke blurting from the exhaust as it bounced down the narrow mucky road and into the field beyond where it took off into the distance, my father perched up on the seat, getting smaller and smaller in the dim light before man and machine disappeared into a dip in the land as we watched from the gable of the house – Onnie, my mother in her housecoat and Eithne clutching the Polaroid camera which seldom left her hands, a present from visiting Yanks –

he's like a child with that thing, my mother said

until he was gone from sight as completely as if they had been rubbed from the world and even if the tractor's successful restoration did not surprise me neither did it do anything to rid me of the gnawing conviction that nothing less than the essential balance and smooth running of the universe's mechanism had now been tampered with in some way that might eventually prove fatal to us all and it is no exaggeration to say that

the sight of that engine spread over the floor would stand to me forever as proof of a world which was a lot less stable and unified than my childish imagination had held it to be, the world now a rickety thing of chance components bolted together in the dark, the whole construct humming closer to collapse than I had ever suspected, a child's fear that sometimes, to this day, takes hold of me and draws me back to that hay barn, just as it did a few years ago when

I was in the village and standing outside Kenny's shop with a carton of milk and a newspaper in my hand, standing on the pavement watching

a huge low-loader pass up the main street, a long, growling beast of a machine hauling itself along in low gear with the driver high up in the cab over the wheels, taking her carefully through the narrow street, making sure she did not strip the wing mirrors off the cars parked on either side of her while the flatbed behind carried something that was dismantled in sections and tied down on both sides with ratchet straps and chains, something that at first sight appeared to be the luminous bones of some massive, extinct creature, now disinterred, with its ribs gathered into a neat bundle around the thick stump of a massive spinal column which time and the elements had polished to such a cool ceramic gloss that if I were to leave my hand on it I would have been surprised if it felt like anything other than glass, and it was only when the whole thing had passed by completely and I saw the back of the trailer hung with caution tape and hazard decals that I recognised the load as a wind turbine which had been completely broken down with the vanes and conical tower separated from the nacelle and stacked lengthwise along the trailer but with enough corrosion around the flanges on the base sections to indicate that this turbine had recently been taken apart as a working project, faulty or redundant or obsolete in some way or other, possibly

burning oil

as my father might have said

so I stood there watching it pass, thinking there was something sorrowful in seeing this felled machine being hauled through our little village out here on the Western Seaboard, something in me recognising this as a clear instance of the world forfeiting one of its better ideas, as if something for which there was once justified hope had proven to be a failure and the world had given up on some precious dream of itself, one of its better destinies, and I was not the only one who'd stood to stare at its passing because three doors up, on Morrison's corner, an old man had stopped in mid-stride and was standing with both hands planted down on the boss of his stick, looking on as the trailer made its careful way through the village, while across the street a few others stood and stared on in spite of themselves, generating a stillness which held for a long moment as the low-loader rumbled by, crossing the square and down the street before turning out of sight beyond the church and off out the Westport road before people became aware of themselves and were now looking at each other querulously and laughing as if they had succumbed to some childish foolery in the middle of the day while, standing across the street from them I wondered where this fallen turbine might be going to, at the same time thinking it was surely a mistake to believe that such things ever go anywhere at all or, more accurately, that there is a place to where such things could go, as stillness and stasis was the very nature of these constructs, much like myself at that moment, stuck as I was in a renewal of that same old anxiety I had experienced as a nine-year-old in the hayshed looking at that diesel engine, the component parts of the world spread across the floor except that now

four decades on

when the idea has come a patient arc through my life I now understood that if I saw the dismantled tractor as the beginning of the world, the chaotic genesis which drew it together and assembled it from disparate parts, then this wind turbine was its end, a destiny it had been forced to give up on, a dream of itself shelved or aborted or miscarried, an old idea which echoed

a radio programme I listened to a while back in which a panel of experts discussed the future of these wind turbines, weighing their environmental impact against whatever their energy efficiency was, the argument going back and forth between various critics and advocates but making little real headway until the topic was turned over to the listeners who by and large, one after another, echoed what had already been said except for one woman, whose hesitant voice cut across the strident tones of the debate when she phoned in to say that

she was living under a hill planted with several of these turbines and whatever about their environmental impact or their worth as a source of clean energy she herself had developed something of a spiritual regard for them as she had only to stand at her back door and look up towards them for a few minutes every day and she could easily believe there was something sacred about them because, grouped and silhouetted against the horizon, their blades stark against the sky, were they not vividly evocative of Christ's end on Calvary, crucified without honour, thieves to the left and right of him and, when turning, weren't they almost prayerful, the hum of their dynamo and their ceaseless rhythm so freely generated by the breeze which was of course nothing less than God's breath across the land, their turning so evocative of all those Buddhist prayer wheels she had met during her years of travel in India and Tibet and it was surely the case also that only machines built to so large a scale and of such pristine alloys could bridge the span between heaven and earth with their song on our account and

was she alone in these thoughts she wondered or

did anyone else have similar feelings about these machines, this technology

which of course they didn't, or if they did they chose that moment to keep it to themselves so that after a few garbled comments with which the radio host laboured hopelessly to place some practical or common sense on her remarks, her contribution to the debate was excused as a quasi-artistic outburst, more in the nature of mystical reverie than reasoned argument, definitely idiosyncratic in a way which allowed it to be harmlessly set aside after a few more words of praise were levied on its heartfelt eloquence and the obvious depth of the woman's feelings

something similar to what I felt that day in the middle of Louisburgh, standing on the sidewalk watching the dismantled turbine being hauled through the main street on its bier without fanfare or procession, the whole thing so lonely and monumental it might well have been God himself or some essential aspect of him being hauled through our little village on the edge of the world, death or some massive redundancy finally caught up with him so that now he was being carted off to some final interment or breakers yard beyond our jurisdiction, some place where the gods were dismantled and broken down for parts or disposed of completely, possibly loaded onto a barge and towed offshore by a salvage tug, out beyond the continental shelf to be weighed down and sunk in some mid-Atlantic abyssal, down between tectonic plates, all these redundant gods lying crushed and frozen in the blackest depths with no surface marker to show where they lie, out of sight and out of mind, among those things in the world that are

burning oil

in some way or other

all of which

reminds me, should I ever forget, that my childhood ability to get ahead of myself and reason to apocalyptic ends has remained intact over four decades and needs only the smallest prompt for it to renew itself once more and for me to get swept away in such yawing deliriums of collapse that I might lose my footing on the ground entirely and spin off into some dark orbit which takes me further and further away from home and into the deepest realms of space, a strange mindset for an engineer whose natural incline is towards the stable construct and not

this circular dreamtime of chaos which

gives such warp and drift to this day so that

it is clear from these stories in the papers that the idea of collapse

needs some expanding beyond the image of things toppling and falling down – plunging masonry, timber, metal, glass – the engineer's concept of collapse, buildings and bridges staggered before crumbling to the ground and raising up clouds of dust because, from what's written here about the global economic catastrophe, all this talk of virus and contagion, it is now clear to me that there are other types of chaos beyond the material satisfactions of things falling down since, it appears, out there in the ideal realm of finance and currency, economic constructs come apart in a different way or at least

in ways specific to the things they are, abstract structures succumbing to intensely rarefied viruses which attack worth and values and the confidence which underpin them, swelling them beyond their optimal range to the point where they overbalance and eventually topple the whole thing during the still hours of the night so that we wake the following morning to a world remade in some new way unlikely to be to our benefit and of course

all this is only clear in hindsight

as if every toppled edifice creates both the light and lens through which the disaster itself can properly be seen, the ashes and vacated space becoming the imaginative standpoint from which the whole thing is now clearly visible for those with eyes to see because up to the moment the whole thing came down it was never clear to me

or anyone else

what was happening

same as when

that story started drifting towards us in mid-March, coming out of the middle distance with its unlikely news of viral infection and contamination, a whole city puking its guts up, the stuff of a B-movie apocalypse seventy miles up the road with

GP clinics and hospital wards across the city reporting a sudden spike in the number of people presenting with stomach ailments, complaining of cramps and vomiting with severe diarrhoea, a rise in numbers so wholly out of proportion with what might be expected for the time of year that initially an outbreak of food poisoning was suspected, an outbreak spread through the city from some large public event or gathering, but when an immediate investigation showed that the cases were evenly spread and did not appear to cluster in any geographic or demographic area it was clear that the source of the illness had to lie in something that was present without discrimination in all parts of the city, a conclusion which

prompted an immediate analysis of the city's water supply and which quickly revealed that it was severely contaminated with the coliform Cryptosporidium, a viral parasite which originates in human faecal matter so that

I can't understand it, what the hell were the city engineers doing

Darragh wanted to know from the other side of the world, his unshaven face filling the screen when he Skyped me that evening, his voice coming with that slight delay as it crossed the distance between us, since

I've been reading about it online – it looks like it could get very serious

it's serious now

and it will all be on the heads of those engineers who fell asleep on the job, how could they have missed it and

Darragh's voice had that note of hysteria to which it is prone whenever he has to grapple with the human slobberiness of the world, a gifted academic mind, or so Mairead tells me, but one that sometimes leaves him with little real notion of how the world actually works so that too often you have to listen to him in this mode, ranting on, sometimes in a language that's difficult to grasp, so I said

yes, those engineers have a case to answer, there should be continual monitoring of the supply but obviously someone slipped up, no doubt there will be an investigation and an analysis of the whole water system but the politicians

let me guess, the politicians will make sure the engineers take the blame for this

blame, responsibility, it's all the same in a case like this, the important thing now is to find the cause and fix it before the whole thing escalates, there's already over a hundred chronic cases and

I'm sorry to have missed it, five years living there and nothing this interesting ever happened so

it was obviously timed for your absence – how is the fruit picking going

not bad, shaking snakes out of trees and filling bags, long hours but the money is ok and there's only a few more weeks of it left before we hit the road

so there's a plan

it might be going too far to call it a plan but there's talk of buying a second-hand van and taking it across country, Ayers Rock the whole lot, then leave it in Perth and fly back home so

how long will that take

we reckon we have enough funds to carry us for four to five months so I should be home in early August, just in time for the business end of the Championship

you won't be missing much if you don't make it, we will be well out of the running by then

Jesus, Dad, don't put a hex on us this early in the year, the Championship doesn't start for nearly two months yet

ahhh

you have to have faith, Dad, that's what we Mayo people do, we journey in hope, true believers

martyrs more like, and your faith hasn't taken as many blows as mine down the years

speaking of martyrs, Mam tells me that you're hobbling a bit, some sort of a limp

it's nothing to worry about, it's just a side effect of the Lipitor, it weakens the tendons in the heel

that's very mythic altogether

it's very painful whatever about mythic, I'll probably have to get the dose changed or recalibrated or something like that

so long as it brings down the cholesterol

yes, that's down to manageable levels now, three point two or something

and you're staying away from chips and cake and all that sort of shit

yes, I've cut out all the dashboard dining

good, we want you around for another few years, by the way, and on another topic, did you make any headway with *Kid A*

I listened to it all right, I liked it – I think – it sounded a lot like unleaded King Crimson though, the same

Jesus, King Crimson, music for engineers, all those dissonant chords laid down at right angles to each other

exactly, my generation demanded more from our music than soft emoting and

you're welcome to it – how is Mam, I haven't spoken to her in a couple of days

Mam's good, she's gone to bed, it's been a long week at school, she's tired

ok so, give her my love

I will, take care of yourself, and one last thing

yeah

don't be afraid to take out a razor and a comb once in a while

will do, bye

mind yourself

bye

and then he was gone, his hand reaching towards me, fingers extended from the other side of the globe as if to touch my face before he shut down the laptop in the flat he shared with five other lads somewhere on the outskirts of Brisbane, the connection broken now and that sense of immense distance closed down in an instant, the world nothing more than the four walls of the room within this house so that it took a moment to get used to the collapse of scale before I got up and walked out to the kitchen to find

something different about moving through the house today

a feeling of dislocation as if some imp had got in during the night and shifted things around just enough to disorientate me, tables, chairs and other stuff just marginally out of place by a centimetre or two, enough to throw me so that now, trying to make a cup of tea for myself, the last two minutes spent searching for the tea bags because the green canister in which they are usually kept is not where it normally sits on the worktop, tucked into the corner beside the boxes of herbal teas Mairead uses for her infusions, but

here it is, finally

stacked away on top of these plates in the cupboard over the sink, god knows why she put it there, why would she want to shift it, she knows full well how these small changes throw me, sending me rushing about the place, pulling stuff apart, never remembering where things are anyway – keys, wallet, phone, everything – can never leave a thing out of my hand without having to look for it, the same panic every morning – the hunt for my keys before leaving for work – turning out pockets and opening drawers, never remembering to put them where they can be found, just throwing them aside without a thought and then searching for them the following morning, a full ten or fifteen minutes wasted lifting newspapers and cushions and jackets until they turn up somewhere obvious, like on the hook over the holy-water font inside the front door, or the bowl on the hall table – who the hell put them there, why can't people leave things alone – every morning this shambolic search through the house, that frustration which is very different to

the anxious feeling running through me now as

some twitchy voltage cutting across me so that it's hard to focus properly on anything, my mind flocked with ideas as if it is filled with electric birds, always in flight, blue shivers which probably caused me to miss the fact that Mairead has laid out some food for me on the table and

looking at it now

looking at it now

a sandwich on a side plate, covered with a napkin and a glass of milk beside it, the whole thing standing there so complete in its own detailed neatness, so perfectly evocative of Mairead herself with all the attentiveness she brings to these little tasks, her capacity for joy in the proper completion of these small considerations so evident in the way it's put together that it feels right to stand over it for a moment just to savour its appearance before lifting the napkin to see that the sandwich is good and simple – cheese with relish between slices of brown bread – a staple carried over from my childhood and which Mairead makes me from time to time as a small kindness, a gesture which touches me deeply at this moment, so much care and attention gathered to the separate parts of it but something inexplicably intense in me reaching towards it, my hand monumental and belated as if it had to pass across a cosmic realm, eons wide, glass and plate absolutely unreachable in a way that cannot be fathomed with all the time in the world to

remember when Agnes and Darragh were children

and it was part of their whole Christmas thing to leave food and drink on the kitchen table for Santa Claus and Rudolph, something to keep them fed on their big night's work, usually cake or a sandwich and a carrot, and it was my job, before going to bed to eat some of it – or at very least to leave teeth marks in it – to show that Santa had indeed sampled our hospitality so that, the following morning, when they had got over the initial delight of their presents they would stand beside the table to examine the remains of the food and the whiskey glass lying sideways on the table because obviously, with a drop taken in so many houses along the way, Santa must have been well slewed by the time he got to our door and it was a wonder at all he managed to leave the right presents in the right houses and there was Agnes standing by the table in her pyjamas listening to me saying all this, weighing it up, while Darragh was already surging ahead, examining the carrot and cake but still not saying anything so that I began to wonder if I had slipped up somewhere in my story and given something away that would spoil the whole thing and I was about to open my mouth again but Mairead was looking at me from across the table, shaking her head, wearing that expression, both fearful and dismayed, which was telling me without words to

stop now, before you go too far

stop now

so I stopped

because every echo of that expression brings me back to that morning when we were just four months married and Mairead stood at this same breakfast table waving a small blue wand over my head and wearing that imploring look I had never seen on her face before, so compromised and uncertain of itself, startling in a woman who, till then, had conducted her life with all the confidence of one who had trusted her first instincts, her way of going about a life which had led her across Europe and through various teaching and cultural posts in Madrid, Berlin, Prague and all the way to the banks of the Danube in Budapest where, after two years working in a language school, she had suddenly turned for home – happily enough, as she admitted herself – but this time taking the scenic route through Northern Europe – Warsaw, Oslo and Copenhagen – before finally fetching up in our local secondary school covering maternity leave for the vice principal, which was when I met her, shortly after I took up work with the County Council and we started a courtship which saw us married a few years later and buying this house which we were settled in only a few months the morning she stood over me

at this same table

waving the stick that was telling us, by way of an unbroken line through its tiny window, that she was pregnant, that we were going to have a child and furthermore that this was something she was so totally unprepared for that she tried to stifle a giggle of fright in an effort to grasp the consequences of what it all might mean – this wand she was holding up between thumb and forefinger as if she were about to cast a spell in the room and draw down a cloud of glittering fairy dust over

this very table here

which at the time, stood in a house that was little more than a concrete shell, an old house going through a radical refurbishment, no doors or windows in some of the rooms, walls and ceilings stripped while the hallway was strewn with timber offcuts and copper piping, a house beginning to evolve around us, a wall-by-wall gain on structure and order, a space in the world we could call our own even if that morning it was in fact little more than a bedroom and a kitchen with the whole place smelling of sawdust and wet cement as she stood over the kitchen table

this same table

with that blue pregnancy indicator in her hand which was telling us with ninety-eight percent accuracy that she was indeed pregnant, because that's what the clear line through its little window was saying, definite as any line drawn in the sand or any surveyor's contour or any of those global parallels

longitude and latitude

which demark those national borders that are drawn up in the wake of long, complex negotiations – the 45th parallel which separates Alaska from Canada or, more accurately, the 38th parallel which separates North from South Korea – a definitive boundary or threshold over which you can venture only if you accept that you are leaving your old life behind with all its habits and customs, a life that has served you well enough up to this but which will not suffice in the new circumstances when

we were both faced with this threshold which most likely had its origins in one of those sudden, joyful fucks on the stack of doors in the bedroom at the end of the hall or on one of the carpenter's trestles in the kitchen, one of those sudden coming-to-grips with each other to which we were given in those days, waylaying each other before moving on to whatever it was we had originally set out to do, an airy ignoring of each other which suited us both, smug and heedless but all demolished by the small baton which Mairead waved over my head with its news of how our lives had taken such a radical swerve away from all the old habits and rhythms we had so easily inhabited up to this but which now, surprisingly, I would relinquish without too much regret because

marriage to Mairead had brought with it a settling of my whole spirit into a kind of banal contentment I was comfortable with, a contentment which had drawn from me some nameless yearning the moment I wedded this spirited woman who stood over me as I sat

with my breakfast and newspaper in front of me

a man in the process of having his life overturned by news his young wife found so disabling but which

I seemed to be taking in my stride, having readily interpreted it as another extension of that ordinary contentment which had come to me in marrying Mairead, so much so that now I found myself marvelling, not at the dullness of my response, but at the realisation that if she had stood there telling me she was not pregnant this indeed would have been shocking news, this would have stopped me in my tracks and caused me something deeper than that mild surprise which kept me sitting there at the kitchen table with my wife repeating desperately that yes, she was pregnant and with that settled there should have been a finality to the moment which would have allowed us to acknowledge it with a tearful embrace and congratulations before setting the whole thing aside for the time being – fuller discussion later that evening – as I was anxious to return to my breakfast and squeeze the last drop of peace and quiet from those few remaining minutes before going to work – all of which was my normal way of going about the morning but

which I now saw, from the look on Mairead's face, that the normal way of doing things would not suffice anymore as a new set of circumstances had just supervened and that I would have to dig deeper within myself to find something which would soothe the startled expression from her pale face beneath the severe centre parting which gave Mairead that ascetic look which so became her as the traveller who had crossed so many time-zones and borders but which spoke nothing of her bright spirit or the generous way her face opened so completely in laughter with such broad disclosure of all her features that it was sometimes impossible to refer back to the pale woman who now

stood there with that blue twig in her hand as

the moment lengthened to a dangerous silence in which it became obvious to both of us that even though we may have had four years of a relationship behind us, we were not yet as skilled as we might wish in coping with news like this, not yet capable of assigning it its proper place and dimension or seeing it in context, because right then we seemed to be incapable of getting past this moment or of putting it to rest for the time being so that we might get on with our day and why

sitting here

at this kitchen table

this particular incident should come to me now it's hard to say, except to confirm that the blue line in that tiny window was

Agnes

or as Darragh would sometimes have it

Agnes Dei

Agnes the Unhinged

the Abbess of the Abyss

Agnosia

Anagnorisis

Agnes, our first born and that threshold in our lives which brought with it all those demands and responsibilities which pushed myself and Mairead into our older selves, our very own need-bearer whose presence in the world was promised in that blue line and confirmed nine months later when she clocked in shortly before noon, tipping the scales at seven pounds four ounces, slightly jaundiced but otherwise fine with fingers and toes all present and correct, latched onto her mother's breast within forty minutes of seeing the light of day and who was fully authorised a couple of days later by her birth certificate which

I saw drawn up before my eyes in a little office down the hall from the maternity ward of the county hospital, a single-page document which told me that now my child was completely realised and that

the seal had been set on her identity as an Irish citizen, who, although less than four days old, was nevertheless the point of all the massive overarching state apparatus within which she could live out her life as a free and self-determining individual, the protective structure of a democracy which she in turn would uphold as a voter, a consumer, a patient, a student, a banking customer, a taxpayer and so on while gathering to herself all those ID cards and certificates that would enable her draw down all the benefits of being born a free child of a republic, accessing education and medicine and bank accounts and library books, all of these rights devolving from

her birth certificate, the source document, which was drawn up for her in a small office at the end of the hall, the cramped space shelved to the roof with files and records and lit by a single fluorescent strip which cast down a hard light on the head of the smiling lady with large arms who took down my details and Mairead's details and then entered them carefully in a newly opened file before she went to a cupboard and took out a blank certificate which we both signed before she entered some final details on it and then, reading it through one last time to ensure it was complete to her satisfaction, took a stamp and pressed the state seal onto it before handing it to me with a smile, where I, affected with a deep sense of occasion, found myself reaching out to shake her hand because this surely was how the moment should be marked and ten minutes later, sitting in the car with Mairead in the back and Agnes in her arms, I continued to stare at this document

the document scarcely less miraculous than the child in the way

it fixed her within a political structure which undertook to spend a percentage of its GDP on her health and her education and her defence among other things and over twenty years later I can still feel something of that mysterious pride which swept through me as I sat there behind the steering wheel, the uncanny feeling that my child was elevated into something above being my daughter or my own flesh and blood – there was a metaphysical reality to her now – she had stepped into that political index which held a space for her in the state's mindfulness, a place that was hers alone and could not be occupied by anyone else nor infringed on in any way which might blur her identity or smudge her destiny, this document which did not tag or enumerate her but freed her into her own political space, our citizen daughter who

are we ever going to leave this car park or are you going to sit all day gawping at that certificate

Mairead called from the back seat and

of course all these high ideas passed into oblivion very quickly or, more accurately, were swept away in the messy flesh and blood circumstance of having a child in our lives, the whole drama of night feeds and nappy changes, the terrors of vaccinations and all those developmental markers which infants have to hit, my heart in my mouth every time the district nurse pulled up outside the house and all that was, hard to believe

the last millennium

ancient history

and of course

none of it on my mind twenty-two years later, the first week of March, when Mairead and I attended the opening of Agnes's first solo exhibition in the Dominic St Gallery in Galway, that exhibition which was her prize for having graduated top of her class in paint two years previously, a gifted artist Mairead assured me whose work in oil had been praised by her tutors as

a sustained attempt to marry the vatic gaze of a hallowed tradition with a technique which strove to find some way out of the redundancy it was so often accused of in a world awash with electronic imagery

or so Mairead told me, as we drove along

recalling the essential feedback points Agnes had received for the degree show which had secured this exhibition while Mairead stressed for me also that this was an important occasion for Agnes not just because it was her first solo show but because it was her first new work since her graduation and as such it would be interesting to see how her themes and technique had progressed in that period of independent experiment, what new paths she had explored and at this point something in me should have been alert to the note of warning in her voice but I ignored it as a coded appeal that I should make a special effort on Agnes's behalf tonight, that I should be especially convivial or at least shed some of my social awkwardness to do her proud and be supportive but, of course, neither of us should have worried on her account because when we walked into the gallery I saw immediately that this was that occasion when

Agnes was never so essentially herself or so self-contained as she was that evening, and that this was yet another of those times when I've looked at her and thought that had Mairead and myself never come together as husband and wife Agnes would still have contrived to exist and be exactly who she was in some other way because she did not appear contingent on anything or anyone and while we might be her parents she was essentially irreducible in the way she was completely at one with herself when I walked into the gallery and saw how, among a fashionable crowd of well-wishers and friends, she still managed to stand alone in the middle of the room with a composite air of being both jilted and the belle-of-the-ball at one and the same time, standing there in the centre of the gallery, hovering above the ground in a black shift, her whole being as Darragh would clarify for me later, an amalgam of witness and pale accuser, exemplary sufferer and Cruella de Vil, a fully achieved study in western gothic, commanding her space with such an impressive aura of quiet disdain that for a moment I was cautious of approaching her for fear of shattering something essential in the exhibition itself, a hesitancy Mairead did not share as she strode across the floor towards her and stood off her at arm's length for a moment before they moved fully into each other's embrace from which Agnes eventually unwrapped herself to welcome and kiss me and draw me into the circle of her friends and well-wishers, men and women in their early twenties, all the young women called Emma or Emily, and all the lads Naoise or Oisin or something like that and of course it took me a while to get my bearings as I found myself caught up in a blur of handshakes and introductions with various snatches of conversation and observations whizzing by which acknowledged, among other things, that

yes, it was an important night and

no, we were only up for the night and

yes, I was proud of her and

no, not too bad, we missed the worst of it and

so on and

so forth

till someone handed me a glass of red wine and I took it with the hope that it might grow in my hand to the size of something I might hide behind while I could see already that Mairead was enjoying herself immensely, moving easily among Agnes's friends, picking up the mood of the evening without having to adjust anything in herself so I took this opportunity to take a step back, literally, to find myself on the edge of the gathering where it was less crowded and a relief to have space and time in which to gather myself before moving away to take a look at the exhibition itself, my eyes needing a long moment to adjust to the light in the room which seemed to be suffused with some sort of ochre mist, something grainy and falling, an effect of the low evening rays reflecting off the walls, or more explicitly off the red script which covered the entire gallery from ceiling to floor along its length, handwriting in various types and sizes, a continuous swathe of text which closer examination revealed to be snippets of news stories lifted from the provincial papers – *The Telegraph, The Sentinel, The Herald,* the *Western People* – all recently dated and all dealing with court cases which covered the full gamut from theft and domestic violence to child abuse, public order offences, illegal grazing on protected lands, petty theft, false number plates, public affray, burglary, assault and drink-driving offences – in short, all those cases that came within the remit of the district and circuit courts, all detailed in descriptive passages crossed with contextualising pieces and direct quotes from court transcripts in which voices of victims and the accused, plaintiff and defendant, sang clear off the walls

when I got him to the ground, Your Honour, I administered

we have stood by him even though he has caused us untold grief

a series of consecutive slaps, Your Honour

I hope he rots in hell, no right father would have done what he did to this family

a strong smell of soot and petrol from her, Your Honour

four types of psychotropic drugs in his system

woke up three weeks later with quarter of my skull gone and fitted with a titanium plate

you will have no luck for this you bastard

and so on and so on, a surge of red script flowing across the gallery, ceiling to floor, rising and falling in swells and eddies through various sizes and spacings, congested in the tight rhythms of certain examples only to swell out in crashing typographical waves in others, a maelstrom of voices and colour and it was quite something to stand there and have your gaze drawn across the walls, swept along in the full surge of the piece while resisting the temptation to rest and decipher one case or another, wanting instead to experience the full flow and wash of the entire piece, my gaze swept on in the relentless, surging indictment of the whole thing, its swells and depths, until I was startled from my reverie by Mairead who appeared by my side to press the exhibition catalogue into my hands with an anxious expression, positioning herself at my elbow where she looked fretful, not a mood I would have associated with her on such an occasion but one which became clear to me when I turned the catalogue over in my hands and read the cover title as

The O Negative Diaries

An Installation by Agnes Conway

Medium – Artist's Own Blood

and I stood there in the middle of the crowd, vacant of every-thing save the single thought – that whatever dreams a man may have for his daughter it is safe to say that none of them involve standing in the middle of a municipal gallery with its walls covered in a couple of litres of her own blood because this, I slowly realised, was what I was looking at, this was the red mist that suffused the weak evening light which streamed in the front windows in such a way that the script itself appeared to project from the walls into the middle of the room, the livid words and sentences themselves hanging in a light so finely emulsified that we might take it into our very pores and swell on it, so that even if the crowd broke up the continuity of the space there was no doubting that the light served to make everyone part of a unified whole that occupied the whole gallery, Agnes's blood was now our common element, the medium in which we stood and breathed so that even as she was witness-in-chief, spreading out the indict-ment which, how ever broad and extravagant it may be on rhetorical flourish, how ever geographically and temporally far-flung it might be, the whole thing ultimately dovetailed down to a specific source and point which was, as I saw it

me

nothing and no one else but

me

plain as day up there on the walls and in the sweep of each word and line, I was the force beneath, driving it in waves up to the ceiling and it was clear to me through that uncanny voice which now sounded in my heart, a voice all the clearer for being so choked and distant, telling me that

I did this

I was responsible for this

whatever it was

definitely something bad and not to my credit because only real guilt could account for that mewling sense of fright which took hold of me there in the middle of that room, something of it returning to me now

sitting here at this table

that same cramping flash within me which twisted some part of me with such sudden fear that before I had made any decision whatsoever I was praying, or rather

I was being prayed as

a prayer

torqued up out of me with an irreversible urgency, speaking itself to completion before the words had properly stumbled through me

Jesus Christ

let it be some vision ahead of her

and not torment behind

responsible for this

just as Mairead grabbed my elbow, a startled look on her face which, for one wild moment, had me believe I may have spoken my plea out loud like a madman because I was now finding myself scrabbling on a knife-edge of panic, a horrible vertiginous moment which I overcame only with a savage effort of will which pushed me in a sudden, awkward lurch across the floor and out the door into the March dusk where rain and the rush-hour traffic clogged the narrow street in which the gallery was situated and those few people who had stood out into the mist to smoke and chat along the pavement now stared at me in such alarm while I tried to gather my wits and steady my breathing that I had a clear vision of how I must have looked careering through the gallery and out into the street, the country man with the big farmer's head on him in the collar and tie, shouldering his way through the crowd with his two fists balled at his side

fit to kill

fit to fucking kill

Mother of Jesus

and so much for the promise to put my best foot forward for Agnes's sake on her big night, so much for making a good impression on her behalf I thought bitterly as I stood there with the rain pissing down on me, nothing but sour embarrassment churning around inside me as

a young man with a wispy beard took a step towards me, concern writ across his face and I can't remember what I said to him or how I replied but his two hands were suddenly raised in front of his face as if someone was going to lash out and hit him – and how ever I responded at that moment it seemed to convince him fairly sharpish that he did not want anything to do with me so he backed off, leaving me alone on the sidewalk outside the gallery where I stood for a further half hour, trying to get a grip on myself, getting soaked through while the crowd gathered up and down the street, smoking and drinking wine before eventually breaking up and spreading out into the gathering night by which time I had calmed down a bit

just a bit

my temper and nerves under control somewhat, helped by the fact that I had gleaned from the snatches of conversation around me that the exhibition was a striking achievement and should, with any luck, be a real success, so I was relieved for Agnes – I did not appear to have done any damage – and could set aside those worries for the moment while I examined once again what I had seen of the installation itself and more specifically try to fathom the shock I had in its presence, why had I felt so deeply about it all, why had I taken it so personally and, most bafflingly of all, how a man of my age could be so overcome by his own feelings, so totally undone as to make him feel very foolish since all I knew, standing there in the rain, was that this was something I did not appreciate one little bit, sifting through feelings that grated and twisted within me, trying to give them their proper place and measure with my back to the cut stone wall of the gallery and I had no need to step outside of myself to know that I must have presented a strange sight to anyone who cared to look, this burly man with a suit and tie on him and the raw winter face of a farmer, standing there as if he was outside second mass of a Sunday, and how ever this may have looked to those last stragglers who stood along the pavement, it was safe to say that no one could have guessed the degree of turmoil and inner vexation which troubled me because never

had the consequences of fatherhood and everything it entailed weighed so completely on me than at that moment with

the anxious worry that I might be responsible in some way for what was on the walls of the gallery behind me, a wringing fear within me which gathered to its tight core two decades of conse-quence, so that it was now clear to me that this whole evening might be nothing less than a full reappraisal of myself as a man and as a father, something I had not reckoned on when I got into the car that evening and drove the sixty or seventy miles to the gallery, that I was travelling towards this moment of reckoning with myself because, like many another man, I had gone through life with little in the way of self-examination, my right to a life of peace from such persecution something I had taken for granted, something I might have acknowledged as the responsibility of others but not the type of inward harrowing I ever expected of myself but which nevertheless I now found myself subjected to in a way which took its prompt from a central, twitching nerve within me which kept asking

had I failed my daughter

had I pushed her towards this – whatever this was – on the walls of the gallery, this was the question that would not resolve one way or another beneath the sifting rain which shadowed the street in both directions, with the conviction hardening within me that having lived a decent life might not in itself be enough – or a life which till now I had honestly thought had been decent – since there was now some definite charge or accusation in the air which made it appear that not having done anything wrong was not enough and I noticed also that

the rain had that steady fall to it which meant it was down for the rest of the evening with the traffic passing in a muted light that was cold and wet and made me realise I was now soaked, particularly across my shoulders and down my back but also, that I could not move, I could not go back inside from shame and embarrassment so I spent another fifteen minutes standing there alone with the wall pressed to my back until Mairead and Agnes finally showed up on the pavement beside me with a look of irritated relief on both their faces, exclaiming

so that's where you are

we wondered where you'd got to and

I tried to avoid the look in Mairead's eye, that look which told me that she was going to set aside her anger and disappointment for the moment but that I would hear about it later on, so I made some foolish play of welcoming them both, hopelessly pressing the excuse that

I've been here all the time, I needed some fresh air, which

was a lie neither of them believed but one they went along with for the moment in their anxiety to move out of the rain, Agnes grimacing and doing a little stamping dance of impatience on the pavement, her high-collared coat, buttoned up under her chin, transforming her from the pale totem of earlier in the evening to someone almost corporate-looking, her whole appearance now that of a young, professional woman who had just dropped into the exhibition on her way home from work and I remembered that this coat was a recent gift from Mairead in both our names to mark this occasion, the prize at the end of a long day spent shopping together, a day which had brought Mairead home glowing with a renewed sense of her daughter's good taste in such things as coats because even if, as she admitted at the time, it would not have been the one she would have chosen for her – so conservative, plain even – and even if she was slightly perplexed by her choice, she was also pleased because for all her support of Agnes's artistic career there were periods when Mairead openly worried about her and wondered would it not have been better if she had not chosen a career which was so governed by luck and uncertainty, a career which was likely to bring more than its share of disappointment and frustrations and

did I know how few practising artists managed to make a living from their work, did I

which of course I didn't

but which sometimes gave me to believe when listening to Mairead going on in this vein, that her all worry was not really for Agnes but was in reality for herself in that it underlined some hesitancy in her own character, possibly evoked a moment in her own past when she might have done something similar with her life but had settled instead for the safer option of teaching, discovering somewhere along the way that for all her travel and adventuring abroad she lacked that courage to make the commitment to something as dicey as an artistic career so that now, whenever Agnes made a conservative choice in something like a coat it was as if Mairead was no longer suffering that rebuke to herself and here she was now, our artist daughter in her sensible coat, looking so sharp that had she been someone else I would not have been surprised to hear that she worked in some sort of financial services job, insurance or something, some career where the value of the present moment was wagered against some unknowable future and standing there in the rain, looking at her, I found myself getting so carried away on this idea, this alternative life to which my daughter might have been born, that it took me a moment to realise that I was being spoken to, Agnes suggesting that we go for something to eat as she was meeting up with friends later for a few drinks but that it would be nice if we could have some time alone together, just the three of us, besides

I'm famished, she said, absolutely famished

as she hadn't had time all day to have a proper meal and had not eaten since before noon, all nerves and anxiety, which might well account for the fevered glow of her cheeks now which blushed up her pale complexion in that same way that makes mothers want to place their hands on children's foreheads and get them to stick out their tongue as she finished pulling on the leather gloves that completed her outfit, that final detail which so clinched the whole look from smart-casual to something much more purposeful and the sight of which galvanised me into a kind of blustering anxiety to move the whole evening on to another place and mood so

yes, something to eat, where can we go this time of the evening, won't everywhere be booked out, we should have thought about this earlier and rung ahead and

Mairead was giving me that look, shaking her head sorrowfully and I hauled up, mid-surge

calm down for fuck's sake, I said to myself, calm down

so I shut up and stood back while the two women consulted and eventually the three of us moved off, following Agnes up the narrow street and across the bridge, through a small alleyway in the shopping centre which opened into a parallel street where there was a restaurant wedged between a church on one side and a theatre on the other, a quiet place where we had the full attention of a waiter who stepped up and fussed around us when we entered, took our coats and bags and led us to a table, one of seven or eight in a small room that was near empty and I was glad to see how happily Mairead surveyed the tables with their linen napkins and heavy cutlery and, as if reading my mind, she turned with a wide smile and a girlish squeeze of my hand to say

isn't this very nice Marcus, very stylish and

her glad enjoyment filled the space around us with its own brightness while the next few minutes were taken up with settling into our seats and picking our way through the menu, gladly taking guidance from Agnes who seemed familiar with the place and what it had to offer so it wasn't long before our orders were taken and we were relieved of the large menus to settle back and review the whole evening which, from what I could gather, had been an unqualified success, with much for Agnes and Mairead to talk about, specifically how the exhibition was likely to play out in the weeks ahead – hopefully it might travel to other galleries, possibly going to Dublin, the work would need that kind of exposure if it were to get any reviews in the national papers – and I chipped in with a few questions to assure them that I was not sulking or upset and that, like a good schoolboy, I had been paying attention and Agnes answered them with that careful measure of attention and consideration which assured me that nothing I had done during the evening, nothing of my fright or panic, had thrown her or damaged her confidence and I was relieved and proud of her also because

her self-confidence was one of those markers I've always held up to myself as proof that I had done a decent job as a father, a true indicator that she had grown strong and self-sufficient and would not be buffeted too easily by whatever life threw at her, nor would she shirk those moments when she would have to stand her ground, moments such as now when she turned her full face towards me and began abruptly

you were surprised by the work, upset

by way of opening the topic

I saw it on your face, it took you by surprise

yes, I conceded, a bit shocked, it wasn't what I had expected, nothing like your previous work and

while the puzzlement in my voice was genuine it did nothing to hide the hurt which I feared would swell up in that surge of self-pity that was boiling within me and which was aggravated by the patient, conciliatory tone with which Agnes began telling me that

yes, it's a bit of a departure all right, I don't think I'll ever fully get away from oils – nor would I want to – but over the last couple of months I've wanted to try something else, an experiment – to step outside the idea of oil painting towards something new and

this is it

yes, she said, with a frown, and however successful this exhibition is, my next work will probably be a return to oil, oil with blood on canvas, some sort of new amalgam possibly, I don't know yet

she said, smiling and

leaning forward in the chair to offer me her full face, her shoulders straining out of the folds of her shift as if anxious to give clear evidence of both her commitment to the idea and her wish to set my mind at rest, all of which undid me so that in a gulping lurch I found myself explaining that

what I found difficult about the whole piece wasn't just the blood

I should have warned you

it wasn't just any blood, it was your blood

it's ok, I took precautions

it's a mutilation

no it's not Dad, it was just a jab for god's sake and she threw up her hands and smiled so

I felt assured now, ready to grasp this moment and press ahead with my own thoughts because

what I found difficult was the mixture of finger pointing and sanctimony in the whole piece, your righteous standpoint over the material, I wasn't so sure about that

you think that's a cheap shot, that I'm standing on some urban stage and poking fun at culchies with

her voice threaded through with that steely edge which always gratified me – a response all her own and so different to what would have been her brother's evasive clowning in such moments – Agnes was always likely to go toe to toe on any point she felt strongly enough on so that

I'm not sure my accusation is that you are taking a cheap shot or

that maybe I'm Uncle Tomming here, gratifying urban audiences with the comedy capers of their country cousins

something like that, cheap ridicule, although I would be disappointed if you hadn't thought of that yourself, you're smarter than that

yes, that crossed my mind, but that's not the same as saying I managed to circumvent it and

the choices you made were soft options, just the sort of stuff that would make us look ridiculous, all those drink-driving convictions, common assault, public order offences – as crimes there was something almost comic about them so that

yes, I agree, there is more comedy than danger in some of them – even the incidents of assault – but all the cases were taken from reports of the circuit and district courts and it was that sense of local reckoning which appealed to me – why, I cannot honestly say, but it was as if there was something manageable about the transgressions and sins that go to trial there – I don't know, as an idea it's still not fully formed, I've given it a lot of thought but it's still not fully clear to me and

she looked serious now and I had a moment in which to consider that maybe I'd got ahead of myself in an attempt to understand the whole thing as these were not words that normally came tripping off my tongue, or more accurately I had never found myself in the sort of places where words of this type were necessary, but now they flooded ahead of me, threatening to carry me off to some sort of disaster so I drew hard on the reins and pulled back from wherever it was I was going because nothing good could come from losing the run of myself at an hour of the evening when it was nearly won, especially now with Agnes herself in such a conciliatory mood and winding up the topic by admitting

there's nothing to worry about Dad, yes, there might be finger-pointing and accusation but it wasn't personal, none of it was at you or Mam for that matter – you're exonerated of all charges – it's an idea in embryo and

she turned her whole face towards me with an expression of such open appeal that I softened instantly as some wiry tension in my gut unravelled to something warmer which drew the edge off the moment so that we could raise our glasses now, allowing us to settle into the knowledge that we had tested the moment severely and could let it rest for the time being, a conclusion confirmed in the relaxed expression on Mairead's face who, till then, had studiously faded into the background but now, sensing the difficult moment had passed, was refilling her glass from the water carafe in the centre of the table and raising

a toast to our daughter on her big day, that it may be the first of many, and

so the moment was solved and we raised our glasses and clinked them together with a lingering note that hung over the table, taking a long time to fade

like the Angelus bell

which still reverbs in my head now, a single note ringing on in the brightness of the day as if the whole world were suspended from it

mountains, rivers and lakes

past, present and future with

the whole moment so complete now and tidied away that we could settle easily into each other's company and turn to safer topics – specifically Darragh and his adventures down under, a subject which drove each of us in turn to different types of disbelief and frustration because

have you seen the head on him

the beard and the hair

that Methuselah look he's cultivating

is it Methuselah or Mad Max

you can hardly see his face now when he comes on screen, just two eyes stuck in a bush

he reminds me of your father with that hair

Jesus, don't go saying that

I don't think he's shaved since he crossed the equator

it's more scarecrow than Old Testament prophet, if that's what he's going for

he say's it's hard work, that whole Waltzing Matilda thing, no time for personal grooming or hard work my arse, the only photos he's posted are of himself and the lads around a campfire in a woollen hat, skulling cans of Four X so

he had to go the other side of the world to do that and

but I think he's moving on to some other job shortly, they've picked all the fruit in the greater Brisbane area and now they're thinking of doing some time on a dairy farm and

what does he know about dairy farming when

as ever, when Darragh was the subject we fell easily to our separate roles – Agnes, the contentious older sister who looked on his antics with a mixture of admiration and jealousy, Mairead, the doting mother who saw something to be proud of in the blithe way he had set aside his studies to take to the road and myself, the father whose patience was sorely tested and who found himself in a constant state of grating irritation with him – a topic of conversation enlivening and productive of so many different themes and moods that to be reminded

later, as we drove home, by Mairead of how completely overthrown I had been earlier in the evening reduced me instantly to a shamed helplessness which she probed in that way of hers, warning me there may have been every chance I had reacted more aggressively than I thought so that it was now advisable that I should bethink myself and come to a clearer assessment of what had happened because

you were frightened

how do you mean

you were, I was worried you might lash out at someone

when have I ever lashed out at anyone

I know, that's what worried me

Mairead said, with the darkness passing in a wet glare on the windscreen as we made our way along the narrow secondary roads connecting the sleepy villages of our homeward journey, me in the passenger seat, unused to someone else behind the wheel of my own car, so finding it doubly hard to cope with Mairead's questions but eventually admitting

yes I was

hoping that the subject would be buried quickly once and for all

I was frightened, both for me and for her, are you saying I overreacted

no, but I was surprised you reacted as you did – what was it exactly that got you so upset

there was blood

yes, it's different to oils, a big swerve away from her previous work, but I still find it odd that you could be so shocked by it

I would have thought it would be shocking not to be shocked by it – when did we become so blasé about such things – and she was so poorly as a child

she wasn't poorly, she was a bit anemic, low in iron so she had to take a supplement which stained her teeth – did you notice how she had them polished tonight, it gave her that shine –

I wasn't looking at her teeth – all that blood – I had an image of her sitting on the side of a bed with a syringe in her arm, that's the picture that came to me

for god's sake Marcus, you've no worries about her

I'm her father, it's my job to worry, do you know how she harvested it

harvested it – you'd swear we were talking about one of her organs

you have a better word

no, but if she said she was careful then I believe her – look, you need have no worries about a woman who wears a coat like that, they are not likely to put themselves in harm's way

that's nonsense

no it's not, so now

I worried that some new sensitivity to shock and fear had opened up in me, some defect or weakness that might expose me to some unanticipated shame with which I would have no ability to cope, something that would have to be met with definite refutation if the grinding anguish which now churned inside me were to be prevented from growing into something more corrosive and

not to worry, Mairead continued, it was only blood, it could have been a lot worse

how could it have been worse

you could have walked into the gallery and found her standing naked

why would she be naked

oh you know, some of these performance artists are pretty out there, she could have been cuddling a pig

a pig

yes, or naked and peeing into a

ok Mairead, I get the picture

I groaned as she

drove on through the wet night, passing through those small towns and villages which slept with their empty streets under a sodium shroud, moving on into the narrow bog roads that were unlit but that had a precarious sense of being raised over the sea of heather and scutch grass stretching out on both sides, driving on through the ragged moonlight in which we seemed to be the only car on the road, Mairead taking it easy because

I've never driven these roads at night

she said, her gaze focused as she kept a steady speed into the bends and sudden turns which

you never realise how narrow they are till you have to drive them at night, so narrow and twisty

there's no rush, just take your time

I thought you engineers would have straightened all these roads during the boom years

we were told we had better things for doing with our money – most of the boom money went into bypassing or linking major urban centres – there wasn't a whole lot spent on bog roads, certainly not a few miles of blue road like this

blue road

yes

what does blue road mean

blue road means that it is not green road

blue road and green road

yes

let me guess, blue and green politics

that's it

and this road got ignored

it did

because green was in power

yes

because, let me guess again – the ballot boxes in this townland keep coughing up blue votes

that's right

and as long as they do these roads will stay narrow and windy and the pot-holes will deepen

certainly not much will be spent on straightening them out – slow down here, this is a temporary surface stretch, these chippings could slide out from under you on a bend like this and

she drove on, keeping a steady speed in the middle of the road, through more bogland stretching away into the darkness, the lights of scattered homesteads winking in the level distance like ships out to sea, miles of bog before stone walls and sod fences began to rise on both sides of the road to close in around the car and

that's odd, she said

what's odd

we just passed a single street light in the corner of that field, one street light all on its own in the middle of nowhere and

I know, did you see what was under the streetlight in the corner of that field

a few cows

there was a half ring feeder

so

so why would you need a street-light over a half ring feeder

how would I know

think about it

it's the light

yes, shining on

feeding cattle

exactly

so someone got a streetlight put in the corner of his field so he can see his way at night to feed them, is that right

yes, that light has been there for years, one engineer tried to get rid of it but word came down from on high that the light was to stay where it was

so now we're stuck with it

we are

that's ridiculous

it's not as ridiculous as trying to remove it now, when our engineer tried to do that he was told fairly sharpish that he could forget about making a budget submission the following year if he moved it

a friggin streetlight, Mairead murmured, in the middle of nowhere

yes, a streetlight and

we finally arrived home just as it was coming up to one o'clock in the morning and when we got inside Mairead went straight to bed as she had to be up for her first class at nine but I stayed up for another forty minutes, took a bottle of beer from the fridge and turned on the telly to watch one last news bulletin before turning in for the night, Sky News inevitably, from which I learned that avian flu was threatening to cross the species barrier in Southeast Asia and that the surge of troops in Iraq was likely to continue for the rest of the year, while the search for a serial killer was now underway in some city after the bodies of two prostitutes had been discovered on waste ground – the same old stories at that hour of the night but still somehow new, after which I turned off the television and set aside the urge to check my email and see if Darragh had dropped me a line, because I knew that if I sat down to the computer so late at night I was likely to get swept away for another hour or so on other news sites or on Amazon or something, sliding sideways into one search after another and all of a sudden it would be three in the morning and I'd have wasted two hours better spent asleep, for which I would have to pay the following day in sluggishness and fatigue, so I checked that my keys were on the stand inside the front door and switched off the lights in the hall and the bathroom before turning into bed behind Mairead with my arm around her and her arse tucked into my belly, drifting off on the warmth of her body, asleep within moments, deep and untroubled and so completely free of dreams that

I got to work shortly after eight o'clock the following morning feeling fresh and sharp, arriving in the council offices just as the two girls at reception, Miriam and Eimear were sorting through the morning mail and pulling on their headsets to answer the phones and there was already a few people in the foyer filling out motor tax forms, trying to get ahead of the queue which would form in half an hour when the counter opened, so I waved to the girls and

took the stairs up to my office at the end of the hall, the small narrow office with its twelve-foot-high ceilings, where I screwed open the blinds on the window which is high up on the wall behind my desk so that light pours down on me from a great height, often giving me the feeling that I am trapped at the bottom of a well and forever unable to see the sky save for this lighted sliver above, an impression which never fails to colour my mood every morning I step into this room so, with my

jacket hung on the chair behind me and the cuffs of my shirt rolled up, I swept my gaze over the desk with its computer and its clutter of papers and envelopes and straight away I lined up five jobs for immediate attention – a penstock outside the village of Kilasser which needed to be opened quickly if the recent heavy rainfall was not to build up on the road surface – a procurement order for six hundred tons of polished granite from Roadstone had to be sorted, a couple of invoices to be signed and passed on to the accounts department and lastly, a message on my answering machine from Charlie Halloran that I should give him a call as soon as possible, a message logged at twenty-two minutes past seven, which was early even by Halloran's standards and which I knew immediately signalled nothing but bad news and while I toyed for a moment with putting it off till later in the morning, I thought to hell with it, better get it out of the way early and not have it hanging over me the whole day, so I dialled him up and cut across him with my cheeriest tone before he could start, saying

Councillor, you're on the ball early this morning

I'm early every morning

he said bluntly

which caused me to sit up immediately because there was no doubt now but that he was on the warpath as he said

you're not the only one who knows what a day's work is –

what can I do for you, Councillor

I'll tell you what you can do for me – Keeva Bridge, what's the story with it, I passed by it yesterday – or rather I didn't pass by it yesterday, I had to turn back, what's happening with it

you know yourself what's happened with it, two months' rain has washed it away, undermined the piers and the whole thing came down under its own weight – there's a crew onsite, it will be repaired in less than three weeks so –

there was a sour guffaw on the other end of the line

it will take a lot longer than three weeks if things are moving at the pace I saw them yesterday

what did you see

I saw damn all, that's what I saw, certainly nothing that resembled work that's for sure, a whole crew of men standing around in hi-vis jackets smoking and talking into their mobiles, that's what I saw at three o'clock yesterday afternoon so

that put me on guard, the frustration in Halloran's voice was sharper than our normal exchanges, the man was obviously riled so I said cautiously

in the middle of the afternoon, they were probably having a tea break

tea break my arse, one lad sleeping in the van with his boots up on the dash – I wound down the window and had a word with another lad leaning on a Stop/Go sign, he put the elbow on the roof and leaned in like he had all the time in the world, all talk, he said there was some sort of hold up, something about the delivery of concrete slabs, I couldn't make out what the hell he was on about so

I had no clue what he was talking about either but I couldn't let Halloran know that so I had to let the conversation spin out till it became clear what exactly he was referring to, saying

there's been a small delay but the men will be on top of it in a day or so and

what I want to know is, are there any arrangements for a temporary bridge – there are eight families in the townland of Aughawill cut off from civilization

we've decided against a temporary bridge, the time and expense

what time and expense – you don't have to be reminded that

the bank holiday is coming up and the first tourists of the year will be driving around in that part of the world and

the new bridge will be done in a few weeks, well in time for tourists, it's a single arch bridge, it's not a listed monument so

it better be done for that weekend, I don't want to have to go on Midwest Radio explaining why there are holdups on that narrow road or seeing pictures of the people of Aughawill ferrying their kids to school across the river in a transport box, making their local representative look like an idiot and

if they're that intent on making you look bad you might want to remind them that they would still have their bridge if their sheep hadn't overgrazed those hills above the river and

oh yes Marcus, I'll remember that, Halloran said with dry sarcasm, better still, the next time I'm canvassing that whole area you can come with me and lecture those people on hill-grazing and crop rotation and whatever else is bothering you, we'll see then how you get on, one last thing – has the Legislator been on to you about this

Moylette

yes

no, Deputy Moylette hasn't been onto me about it yet, at least not so far as I know

it's only a matter of time, that whole area is right in his heartland, I'm surprised you've not had a concerned call about it from him – how about Lavelle, has he called, I'll bet he's called

no

it's not like him to be so slow, I would have bet on him being on to you by now

well, I look forward to calls from those two men

yes, ok, I'll leave it at that – do what you can about that bridge, get it sorted

I'll look into it, thanks for calling

bye

bye

and the line went dead as he hung up and I sat back in my chair, gathering my thoughts because Halloran the fucker had now given me something to think about – what the hell was happening out on the bridge, what delay was he talking about and how come Keville, the site engineer hadn't contacted me about it – these were the thoughts I sifted through after that conversation, taking my time before making a phone call because I knew well from past experience that the worst thing I could do at that moment would be to lift the phone and start bollocking someone at the other end, no surer way of fucking things up or of making a bad job worse, so I sat back in the chair and closed my eyes and considered the problem from as many angles as possible – first of all from the engineering angle and what exactly this hold-up was and then the political one, that aspect which specifically concerned Halloran with his vigilant need to keep his own patch tended and to keep himself positioned in such a way that any credit for its repair and restoration would come to him because it was well known that Halloran's ambitions beyond a council seat made him a real threat to Moylette, the sitting deputy, and it was only when I put the two names together in my head that I knew I would have to contact

the site immediately because the last thing I needed now was a call from another politician, talking to him without the full story, so I dialled up Keville and got him after a few rings

hello, yes

Keville's voice rising over a barrage of background noise, an engine roar swelling nearby as a jackhammer kept up a series of short metallic bursts with Keville yelling again

hello, hello

hello Andy, Marcus here

Marcus, how's it going, give me a second till I move away from here and

I could envisage the whole site now as it was only a few days since I had driven out to it so it was still clear in my mind, the bridge cordoned off behind orange mesh wire, the machines and the crew in hi-vis jackets with the smell of raw stone and concrete and diesel coming down the phone towards me and

Marcus

yes

can you hear me

Keville yelled, with some distance between himself now and the jackhammer so

Andy, I said, is there some sort of a delay on the job, have I heard right, to which

there followed then a fragmented story which did indeed confirm the gist of what Halloran had told me, there had been a single day's delay due to a power outage in the Roadstone yard that had knocked out their concrete production for a full twenty-four hours – and no, they had no backup generators – but that he'd got an assurance that they would deliver the pre-cast slabs later today and that the mobile crane was already in place and ready to go so there would be no time lost on that and no surer thing, he had been onto Roadstone already this morning and they had given him their solemn word that they would be there this afternoon at the latest and

I let him go on in this vein for a couple of minutes or so, repeating himself and letting him run the story on towards the assurance that he could handle it himself, which was what I wanted to hear from him, this being one of the first jobs over which he was the site engineer, but I knew to listen to him that any hope of bringing the project in under time and budget was now likely to come a cropper, his frustration and sense of injustice mounting with him ranting on for another few minutes while I sat there listening, hoping he would finally hear my silence through his frustration and realise that I was not happy with the situation and sure enough his voice begin to fray and take on that burred edge of anxiety which threatened to tip over into self-pity as he blurted

there's not much more I can do

no one is blaming you Andy

if I could cast the fucking things myself I would

calm down

I've only the one pair of hands, you can count them yourself so

I cut him off then for fear this running temper of his might spill over completely and then we would have a different sort of crisis on our hands so I said

look, get it sorted out as soon as you can and call me when those slabs are unloaded, I don't want another politician coming on the phone and blindsiding me with stuff I should know and

someone's been on the phone

I had a call from Halloran this morning

the Councillor

yes, it was him who told me about this delay – I shouldn't have to hear it from him or

how did he know about it

you must have spoken to him yesterday

I didn't speak to anyone

it was one of the lads on the Stop/Go signs, talked to a man who wound down the window and asked a load of questions, sometime in the afternoon, around three o'clock and

there was a long, thickening silence on the other end and I could feel Keville's rage fizzing as he listened because

that's how I heard about it – so be careful who you talk to and keep me abreast of things and

I hung up and the office contracted around me, grey light swelling up to the ceiling and the vacant hollow in my belly reminding me that I had set out that morning without any breakfast, so I checked for money in my pocket – two twenties and some loose change – before I walked out of the building and across the grassy mall towards the café deli on the street corner where I bought a chicken sandwich and a large cup of strong coffee which I took back to a bench under a large maple tree, a cool enough spot for the time of year but bearable for the length of time it would take to eat the sandwich and drink the coffee, so I sat down after I wiped the seat, finding myself facing into the low, watery sun over the columned building across the street in front of which stood a handful of people, wigged and gowned in close consultation among themselves, leaning towards each other for a long moment before they finally broke apart, two of them turned back into the building and the other two walked up the street and I remembered the court was sitting and that this building with its costumed players was the very source of Agnes's work which had caused me so much upheaval the night before and which, till then, I had not given a thought, apparently having done a good job overnight of pushing the whole thing to the back of my mind, but now, sitting there the whole evening came back to me in a red surge, all those anguished feelings returning in paler versions of themselves to swing through me there on the bench so that for a loose, churning moment

I did not know how to react, whether to stay seething on the bench or to enter the courthouse with some ludicrous idea of holding someone to account for what I had experienced the night before, an idea which almost raised me to my feet and carried me forward on a surge of anger, already seeing myself plunging through the swing doors of the court and into the inner chamber where I would pull some defendant from the dock or judge from the bench – I would not be choosy – and give him a battering there on the floor of the court

and

and

I whiled away a few minutes with this pleasing fantasy, honing its climactic moments to an escalating scene of chaos and outrage which spilled out of the chamber and into the street, a scene which, for all its alluring comedy, left me with little proper idea of how it might resolve, what it all meant or what good it would do me, just a few more minutes sitting there savouring its dismal pleasure till it was clear then that the images of the previous night were going to vex me for the rest of the day leaving little hope that I would be able to immerse myself fully in the work which lay on my desk, but nevertheless so intense was my desire to bury those memories and the fears they drew with them that I drained off the last of the coffee and returned to the office in a purposeful mood where, for the next few hours, I ploughed grimly through the jobs lined up on my desk – settled the issue with the procurements office, despatched a two-man crew to open the penstock in Kilasser and agreed the price of granite from a quarry in Ardrahan, sixty miles away, by faxing them a cheaper quote for the same stone quarried on the other side of the world in South China then shipped to Turkey for polishing before it ended up in West Mayo at two-thirds the price – jobs I ploughed through before late afternoon when

Casey, a road engineer put his head around the door, looking for advice on how to deal with a difficult residents' association that would not see sense and

I can't get them to budge, he said, three meetings with them and they won't listen to reason or

what's the problem exactly

the problem is this mile of road running through the village, these people want a fine chip surface which is totally unsuitable in a residential area with a school and a pub in the middle of it and

you outlined the engineering reasons against it

of course I did, the engineering reasons and the safety reasons – the surface they want has a breaking distance nearly twice that of the coarse chip surface and it's dangerous in a built-up area, plus you won't be able to keep it gritted when the frost comes

not to mention surface water

and surface water – the least drop of rain and you'll have cars aquaplaning all over the place

I know those people – they haven't a good word to say about each other but when it concerns the village they pull together and

of course Halloran is egging them on

I'll bet he is – that village can have their road surfaced with polished glass as far as he's concerned, Halloran is harvesting fifty or sixty votes along that road

that makes sense, I can understand him keeping them sweet but you'll never guess why they want this particular surface

why

the fucking tidy towns competition – the smooth road surface looks a lot nicer than the normal coarse chip finish which should go on it – when it's lined and striped and with cats-eyes running along the sides and middle it will be worth ten extra points in the tidy towns competition and

ok, I said, now wanting to draw a line under the discussion, here's what you do – call one more meeting with the association and hand each board member a letter which repeats the points you've made and tell them that this dated letter is going on file and

it's going to take more than a filed letter

let me finish, give them a moment to think about it and if that doesn't shift them tell them how you see this panning out – tell them that sometime in the near future, this year or the next – they will be presented with an accident report drawn up by the Gardaí or the NRA which lays the blame for the collision at the feet of whoever it was decided to lay that surface on a straight road going through a village with an 80km speed-limit and

Casey's face opened in a broad smile

shift responsibility onto them

exactly, they won't be half as anxious to press for that surface if they think there's a possibility of their name being brought into adverse legal proceedings

it would give them something to think about right enough

and the letter puts you in the clear should there be an accident

that might do it all right, Casey said, opening the door and nodding his head as if he could see the problem solved already, I'll give it a try anyway, thanks Marcus

no bother, let me know how you get on

I will, mind yourself

and he pulled the door and was gone, leaving me to savour the assurance that I had done a decent job of playing the older, wiser head, passing on the tricks of the trade, a good feeling that held till the end of the day when I dropped a load of invoices into the accounts department across the hall on my way out onto the mall where

a few walkers were crossing the grass and two young lads in school uniforms were kicking a ball to each other, the whole evening having that end of winter feel to it without it being properly spring and for some reason I decided to take a quick spin up to Keeva to see how the bridge site was going, it was a nice drive and it would be no harm to have a look at it, bring myself up to speed on how things stood, so I sat into the car and turned on the radio, tuning into

hearing it now

Midwest Radio

the lonesome lilt of country music coming across the airwaves, something odd and misplaced about the teary melodies and lyrics swirling around the kitchen at this time of day, the mood of the song better suited to late at night when darkness and that lonesome distance proper to country music takes hold but of course

it's me and not the music that's misplaced, being so seldom at home on a weekday like this, it's difficult to say what's normally played at this time while

sitting at the table and

letting the song wash through me like a steady tide from a world of manageable heartache, a world where bad feelings come with melody and are capable of being rendered down into verse, bridge and chorus, which can be sung away to your heart's content with that just measure of regret which allows you to feel that, for all your loneliness, you are still part of the wider human drama and that this is a genuine kinship, more valuable and heartfelt than hearing the news or reading the paper, listening to

Hank or Waylon or George and

knowing that we are all part of the world's heartache, its loss and disappointment mapped out in the songs of

Hank and Waylon and George so

it was shortly after half four when I got into the car and drove to Keeva, the evening closing in and the distant hills beneath the clouds drawing near in the rain which began to fall, steady at first for the first couple of miles, but pelting down in great blue swathes by the time I arrived at the bridge, the clock in the dash telling me that it was ten to five, twenty minutes past knocking-off time and sure enough the men had tidied up and gone home, which was a good thing as I preferred to inspect the site on my own, so I pulled over to the side of the road, just outside the bollards and caution tape that cordoned off the bridge site and rolled down the window to have a look as it was now too wet to step out and walk around, the rain drumming down on the roof of the car and the wipers swinging across the windscreen, but I could see enough to know that the whole project was back on track as Keville had promised, with the concrete slabs now set in place, laid across the span between the piers, resting on the steel beams, all the structural work completed so that if the weather held, it would take less than two weeks to finish it properly, pave and face it and surface the approach roads from both sides, two weeks all going well, the whole thing completed for the bank holiday weekend and Halloran and Lavelle happy and not ringing me up and annoying my hole and just as I was thinking this

I saw a shape coming towards me through the rain, a yellow blur at first across the windscreen before it tightened into a man in oilskins and wellingtons with the rain hopping off him, the last thing I wanted to see at that time of day but nevertheless, I wound down the window and he put his hand on the roof and leaned in with the raw face of a man used to being out in all sorts of weather, now looming in the window towards me to say

that's wet

that is wet

it had to come sometime

what has you out in it

I saw the car, I knew it was you

you don't miss a thing

no, not a thing

the forecast isn't great, there'll be no let-up till the middle of next week

isn't that a bastard he says, with the rain still running off him

so long as we get it now and not in summertime

it's a bit early to say that

I suppose

and with that my patience was at an end so I thought it was time to cut to the chase and put it up to him

you didn't come over here in this rain to talk to me about the weather

you noticed that

I'd notice less

I'll bet

what's on your mind

I was thinking

what were you thinking

I was just thinking that you nearly have the bridge finished, another week or two and you'll be out of it and

it's going well all right, what's your interest in it

I was just thinking that all that stone from the old bridge, you're going to have to dump it somewhere

I suppose

well, it would save you time and money if you were to tip it there in the bottom of that field, it's only across from the site and you could just pull in and leave it inside the gate and

I knew straight away what was on his mind, cut granite at one-fifty a ton, a couple of loads of it tipped into his field would be a tidy asset and

you'd make sure it wouldn't go to waste

I was only thinking like

you were

and him grinning in at me now, knowing full well that his offer was indeed to our advantage but that it would also be a considerable boost to himself, fifty to sixty tons of cut granite tipped into his field so that he could be working away with it however he pleased or sell it on at a tidy profit, both of us knowing that it would be a lot cheaper to tip it on his land less than fifty yards from where it now lay, instead of loading it up and hauling it the twenty miles to the landfill site the far side of Castlebar, but still, I was not willing to give in, something about his naked opportunism had riled me, some part of me bristling so that I knew straight off that I would not relent today, not this evening at any rate, which was not to say that I wouldn't sometime in the future because I knew that what he'd said made sense, but even still, this was one of the things that sickened me about this job – every cunt wanting something – and even if I could make the whole thing legitimately difficult for him, citing all sorts of insurance clauses about vehicles under public contract entering on private land and all those by-laws covering fly dumping, I just finished up saying

leave it with me, I'll see what I can do

sound he said, and smacked the roof of the car as if the matter was settled

how is your neighbour, I didn't spot him when I pulled up

Thomas

Thomas, the curtains were drawn

you wouldn't know with that man, he mightn't have surfaced yet, he keeps his own hours

is he still dancing

he is, he'll be in Digger Jay's tonight

no sign of him bringing a woman into the house

no

he'll do nothing foolish, the same Thomas

you can be sure of that, I'll let you go

we'll talk again

sound

mind yourself

and he headed off, not a bother on him, the rain still pissing down as he faded away in the rearview mirror, the yellow oilskin becoming a smudge of light as I turned the car and headed back the way I'd come, the road taking me past his house, which was all cluttered up outside with sand and blocks, and a mixer with a shovel leaning against it and I saw that he was putting an extension onto the left gable, a substantial addition which was already tiled and plastered, the scaffolding still up and the blue tape on the window frames while off to one side a large pile of topsoil showed where he had dug into the slope behind the house to find space for the extension so that now there was a low, sheer-faced ledge where the slope ended sharply and it was easy now to see what he planned to do with the stone – he'd use it to face off that bit of a ledge so that the soil wouldn't subside onto the house if it took water, the heavy stone would buttress the slope all the way around the back of the house and whatever was left over could be used to landscape the garden that fell away from the front to the road and I could see what was in his head now, how

he would drive into the field with the transport box and bring the stone around the back of the house where he'd work away on it during the dry months of the summer, tapping and dressing and pointing it, building it up layer by layer so that if everything ran in his favour he would have the whole thing done before the weather turned at the back end, the wall capped and pointed and a couple of grand saved into the bargain, the whole project so clear in my mind that

even if I half admired the kind of opportunism which had

brought him out into the rain to meet me I saw there was something mean in it also, that small mentality which enabled small minds to thrive on such opportunities or to spot them in the first place, something in the whole thing which made me resentful so that now

I was pissed off with the whole fucking thing

him and his extension and the granite and the whole fucking lot, this shite swilling through my head, as if there wasn't enough there already and

these were my thoughts

driving home that evening, not bothering to turn the radio on, just listening to the road as it sped by under the wheels with the rain rolling away now and the evening opening out into bright sunshine for the hour of daylight that remained, so that coming round the bend at Belclare the road turned into the full glare of the sun going down over Clew Bay, a silver streak over the sea from the horizon, nearly blinding me behind the wheel so that I had to pull down the visor and coming around by the Deerpark the side of Croagh Patrick was so clearly present, so close, it appeared as if I could put my hand out to touch it, all the glad sights of a spring evening giving me the idea that Mairead and I might go for a walk together after we had something to eat, which

we did, pulled on light jackets and set off as night was beginning to close in, starting off along the main road and then skirting the village by the sea path across the Black Hill, the breeze crisp on our faces and as we walked Mairead told me about a documentary she had watched recently, telling me

there's a nomadic tribe in Mongolia who cross the Gobi desert, herding their goats and sheep and horses, and pitching their yurts on the outskirts of towns and cities to trade with the settled communities, nothing odd in any of that but, what was really interesting, was that at the centre of the tribe there was a holy-woman or witch-doctor who had the usual tasks of healing and invoking the gods, all the shamanic and medicinal duties, a vocation that had come down to her through the family, the line of apostolic succession, which meant that she had this other function also of keeping the tribe's world in balance and harmony by living her life backwards and

how do you mean backwards

I mean she walks backwards and talks backwards and rides her horse backwards, she gets up in the middle of the night to eat her dinner and she goes to bed when everyone around her is beginning their day and

why would she do that

this is fascinating – it's their belief that if everyone is walking and talking and doing things in the same direction then there is real danger that the whole world will tip over, so one person is needed to work the opposite way to keep the world balanced and

that makes sense, it's basic engineering, any load bearing structure will topple over if it doesn't have balancing counterweight, cranes will topple over if they are not properly weighted

I don't think they understood it as engineering

probably not, but that's what it is, some mechanisms have to be counter-geared to keep them tensioned

all I could think of was that only a woman would get a job like that

maybe only a woman could do a job like that, one weighty and contrary soul to keep the world in balance

I thought of Darragh when I saw it, it's just the sort of thing he'd be good on

yes, he'd make hay with that all right, he might even see himself in that role already, the way he goes on

you're too hard on him

he's hard on me as well as

we came in the Westport road under the street lighting, about five miles in all so that by the time we got home it was well dark and I was pleased there was no twinge in my heel, that pain coming and going with a mind of its own, so I took a mug of tea into the office where a quick check told me that Darragh was online so I dialled him and he came on after a moment, his bushy head filling the screen, telling me after saying hello, that

I saw the photos

what photos

the photos from the exhibition, she had them up on her Facebook page whose Facebook page

Agnes the Unhinged, the Abbess of the Abyss, Anagnorisis

Darragh, that kind of name-calling is very wearing –

he held up an apologetic hand

no disrespect meant, Dad, just a bit of sibling sparring, all I'm saying is it seemed like a pretty exciting evening, Agnes standing there like a pale accuser decrying the whole world, it must have been strong stuff

it was different, that's for sure

I'm not surprised you were upset

how did you know I was upset

Agnes emailed me a full account of the whole thing, it seemed like a real occasion

yes it was, lots of people there and they seemed to be enthusiastic about her work

which was a far cry from the usual oil-on-canvas

yes

a bit of a shock

you could say that

her account was very vivid, a great colour piece – if the visual arts thing doesn't work out she has a bright future as a writer

which was exactly the kind of threat Agnes held over Darragh, the likelihood that her dogged abilities would outshine his real but fragile talents and that one day he would find himself conclusively shamed by her willingness to apply herself and wring the most from her lesser gifts, because while his own sporadic commitment to his studies would always enable him to get by without ever fully achieving what he was well capable of, too often he shielded himself from Agnes's threat behind an antic persona of sniggering and scoffing, so frequently lapsing into a language that went completely over my head that it was easy to get the impression he was speaking from a different realm of understanding altogether, a credible enough idea in the present circumstances since he was now talking from the opposite side of the world, his voice burred as if the words had travelled through some warping disturbance in the ether between us which was pushing them out of shape, not that it got in the way of those things we discussed, our conversation skimming through sport, politics and local gossip, those things we felt sure of – Hatton would not go the distance with Pacquiao, not at ten stone, and Mayo would find it hard to get out of Pearse Stadium with a win this summer – and those things we felt unsure of – would Kenny's leadership of the opposition hold till the next general election, since it seemed likely he would have his work cut out defending no-confidence motions in the months ahead, twenty minutes talking as two men putting the world to rights before he asked

are you still watching *Battlestar Galactica*

yes, it's halfway through the third season, are you keeping up with it

no, getting to a telly is a bit haphazard here and I haven't got around to streaming it – are you taping it

I think so, it's on the box somewhere if someone hasn't deleted it

great, I'll look forward to watching that when I get back and how's Mam, did she have a good time at the exhibition

Mam's fine and she had a great time, herself and Agnes, we would have stayed up the night but both of us had work the following morning so the three of us went for a meal after the opening and then drove home, it was after midnight when we got back – she's lying down now, taking a rest after all the excitement and

there's nothing wrong with her

no, she's just a bit tired after the whole thing, it was quite stressful

give her my love

ok, will do, take care of yourself

bye

bye

and I watched the screen cloud to a fizzy interference as it shut down, leaving the room to dark silence and a burnt feeling behind my eyes as if the light from the monitor had scalded them to the core, the kind of feeling you imagine you would have just before the world goes up in flames, some refined corrosion eating away at the rods and cones, collapsing their internal structure before they slope out of their sockets and run down your cheekbones, leaving you standing hollow-eyed in the middle of some desolation with the wind whistling through your skull, just before the world collapses

mountains, rivers and lakes

acres, roods and perches

into oblivion, drawn down into that fissure in creation where everything is consumed in the raging tides and swells of non-being, the physical world gone down in flames

mountains, rivers and lakes

and pulling with it also all those human rhythms that bind us together and draw the world into a community, those daily

rites, rhythms and rituals

upholding the world like solar bones, that rarefied amalgam of time and light whose extension through every minute of the day is visible from the moment I get up in the morning and stand at the kitchen window with a mug of tea in my hand, watching the first cars of the day passing on the road, every one of them known to me

name, number-plate and destinations

one after another, beginning at half seven with

Frances Dugan in the green Mégane, off to her job as a receptionist in the Clew Bay Hotel – I went to school with her husband Philip who is about to start chemo – and

Sarah Moran going in the opposite direction to begin her eight o'clock shift in Allergan and

Mark Ruddy in an '07 Pajero returning from the night shift in Baxter and

the school bus going back to collect the kids from the furthest edge of the parish and

Máirtín Dubh in the green post van, followed by

Shamie Moran in the milk lorry, seven thousand litres of milk sloshing around in the tank behind his head with

Jimmy Lyons behind him in his blue Passat – in half an hour he will throw open the gates of the builder's yard on the Kilgeever road, so that

five mornings a week I watch these early starters from the kitchen window with a mug of tea in my hand and when I see Jimmy's Passat turn left onto the main road I know that it's nearly half seven and that I had better get a move on if I'm going to make it to work on time, knowing also that Mairead has still got at least forty minutes in bed yet, a thought which always pleased me, as if those minutes were my gift to her each morning, a thought which often recalls me to

the early years of our marriage when Darragh and Agnes were very young and I would wake and get ready for work while the three of them were still fast asleep in a house that had no sound but myself going about the first tasks of the day – washing, shaving, dressing, setting the table for their breakfast, mugs and bowls, pulling on my boots and jacket – the peace and quiet of early morning making it my favourite part of the day, Mairead and the children asleep, breathing in their separate rooms, a gentle flowing current which brought the house alive even in the darkest winter mornings when

I was sometimes filled with a marvellous sense of how important and serious it was as a father and husband to be up and about so early, with work to go to and a family to provide for, to have such responsibilities, grabbing my keys and jacket and out the door with Mairead and the kids still asleep in their beds, off to work to make a future for them, a glorious undertaking which I took so seriously then, sometimes feeling that I, alone in the world, was tasked with such a job which in one sense was the truth as I alone had the job of caring for my particular family, but which of course was the most banal thing in the whole world as there were millions of men every-where who, at precisely the same time, were doing the same thing, getting up and going out to work, these morning rhythms which start the day and hold all our smaller rituals in its embrace as when now, the children gone and Mairead and myself alone here in this house we

come home from work and sit together at this table to eat while listening to the news on Midwest Radio, the local news followed by the death notices for the area, telling us that the death has occurred

in the family home

or after a long illness

or after a short illness

or suddenly

or in England

or peacefully at their home in

all the innumerable ways and places in which anyone can die

none less fatal than the other

man, woman or child

taking leave of this world how ever we do, one way of dying no less effective than the next, the names of the deceased rolling by with the announcer telling us that all donations should be sent to Our Lady's Hospice Ballina and house private, which is Mairead's cue to switch the radio off before an advert for some

furniture sale in Swinford or

night club in Crossmolina

or Peter Duffy, Tool and Scaffolding Hire comes on and

this is one of our rituals

Mairead and I, sitting at the table and tuning into these death notices, joining that community of listeners who are doing the same thing, half the county sitting at their kitchen tables with mugs of tea in their hands and their ears bent to hear who has died or gone with the majority as my father used to say, wondering will the list of names throw up someone we know, a name to take us by surprise, a name which shocks us or a name to sadden us, someone young or someone old, someone who has died suddenly or someone who has finally succumbed after a long illness, someone we met only last week, someone we hadn't met in a long time

someone

who's crossed our lives in one of the innumerable ways in which we come together from time to time with never any suspicion that this may be the last time we meet or speak or do some favour for each other and

it was surely something of this sort my father honoured when-ever he would sit down to listen to these same death notices, a habit which for years filled me with impatience because there seemed no purpose to it when, at five o'clock, he would stop in the middle of whatever he was doing and turn up the volume on the radio to listen to the roll call of the dead, name after name in alphabetical order until the last one had sounded and the announcement tailed off with the assurance that

Midwest Radio would like to extend their sympathies to the families and loved ones of the dead and

only then would he resume whatever it was he had been doing, his duty done, honour and respect given to the last mention of lives gone forever and if initially I was impatient with what appeared to be a needless interruption and bristled to be rid of it, with the passing years and without ever knowing quite how it had happened, I too began to stop whatever I was doing to listen with the same attentiveness as my father and it was only after a while I realised it was not merely the dead I was honouring but that I had willingly taken my place among all those other people in the parish who were doing exactly the same thing, sitting in their kitchens and listening to that rolling litany of names tapering out to infinity since

death and funerals was one of those topics my father and mother enjoyed sparring over in their later years, all the more so if they thought they could scandalise their grandchildren with a dose of irreverence and black humour, their life together now a complex two-hander, with a lot of give and take and

one time my father was teasing Onnie about her death, telling her that if she was going to die before him he hoped it would be during the winter months because if it happened in any other season of the year he would have no time to bury her, he was a busy man – cattle and hay and turf and everything else – he wouldn't have time to arrange a funeral for her, the best he could do would be to light a fire in the bottom of a tar-barrel, that would be the best he could do, stuff her into it at the gable of the house and Onnie listening to all this, smiling over at him, saying

I don't mind what you do with me, when I'm dead I'm dead and the dead don't care so

you'd want to be checking your rosaries now and saying your prayers because time is

I'm not afraid to die, she countered, I've made my peace with God so I have no fear of meeting him and

Darragh's face knitted into an expression of complex surprise, but he held off on any comment till we were driving home that evening, shaking his head to underline his bewilderment when he wondered aloud

what sort of a life would you need to have lived in order to be able to say something like that without sounding foolish or arrogant

I doubt Onnie ever gave much thought to the sort of life she lived, she just lived it, got on with it and now

Darragh's voice broke up with a dry laugh

I can see her now, standing before God on the floor of heaven, saying, is that all you got bitch, is that your best shot

you think she'd adopt that tone

she can adopt any tone she likes, that's the gist of what she is going to say, she is going to kick ass, laugh judge and jury out of his own court

I hope their meeting won't be that combative

that's what God hopes also but He won't know what hit him, she'll flatten Him and then moonwalk out of there with the keys of the kingdom in her blue housecoat

that would be worth seeing, granny moonwalking with her stick

no, come the resurrection Onnie will be restored to the full of her health, throwing away her stick will be part of the deal, she'll probably be reborn as an action movie heroine, telling Him you can kiss my arse, her parting words and

even if Darragh's admiration was delivered in a language I could hardly understand, his grasp of my mother's proud humility and her fearless assessment of her own life was hopefully a lesson of some kind to him, certainly it had made some sort of impression as his face was still fixed in such an expression of wonderment when he got home that Mairead took a look at him as he passed through the kitchen, asking

what happened to that lad and

it was only when I opened my mouth to explain that I had any clear idea myself of what had come to pass, telling her that

Darragh was shown that there are more things in heaven and earth than he has dreamt of, Onnie broadened his mind for him, she broadened mine as well so she did

she was in one of her philosophical moods

she was a lot more plain-spoken than that, she gave him something to chew on for the rest of his days

good god, all that in one short visit

all that in two sentences with

the Angelus bell still ringing in my ear

the last reverb of its tolling vibrating within me a full twenty
minutes after it sounded and

why these bleak thoughts today, the whole world in shadow,
everything undercut and suspended in its own delirium, the light
superimposed on itself so that all things are out of synch and kilter,
things as themselves but slightly different from themselves also,
every edge and outline blurred or warped and each passing moment
belated, lagging a single beat behind its proper measure, the here-
and-now beside itself, slightly off by a degree as in

a kind of waking dream in which all things come adrift in their
own anxiety so that sitting here now fills me with

a crying sense of loneliness for my family – Mairead, Darragh
and Agnes – their absence sweeping through me like ashes

sitting here at the table and

something in me would be soothed now if, at this moment,
Mairead or one of the kids were to walk through the door and smile
or say hello to me, something in me would be calmed by this, a
word or a smile or a glance from my wife or children, to find myself
in their gaze and know that I was beheld then, this would be something to believe in, another of those articles of faith that seem so
important today, a look or a word, enough to hang a whole life on,
something to believe in during

these grey days after Samhain when the souls of the dead are
bailed from purgatory for a while by the prayers of the faithful so
that they can return to their homes and

the light is awash with ghouls and ghosts and the mearing
between this world and the next is so blurred we might easily find
ourselves standing shoulder to shoulder with the dead, the world
fuller than at any other time of the year, as if some sort of spiritual
sediment had been stirred up and things set adrift which properly lie
at rest, the light swarming with those unquiet souls whose tormented

drift through these sunlit hours we might sense out of the corner of our eye or on the margins of our consciousness where

you need to have faith in these things, a willingness to believe and elaborate on them so that

it always gladdened me to find that the part of me that was always a true believer has not died, that part of me Mairead calls the altar boy and who, after all these years, is still alive within me and clutching his catechism, still holding to the truths which were laid out in its pages

who made the world

God made the world

and who is God

God is our father in heaven

and so on and so on

to infinity

the whole world built up from first principles, towering and rigid as any structural engineer might wish, each line following necessarily from the previous one to link heaven and earth step by step, from the first grain of the first moment to the last waning scintilla of light in which everything is engulfed in darkness, the engineer's dream of structured ascent and stability bolted into every line of its fifty pages, so carefully laid out that any attentive reading of it should enable a man to find his place with some certainty in the broadest reaches of the world, a tower of prayer to span heaven and earth and something which a part of me has never grown out of or developed beyond

the altar boy with his catechism

instead of

the man of faith I tried to become at one time

that difficult, comic interlude in my life, which I spoke of

four or five years ago – hard to recall the exact context in which the subject arose or why I chose to bring it up, but it was probably something Darragh said that panicked me into revealing it, the subject welling up inside me before it came blurting out one evening when we were alone in the sitting room, my two years in the seminary sounding incredible in the father-son intimacy of the moment – incredible in any circumstance – and being seized upon with a clinching spasm of fear when I saw the shock immobilise Darragh's face for an instant as a long frozen moment stalled between us before he paled further and tipped sideways on the couch like a large doll, hooting and guffawing with genuine laughter for a full minute before he could pull himself up and give the news a more considered reaction, finally saying

it makes sense though, that explains a lot

does it

yes, you're an engineer, maths and physics and suchlike, but it was always a bit of a mystery where all your references came from, all the poetry and philosophy that overtakes you from time to time, but now I know, it was all part of the old ecclesial schooling, am I right

yes, the great books were part of the training

and you had two full years of that

yes

so what caused you to throw it up, was it the dark night of the soul, Christ no longer visible and –

it would be nice to think it was something that heroic, that my soul had been put to the test, but it wasn't like that, it was more a gradual leaking away of conviction

maybe it was a mother's vocation, that's why it didn't stick

no, it wasn't a mother's vocation, it was all my own doing

and were you a pious child, your little face always turned to the heavens

I was an altar boy

every rural lad was an altar boy, surpliced and soutaned and swinging a thurible, it didn't always grow to a vocation

true – but with me there was an element of astonishment, a sense of participating in something grand and mysterious and I wanted a deeper part of it and that took me to Maynooth

where God finally showed Himself to you but gave you the two fingers instead of the guiding hand

it was more of a voice telling me to cop myself on

you were only codding yourself

something like that

he had great patience, Agnes – did you know this

know what

Agnes crossed the room, flinging herself in a tired heap into an armchair where she picked up a magazine and began to flick through it

that dad was nearly a priest

what

Dad – Fr Marcus Conway, a man of the cloth, a sky pilot

no way

yes way – which order did you sign up to, was it one of the preaching or teaching ones

neither, it was just to be an ordinary parish priest

that's a pity, I could well imagine you in one of the preaching orders, a man who laid down the party line – possibly the Dominicans, you'd be good banging on with the *Malleus Maleficarum* and

though they were younger at the time both of them were always keen to display their wit and reading, the title for house brainbox still up for grabs back then as

it explains a lot though, Agnes said

so I'm told

something I could never understand – how a farmer's lad like you ended up with someone like Mam, more exactly how an engineer won the hand of a cultured girl like Mam

yeah, Darragh said, how does a stint in a seminary equip you to go about wooing a girl steeped in French existentialism –

that's my point, Agnes continued, ok, my theory is that God took pity on Dad – He foresaw that he was going to try it on with her, but He knew also that as things stood he didn't have a chance – she was way out of his league – so He lured him into a seminary to tool him up with poetry and theology and philosophy so that he wouldn't get steamrolled when he finally met her but

I don't buy that, Darragh replied, clearly irritated by the way Agnes had made such headway with the subject, irked at how quickly she had picked through its possibilities and

how would reading Aquinas and the church fathers make headway with Mam

even if that was all he ever read – which I'm sure it wasn't – it was still enough to enable him to fight his corner when he met a young woman who could quote Sartre and de Beauvoir, chapter and verse, in the original French

I don't remember our courtship being so gladiatorial

of course you don't, that's because God took you under His wing and tooled you up with *The Song of Songs* before turning you loose – all that time you thought you were in a seminary to get close to God, but in fact you were only training for the day when you'd meet her –

she's right, Dad, you had to be made worthy of her and that's how it was done, two years of schooling in the broad humanities so that you would be fit for her when you met and when your training was done, God absented himself from the scene, gave you the back of His hand and a shoe in the hole and

that's what happened, Darragh concluded his nose now well out of joint on account of Agnes's better read on the whole thing

that's my take on it, she concurred

and two years after you sign up, God shows you the door dressed up as a crisis of faith so you jump back over the wall, your head filled with all that good stuff for when you meet this educated girl who's travelled the world and who, if you don't play your cards right, will tell you to piss off in three different romance languages and

I was relieved my admission hadn't phased or embarrassed them, and the deft way they had made light of the whole thing gave me hope that there was something in the experience that would stand to them down the road, but it

was strange also to me that the conversation revealed nothing of the confusion and anguish I had experienced at the time, not to mention my foolishness on realising that a child's awe and trepidation would never evolve into a faith and that I had made a mistake that would cost me two years, a stretch of time which back then felt like an epoch but that now, from the distance of middle age, seems little more than a brief but gloomy interlude spent among the rooms and corridors of that seminary with its grottoed walls and parquet floors, one among a large drove of pale young men drawn from all over the country, some genuinely intent but more, like myself, there in a mood of hopeful bafflement to bury myself in some stumbling quest for a god whose presence resolutely faded the harder I strove towards him and who did nothing to acknowledge my search, so that my faith petered out in time

ordinary time, festive seasons, days of obligation

a gradual leaking away of all conviction which now appears to have been mercifully rapid but which, at the time, manifested itself in length and breadth as a kind of ashen desert, which left me scalded in spirit, but merciful enough to leave unscathed that part of me which found something comic in my quest so that I stood blasted and sore but laughing at myself in a wasteland that stretched through the parquet corridors of the seminary, where the walls echoed with my own laughter –

what the hell was I thinking of

and along which there was nether a single nook nor corner in which I could get away from myself and even if Agnes was correct – she was – and I did acquire enough reading to give me some chance with Mairead – a stiff dose of poetry, the geometric conceits of the metaphysicals always appealed to her sense of symmetry and balance – it would be quite some time before its worth became obvious, hidden as it was beneath a burning skin of shame so that when I returned to the home place after two years with neither dog-collar nor parchment – the spoiled priest slinking home – it weighed heavily on me that I may have brought some ignominy on myself or my family, but with nowhere else to go and nothing to do I did indeed return, where, after a few weeks

the offer of a job as a gardener with a pharmaceutical company came up, a firm that had just opened a facility in Westport – manufacturing solvent for the cleaning of contact lenses – and I spent a full year there with three other gardeners raking gravel and tending verges around the warehouse and laboratories, shaping those flower beds and rockeries that were their corporate pride and joy and for which they would win several awards after

I left to study civil engineering the following year for no reason other than my father pointing out to me at the time that the country was in such a bad state I might as well be in education for a few more years while things were as they were, either that or go to London or

America, which he advised against, pointing out that since I had no trade or qualification

I would probably end up labouring on the pick and shovel and he did not want that for me, no he did not, so it was better to work out the rest of the year as a gardener which was good honest labour with enough fresh air in it to clear my head and sort myself out so that I could go back to study in the autumn because, as he put it

there's no use staying in this place, the few head of cattle and the bit of land, it's too small to make a living on but it's big enough for a man to go around codding himself that he's busy and has things to do, slobbering with buckets and calves and feeding, but in the end that's all you'd be doing, codding yourself, so my advice is to get an education, see a bit of the world, this place will always be here and

my father's voice with its neat way of invoking the world as a properly ordered and coherent place in which a man could find his way or take his bearings from certain signs and markers if he only did not allow his vision to become cluttered up with nonsense or things to assume outsize importance in his life, his way of

fixing an accurate scale and placing of himself in this world as

he would show me time and again, most memorably, later in his life when his work as a farmer and fisherman was well behind him, that Sunday afternoon when we went out on the bay for a trip, Joe Needham and ourselves, just the three of us taking the trawler for a quick run up to Clare Island where Joe had set pots for crabs and lobsters and

it was a beautiful summer's afternoon when we set out, a high, clear sky over us so that you could see the whole of the bay in every direction, from Westport Quay in the east, out to the horizon beyond Turk and Clare as we passed back the coast, keeping close to the shore so that the sea opened out to its full reach ahead of us and we could see across to Mulranny which, in the afternoon heat, was a blur, a distant shadow of coastline where sky and sea came together and once again the whole expanse of this blue day recalled my childhood conviction that there was nothing greater than the sea, no other width or breadth which could surpass or encompass it because the older I got and the more I had advanced in my work as an engineer the more certain I had become that

out there, on the blue bay

was where my sense of scale and ratio was established during my childhood, specifically during those summer months when my father and I would set off from Carramore Pier in his small currach to set pots for crab and lobster along the shoreline, a dozen pots stacked in the bows of the currach which we would string out beyond the low-water mark, pink and blue buoys riding the swell behind us as we drifted out deeper on the tide, and it was most likely during these lull periods when I would sit in the back of the currach trailing lines for mackerel or pollock and watching the land recede into the distance that I came to a full sense of the world in its broadest span, the sky overhead and the calm surface of the sea spreading out all around us while my father sat smoking in the middle of the boat with his boots pushed out in front of him, letting the currach drift on the tide, happy as I could imagine any man to be

in the swelling immensity of the bay, with the lines cutting the surface of the water behind and it must have been one such mood he woke from one day to tell me the story of how, when he was a child himself

a massive ship came into Clew Bay, a ship from god-knows-where with no recognisable flags or markings on it, a huge ship which bow-to-stern was over a mile long and with four massive funnels on it coughing up big balls of black deatach and armed with cannon and other artillery along its sides when it anchored in the middle of the bay for a full day before it fired two shells onto the mainland, whether as warning or salute no one could say, but one of them destroyed a cart-house in Durless and it was never known where the second one landed or if it did land because for all he knew it might still be orbiting the earth or still flying off into space fifty years later, after which the ship unloaded enough raw timber onto boats from Westport Quay to roof seventy houses, but only after it had been cut into workable lengths – a big job in itself as this timber was so dense and close-grained it destroyed every saw blade that was set to it, shearing teeth and buckling so many, one after another, that Kelly's timber yard had to send to Sheffield for specially tempered blades before the job could be done, the heavy balks of timber now running smoothly through the bandsaw, but any man who ever worked on the cutting of that timber never had the full of his health afterwards because there was nothing but blue dust out of it, which lodged in their lungs and sent several of them to early graves, five or six men with young families left behind them, drifting away into oblivion the same way the ship itself left the bay, turning on its own central axis with its massive diesel engines churning and pushing it out into the Atlantic beyond whence it came and to where it returned and

my father told me that story one day in one of those quiet moments when we were drifting from shore on a neap tide and the box in the bottom of the boat was filled with mackerel and of course it was all nonsense

pure fucking nonsense

but there's never been a time since, with a clear sky overhead, that I don't look out on the bay without the image of that ghost ship with all its timber and artillery floating across my vision and a part of me wondering to what purpose my father told me that story, what did he think I might gain from it, how was my world enriched by knowing it and if, with the passing of years, I would come to know that it was just one among a myriad number of such stories he had to tell when the mood took him, it was also of a piece with the man himself because even as a ten-year-old I knew there was something storied about himself also when

at the age of sixteen, he had won a five-mile currach race along this very coastline, beating older and hardier oarsmen by a distance which passed into local myth in a race that proved him to be not just a better oarsman but also a better seaman, with wisdom and courage enough at sixteen to set aside the conventional wisdom of taking a wide sweep around the shoreline so as to avoid the onshore currents which would pull across the boat and push it onto the rocks, choosing instead a line tighter to the land which was more dangerous but sheltered from the offshore winds which he rowed under, sitting on the middle beam and pulling from his shoulders as his father had advised till, fifty minutes after leaving Roonagh he came into sight from Old Head Pier rounding the Priest's Lep with his two hands on fire at the oars and blood seeping up between his fingers when he ran his boat up on the slipway and near tore the bottom out of her, far gone now in a delirium of pain and fatigue, but so far ahead of the following boats that he had time to drink a jug of milk and rinse his shirt out in the tide before the second boat had come ashore and

if, at ten years of age, I had no real sense of how difficult that race had been, alone out there with nothing but your two arms and blank determination to keep pointing the bow of the currach in the right direction, it was easy to imagine the flooding relief of a brutally extended effort finally coming to a close as he rounded the point a full five minutes before anyone else would come into view and it says something about my relationship with him that it was the way he wore it so absently that impressed me rather than the achievement itself, because he never once mentioned it to me in all the time we spent together, so that even after I did hear about it from men who, in old age still remembered it with wonderment, I never asked him about it, as it seemed to me his silence on the subject only added to its grandeur and I did not want to take from it in any way with questions so that

years later, when his days as an oarsman were behind him but there was as yet no sign of the madness that would overtake him at the end, we took that Sunday trip in the trawler up towards Clare Island and he stood in the wheelhouse with Joe Needham who showed him all the instruments and the navigating equipment and it was no surprise that he took a special interest in the plotter and how it mapped out the rise and fall of the seabed beneath the keel and I could tell, just by the way he examined it that he could not let this go

could he fuck

because he saw in this new instrument a challenge to the triangulating system he had used to navigate by, the old method by which three landmarks were aligned from sea so as to position the boat over those raised parts of the sea floor where crabs and lobster fed and I wondered why, at this age of his life, when he was now an old man and his work as a fisherman was behind him, he could not

ignore this challenge and let it pass, because we both knew there
was a lot more at stake than the accuracy of a piece of folk wisdom
or an antiquated system of navigation but I knew by looking at him
that he could not let it go

he just couldn't fucking do it so that

twenty minutes out from land, on a heading straight for Clare
Island, he calculated that we would soon be over 'The Maids', a
sudden rock shelf visible only at very low tide, a feeding ground
on which crabs and lobsters thrived, and he stood at the stern of
the boat looking back towards land because the old way of finding
this particular marker was to head straight out from the bottom of
Kerrigan's land and bring the spire of the Protestant church in the
north out with you till Matthew Ryan's hayshed in the south came
into view around the end of the headland and with these three
markers drawn into alignment you should be over 'The Maids' as I
knew them myself and still know them, having heard of them since
childhood but not till now, when they were being put to the test,
had I ever wondered how much faith should be put in this old way
of finding them because while part of me had a real appreciation of
such inherited wisdom another part of me was never sure just how
wise it was to invest so much in it but now

my anxiety in all this was only a small wager – this old technique
was not something I ever had to live by, unlike my father who now,
at a time in his life when he could have passed up the challenge
with honour, still found it necessary to test what he knew and had
lived his own life by so that now, with him standing at the back of
the boat and scanning the coast, my heart was in my mouth because
there was no knowing how he'd react if his old system was at variance
with the sonar and my sense of what was at issue was so clear to me
it reached down into my very soul because, what really hung in the
balance was the possibility that a good man, through no fault of his
own, but by way of received wisdom and immemorial faith, may have
lived an important part of

his life warped in error and foolishness, misguided over the
seas and if that was now shown to be the case then might not
that same foolishness have been handed down to me some way or

other – what's bred in the dog coming out in the pup – and been responsible for some of the misdirections of my own life so

now

he shouted from the stern

we should be over them now

and sure enough, standing in the wheel house, I saw the graph rising across the screen, the ocean floor coming up to meet the keel in a crest of shallow peaks, my soul rising with it, a gladness which must have been contagious because Joe Needham was chuckling and slapping me on the back as if I were responsible for the happy outcome, both of us relieved – thank fuck for that – and I went out to the old man and confirmed that yes, we had hit the marker and he contented himself with a nod, pointing out to me the relative positions of the church and the hayshed, markers which were ten miles apart in a straight line which traversed the parish west to east, a meridian known only to a handful of fishermen along this coastline and

that summer Sunday, with its blue sky arched down to the horizon beyond Clare Island my father showed me how he had so precisely fixed and located himself within the world's widest shores, an incident I would recall often not because of what he had shown me but because I, with all my schooling and instruments, could never lay claim to such an accurate sense of myself in anything whatsoever, not even as

an engineer, whose life and works

concerned itself with scale and accuracy, mapping and surveying so that the grid of reason and progress could be laid across the earth, gathering its wildness into towns and villages by way of bridges and roads and water schemes and power lines – all the horizontal utilities that drew the world into settlements and community – this was my life, an engineer's life, which, even if governed by calculations, was never one in which I was so accurately placed as my father, not then and not now either as I had thought that by now I would be carrying myself with more certainty – some part of me believing that with wife, work and family a wisdom of sorts would surely have come also and brought certain assurances or clarities but instead it seemed that all my circumstances had gathered to a point where they were unwilling to present themselves as a clear account, but settled instead into a giddy series of doubts, an unstable lattice of questions so far withholding any promise I might inherit

my father's ability to comprehend the whole picture across all those contours and cycles in which our lives were grounded – family, farming and fishing and most memorable of all, politics, as he would show me in the run-up to the 1977 general election, that counter historical upheaval which was not only a watershed in the nation's fortunes but which marked also my own political blooding as well over

thirty years ago now, hard to believe, and certainly not anything so predictable that morning I went out to start milking shortly after seven o'clock, a beautiful May morning with a cold mist rising off the land to meet a low sun as I came around the side of the barn with a galvanised bucket in my hand to see all the telegraph poles along the roadside hung with election posters that had gone up overnight, the face of a new candidate staring down at me from within a green and gold border, high up on every pole, this face echoing away into the mist back as far as the crossroads and

I, standing there in the door of the cowshed with the bucket in my hand, was not to know that the way this candidate's face paled off into the dawn was this moment's way of telling me that at some time in the future I could look back and mark this morning as the moment in my life when I came to political consciousness, having turned eighteen earlier that year and my father having made sure he'd contacted the local Peace Commissioner to enter my name on the electoral register putting me among that large swathe of young people who would be voting for the first time in this election and who were judged by commentators to be an unpredictable element in its outcome so that

I, with a keen sense of my involvement in this historic moment and an anxious interest to measure my political wit in these charged circumstances persuaded my father to sit down with a constituency map of the country and, holding as many variables in mind as possible – all the likely swings and divisions of the electoral system – we would separately try to prophesy the result, going through the constituencies one by one and marking them as we thought they would fall when the votes were counted, all the gains and losses of an electoral campaign, and when the forty-two constituencies were complete I found that my prediction differed little from the current political wisdom, which foresaw the coalition government being returned with a loss of two or three seats at most across the whole country, a solid outcome that would see the nation returned to the sullen rule of the law and order party, an outcome which gratified me in one sense as I was happy to find my own result chiming with the majority of the media's political analysis but which also had a disappointing lack of drama about it as well, a quality squarely in keeping with the personality of the outgoing government – steady and dogged and fixated on questions of security – but an outcome totally at odds with my father's analysis which

when he pushed his paper across the table towards me, showed that he had weighed the opposition with a tidal majority of twenty-two seats, such an outlandish result and margin that, for a moment, I thought he had not taken the exercise seriously but had merely struck through the constituencies carelessly to have done with it and come up with this result which I was careful to recheck no fewer than three times but which, how ever way I did it, still refused to yield little of its ridiculous margin except one or two seats either way, no serious adjustment no matter how it was looked at it, twenty seats or thereabouts, an epic margin which, in the unlikely event of its fulfilment, would reconfigure the whole political horizon into the long-term future, but so utterly fantastical and beyond all likeli-hood that it was not made any more probable by my father getting up from the table without a word of explanation except to tap his finger in the centre of the map and say

big changes, mark my words

something of which he might have been referring to a few days later when a car pulled up at the gate and three men in suits and with party rosettes in their lapels came across the gravel towards us, two local men whose party affiliations we knew well and who were now leading the new party hopeful – the same candidate whose face I had seen in the morning mist and who now, in the flesh, presented himself as a tall man, well over six feet in a pinstripe suit, a man with an imperious air and an unusually long neck, a man who, even if he had not yet acquired the famous habit of speaking of himself in the third person had already about him an air of providential certainty, such was his bearing and his innate ability to look down on the world from a height as

the two men introduced him and he shook both our hands and asked me my name, correctly guessing that this would be my first time voting as he handed me a leaflet, this man with the side parting in his hair, listening while his canvassers gave a brief resume of his stellar career as a county councillor, ticking off all those local achievements which could be credited to his name – road surfacing, the new health dispensary, the extension to the local national school and the water filtering plant – some of the facilities he had agitated for and been present at the opening of – a broad swathe of achievement in local government which was all well and good they conceded, but it was now time for him to step up to national level where the power and influence resided, something which of course could only be of benefit to this western part of the constituency because, as was well known, it was ten years, more even, twelve, since this part of the county had a Dáil representative and it was past time there was a strong voice from this area to vent local concerns so that any stroke at all after his name on the ballot paper would be welcome and

I stood with my father at the gable of the house, sifting these weighty issues and savouring a fine sense of importance that the nation's political process had come courting me and my vote, that it had taken the time to cross the country and shake my hand and make its case before me as it would any other man whose name was on the electoral register and who wielded the single transferrable vote and the idea that I was a citizen with consequential stake in these matters had such lasting effect upon me that, from that day to this, I have never failed to vote in any election and that while I may not hold to the one-true-political-faith anymore and I have, through the years, voted left, right and centre, each time doing so with some shade of that solemn meeting at the gable of the house renewing itself and prompting me, time and again that sense of consequence which attends putting a stroke on a ballot paper coming to me in the privacy of the voting booth as it did when

polling day came around on June 16th and our local national school was made over as a polling station with all its gates and the concrete wall surrounding the playground covered with the banners and posters of both parties, blue and green, jostling and overlapping each other on poles and pillars where men I knew since childhood stood with rosettes in their lapels handing out leaflets, pressing them into my hand on the off-chance that my decision might still be in the balance and could be swayed one way or the other by a leaflet at this last moment as I went into the middle room of the school and stood over the election officer, watching as he turned the pages of the register to find my name recorded there in blue ink before using a pen and ruler to strike through it with a single line as if obliterating it for all eternity before he handed me the stamped ballot paper with its list of candidates, which I took to the curtained cubicle at the other end of the classroom and ticked off my preferences, one, two and three in the boxes opposite the candidates' names before folding it once across the centre and dropping it through the slot in the black ballot box

the single transferrable vote

amen

the electoral instrument so ingrained in the political psyche that it must surely be possible now to isolate its neural correlate, a twitching cluster of synapses to which we could point as proof that democracy in all its shades and hues inheres in our very souls, land-slides and single-party rule, minority governments and coalitions, hung Dáils and all part of the very fabric of our being, after which

I stepped outside, my vote cast, my first say in the fate or destiny of my country and even if I did try to wear that responsibility lightly there was some urgency in the air which went beyond the result of a general election, something which later that night was not soothed by the nine o'clock news bulletin which confirmed that polling booths around the country were reporting an unusually high turnout, well over seventy per-cent which was impressive even for a country whose electorate were always keen to exercise their franchise as the whole thing became clear the following morning when, within a few hours of the first ballot boxes being opened, tallymen in counting centres throughout the country began reporting a massive swing to the opposition, a double-digit surge which looked likely to sweep them to single-party government with an unprecedented majority of nearly twenty seats, a majority near-as-dammit to my father's prophecy, which had me listening open-mouthed to the coverage throughout the day, when so many sitting TDs of the National Coalition began the inexorable process of losing their seats across the country, north, south, east and west, swept aside in both urban and rural constituencies by a tidal wave of electoral rejection which was now taking its full revenge on the government for four years of rising unemployment figures, inflation and a whole ream of other grievances so that

by midday a steady marching pace was set for the cull which swept through the country, dropping a slew of sitting deputies in marginal constituencies who went down to small percentage swings, back benchers and cabinet ministers toppling also in a steady rhythm, the government's officer class totally decimated by the time the leader of the National Coalition came on television later that night to concede defeat with his face fixed in an interminably long and silent opening shot before he finally spoke, his voice ragged with shock, telling the nation what it already knew, that the people had spoken so unequivocally it had left him with no option but to resign and hand over the reins of government to the opposition with all best wishes for the future, a resignation stiff with grace but that did not fully plumb the depths of the electoral disaster his coalition had undergone, so that we had to wait till early the next morning

before we got the full figures, the results of those late counts that had continued on after the close of broadcasting, the definitive nature of the victory clear and impressive now as commentators picked through the bones of the carnage, none of their reports quite catching the proper sense of epochal change which hung over the country that morning, something greater than a change of dispensation, something with a hidden force biding its time within those astonishing figures, reluctant to disclose itself just yet so that for a while commentators confined themselves to speaking in terms of a sweeping tidal movement that had carried the opposition party to power and while the image was clear, its broad application rolled over that grain of unease which grated at the heart of what had happened and around which some coherent anxieties would make themselves clear in the coming days as the drama of the opposition party being swept so triumphantly to power gave way

to a whole new set of considerations – what would this single party majority do now, this assembly with all its new faces – no less than seventeen new deputies – how would they comport themselves in terms of building a government, how would it fulfil the extravagant assurances of its election manifesto and to what degree would it fall short of all it had promised on the hustings, all of which to my mind, was slightly distant and beside the point as my own immediate attention dwelt on the fact that with my first vote I had positioned myself on the winning side, not merely in party terms, but also with regards the specific candidate I had voted for – the tall man who'd shook my hand and canvassed my vote at the gable of the house had topped the poll over the heads of the other oppositional candidate whom, early in the afternoon, he had vanquished on the third count, taking his seat with an eventual surplus of over a thousand votes to be bounced on the shoulders of party workers and volunteers who punched the air and sang

Take me Back to Mayo

rowdy well-wishers caught up in a dizzy moment of victory who would repeat the celebration a couple of weeks later when the 21st Dáil assembled and he, wearing a white suit and a polka-dot tie in the manner of a lounge singer, would be shouldered across the threshold of Leinster House by the same scrum of party workers, well wishers and volunteers, but not before he took a moment to remind the assembled media of the prophet who said

the Messiah would come out of the west

an incident which, when it found its way back across the country to our constituency would cause my father to mutter

there will be telling on this yet

which was true because over time it would come to light that a whole new generation of deputies would deduce from the spectacular nature of this victory with all its biblical swell and destructiveness, that the result was surely a temporal extension of God's will, certainly nothing but such transcendental endorsement could account for the hubris and greed that entered the political arena after that election, which as yet was

all in the future, and not yet capable of casting any shadow on the epochal victory itself nor on my own satisfaction at being on the winning side so that when, two weeks later, the victorious candidate headed an open-air rally in our town to thank the people for their work and support, I was among the large crowd gathered on the square that summer's evening, standing with my back to the chemist window and listening to the tall man tell us in a confident voice that he was going to Leinster House with a mission to redress those decades of neglect that had turned our region into a wasteland of unemployment and forced emigration with so many families torn apart for the want of viable income, and so it would be his mission above in Dáil Éireann to rectify this beginning with a campaign for improved infrastructure across the whole area, with roads and other services needing a total upgrade if the place was to prove attractive to any kind of inward investment – roads and sewage and phone lines – these would be his immediate focus and he would be second to no one in his efforts to see this mission through to completion because he knew full well that the people of West Mayo would be the judge of whether he was as good as his word because in five years' time he would have to stand before them once again and if he had reneged on any article of the pledge he was making here tonight to the good people of Louisburgh then he knew full well what to expect if he came looking for votes in this part of the constituency, he would be shown no mercy and would be told to step aside and make way for a better man, so this was the promise he was making here tonight and

so on and so forth

and

even if we heard that speech at five-year intervals – the staple address of every electoral cycle – or a close variant of it, from this same stage in the middle of the village, neither its bludgeoning repetition nor any other aspect of that dramatic election ever, in my eyes, took the shine off my father's feat in so accurately forecasting the outcome, his lighted intelligence running ahead of history to see something of the world before it was properly revealed, one of those moments when it was easy to suspect him of knowing his way with a sureness of step I would never possess, a sound judge of men among other things as his suspicion of the tall man would prove well-founded when, years later, several cross-party tribunals would make adverse findings against him on planning issues and party funding, his fortune made but his reputation ruined in the end, scandal and suspicion mounting so high around him that his very real political gifts and sensitivities were completely obscured, not that he gave a shite one way or another, he was well retired by then, his money made and his time taken up with a late vocation for landscape painting, sentimental watercolours depicting a Mayo landscape of rolling drumlins and single arch bridges, hedges and boreens, the same topography in which he had licensed so many gravel quarries and cement works and

can hardly breathe now, so humid

something dragging in my chest ever since coming into this kitchen, something to do with that overcast sky out there, pressing upon me as if the clouds themselves had dropped into my chest, lodged there and making it difficult to breathe with my lungs struggling to gain some sort of hold on the air, nothing but a vacant hole in my chest as if it had been cored to the bone and of course

it's that awful hour of the day, this soft hour bracketed between the Angelus bell and the time signal for the one o'clock news, the morning's best energies spent but still too early for the dinner, no proper work getting done and nothing on the radio but songs in three-quarter time as if the whole world was exhausted or washed out the same as

Mairead was the Friday I came home and found she'd been sick since morning, nausea and a fever for the first couple of hours but worsening to cramps and puking in the afternoon, keeping her in bed with the curtains drawn, a livid flush on her cheeks and a gloss of sweat on her face, her voice a thready rasp of itself, whispering

it's been like this all day, I can't hold anything down and

it was a shock to see her like that, lying there with all the energy twisted out of her, this woman who never took to the bed for any reason whatsoever and

do you want me to call the doctor, you're burning up as

I laid my hand on her forehead which, in spite of appearances, felt cold beneath the sweaty sheen so

no, it's only a bug, it'll be gone in the morning, all I need is a bit of sleep and

you're all right besides with

her face narrowing into a tight grimace when

I've got these cramps that come and go through my stomach, I've had them all afternoon and they are not getting any better – if I could just get some sleep before

her misery came to a head later that evening when I was in the kitchen and her voice called weakly from the bedroom where I found her leaning over the side of the bed vomiting a green wash into a basin, her body purging itself in a spasm of spew, a rinse of bitter filth sluicing up out of her as if it were being pumped from deep within with such twisting force she was now almost out of the bed, resting her hand on the floor, bracing herself over the basin as she continued to disgorge, her body now almost head down on the floor and which, after another bout of puking, I finally drew up and settled back within the pillows where she lay trembling and snuffling wetly so

that's it, I said, I'm calling the doctor

no, she rasped, not yet and

the look of pain on her face sank beneath a look of shame and alarm which lifted up her chin as she said weakly

I need to go to the bathroom and I need you to change these sheets

ok, I'll throw them in the washing machine

no, not the washing machine, throw them out and the duvet cover also she said

her voice now with an imploring under-note to its breathlessness which I did not understand till she glared meaningfully into the middle of the bed, her shame now burning under a tide of rage which drew her up with gritted teeth to say leave the room

you're not able to get up on your own

for Christ's sake leave the room or you will regret it she

barked, an outburst which momentarily drained all her strength away, pushing her back between the pillows with a heavy gasp as I turned from the room and pulled the door behind me, returning only when I heard the shower running in the bathroom to pick up the sheets, duvet cover and nightdress which were gathered into a tight ball in the middle of the floor where the air was thick with the smell of vomit and that other filth which had been drawn from her body, now bundled up in these sheets which I pushed into the wheelie bin outside the back door and then waited with a change of nightdress for her when she stepped out of the shower, which she did after a few minutes to stand swaying on the tiled floor, heat-blushed and dizzy, with steam rising from her pale shoulders as if she was some new-born thing, so I took a towel and dried her off before slipping the nightdress over her head and then did something I had not done in the longest time – gathered her up in my arms and carried her down the hall to Agnes's room which was already made up, to sit her on the edge of the bed where she balanced breathless and trembling, swaying to one side as I looped a towel around her head and dried her hair as gently as possible then ran a brush through it so that when she lay back into the pillows her face was opened with a fevered heat coming off her in scented waves, gasping

thank you

her eyes closing as she spoke, all her strength needed to draw the two words up from inside her and

I'm ringing the doctor now, this needs to be seen to

yes and

her exhaustion pushed her off to sleep as I made the phone call to the clinic where the receptionist told me that Mairead's GP was on leave but they put me on to a woman with a quiet telephone manner who requested that I detail clearly all the symptoms and how long they had been in place – all the vomiting, the cramps, the diarrhoea, the fever – after which she said she would be at the house in twenty minutes, which indeed she was and there was a pleasing difference between the calm voice on the phone and the wild-haired woman who sat on the side of Mairead's bed taking her temperature and pulse, a young woman in an oversized mac with the cuffs rolled up over her wrists and whose face it took me a long moment to recognise, but eventually it came to me, a neighbour's child, one of the Cosgraves of Derreen who now

sat beside Mairead, running through the steps of her medical examination – pulse, heart, blood pressure, temperature and drawing off two phials of blood from her arm – her hand on her forehead while Mairead held a digital thermometer between her swollen lips, swimming in the ebb and flow of her own fever, the great pulsing throb of her discomfort which seemed now to envelope her and into which this young medic now placed her hand and lowered her head to ask

when did you say you went to Agnes's opening

two days ago

and you had a meal after

yes

as she stood up, pulling the stethoscope from around her neck and casting her hair behind her shoulders

so was it a good night, did you have fun

yes, we did, it was a bit of a surprise and

it's been a while since I've seen Agnes, she was a couple of years behind me in school and

you're one of Padraig's girls

yes, the oldest

I knew the face, but I didn't know which of the Cosgraves you were

there's a few of us all right

how's your father, I see him now and again on the bike and

he's great, fit and supple, still cycling into town, my mother worries about him, he's going deaf in one ear so she worries that he can't hear things coming behind him, but other than that he's great … so that's what Agnes is doing now, painting, and her brother

Darragh

yes Darragh,

oh, we don't know what that lad's at, all we know is that he's in Australia, travelling and growing a beard, that's all we know about him

Darragh was younger than me, Agnes is the one I remember most, tell her I said hello as

she turned towards Mairead in the bed who was now lying with her eyes closed, totally oblivious to what we were talking about and the young doctor laid her hand one final time on her shoulder before getting to her feet and leaving the room with me following her out to her car on the side of the road where she threw her bag into the back seat with a startlingly swift motion, saying

from what I can see, this is a case of food poisoning – all the symptoms add up, the fever, the vomiting and the cramps, all the classic symptoms and if that is the case then there really is nothing you can do about it but ride it out with her, give her plenty of water to keep her hydrated but that is all that can really be done for her and I'll get those samples off to the lab first thing on Monday so

food poisoning after two days

yes, it can happen

what about the diarrhoea, she would not want that and

she shook her head because

no, I could prescribe something for that but I don't want to at this early stage, that might only dehydrate her and that's not what she needs at the moment, I want to give her a few days because the symptoms should abate and she should start to feel better within a day or two, so just keep giving her cool drinks and let her rest, there really isn't a lot more that can be done, I'll call again tomorrow and

she handed me her card with her home number on it and gave me a sympathetic smile once more before she got into her car and pulled away onto the road and

that was it for the weekend

I was now Mairead's carer, ghosting through the house with drinks and clean sheets, mopping her brow and trying to strike the right note of care and compassion at her bedside so that she could feel my presence through her fever, hovering there, willing her to feel my attentiveness even if she was mostly oblivious to my presence, trembling as she was within a humid haze, sometimes dozing for hours so that for long periods I had little enough to do except stand beside her bed looking down on the contours of her body beneath the sheets while in those short, lucid moments, when she was able to sit up with the pillows to her back she could only lie there in disbelief, her whole being raw with the sensitivities of what she was going through, this woman who, in all our years together, had never been sick for any length of time

now lying in bed with her pulse slackening to a distant thread in those moments before she was hauled over the side of the bed, racked with such convulsive bouts of spewing I feared she might be washed from her body completely, bone and soul gone, leaving nothing beneath the sheets save some dry, lifeless husk which would serve for kindling, so for the two days of that weekend

I stood by the side of her bed, frequently at a loss as to what exactly I should do, her face glossed with sweat, skin glowing in the weak light of the bedroom and something deathly about the way this illness closed her eyes, leaving her face so unguarded it allowed me to stare at her and notice for the first time how her avian features – nose and cheekbones converging on some vanishing point ahead of her – had been further refined in her daughter's sharpness, how she had held her looks and shape into middle age so that the contours of her body still held close to the figure of the serious girl I'd met over twenty years ago, the girl composed of languages and foreign travel, her body with no fat on it to hinder or weigh it down and so lightly built for the job of always teetering on the first step of the next journey, always drawing her on, but now this same body was that narrow place in which a fever had taken hold with its purgative heat scourging it from the inside out and which

would account for the filthiness of the whole process, the sweat in which she was constantly bathed, the bile that rose out of her gut and the diarrhoea that racked through her stomach and bowels in sudden spasms, leaving her mortified as her whole being stank, no matter how carefully she washed herself after each trip to the bathroom, sometimes no sooner back in bed, showered and in clean pyjamas, than she would begin to sweat once more from every pore and crevice of her body, till in no time again her bed and clothes were damp and stale, with her hair slicked over to the side of her head, the room filled with a stench beyond what was human, as if her very soul was being drawn from her body, out through the pores of her skin so that

it was a genuine anguish to witness her shame in all this, that raging helplessness over which there was nothing I could do since this illness seemed to have taken hold of all the rhythms and pulses of her body, clinging to all its currents and shifts while

her suffering now spread through the house like the micro-climate of a different, more rarefied realm, up and down the hall and through all its rooms, that separate latitude within which the sick thrive so that whenever

I walked down the hall towards whatever bedroom she was lying in I sometimes experienced those few steps as a long journey southwards which crossed borders and time zones, traversed deserts and mountain ranges to where I would eventually find her, my quarry, stricken under a pitiless sun, gasping and parched in some benighted jurisdiction which suffered a rapid turnover of governments, spiralling inflation rates and despicable human rights records – only such radical change of topography and circumstance could account for that gaping sense of distance she inhabited during the first couple of days

Friday, Saturday and Sunday

with their patient, attritional wasting which seemed to consume her down at the very smallest grains of her being, drifting from herself on clouds of her own breath, each laboured exhalation peeling away another layer of her into the ether, this illness which had settled into the most sheltered niches of her organism from where it could achieve the most finical, attentive wasting so that

by Sunday afternoon, when she was propped up with her eyes closed and her mouth ajar, trying to hold down those few mouthfuls of water that were already stewing to bile in her stomach while the room around her was warped in her heat haze, doors and windows drifting in her ambient temperature, everything lopsided and out of shape, her head thrown back to give me a clear picture of how this illness was draining the flesh from her face, drawing out the bone structure beneath, her jaw and cheekbones jutting sharply while the radial pattern of her fingers began to show through the backs of her hands resting on the duvet cover, her extended fingers fanned out from knuckles to wrist which peaked over the plane of her narrow forearm, all her bones now poking through her flesh until

a call from Agnes on Sunday evening clarified things for me after

she had listened quietly to my account of Mairead's illness, she told me that

the city's local radio station was reporting that a city-wide health emergency was coming to light since a glut of people had begun presenting at GP's surgeries and A&E with precisely the same symptoms as Mairead, so many cases that the numbers could not be ignored with the result that the city authorities had, at an extraordinary council meeting the previous day, put the whole municipal area under a boil-water notice until the proper source of what they described as a viral contamination was traced and eradicated while at the same time – with admirable speed she had to admit – lists of safety measures were already published in the local newspapers and on handbills that were pushed through letterboxes or were available on the City Hall website and in churches, supermarkets, libraries and community centres or broadcast with the hourly news bulletin on local radio – every channel of communication utilised to carry the word to homes and business places, to wherever the city's population might gather in work or worship or entertainment, all angles covered so that

my guess is that it's this virus thing is what Mam is suffering from, remember she was the only one of us who drank water at the table that night

yes, she insisted that I have a drink, she would stick to water, she wanted to drive but

I could come home tomorrow, it might do her good if she saw

no

the word blurted out of me before I could stop it because

there's nothing you can do for her and I'm not sure she'd want

you here right now, this is an important time for you and she would
never forgive me if she knew that I had hauled you away from your
work so

it might cheer her up to see me

the best thing you can do for her now is get on with your work
and talk to her in a few days when she's better and

I feel terrible, this is how my big night turns out

for god's sake Agnes, these things happen and they're no one's
fault, just keep in touch and don't worry, this'll blow over in a few
days but

I could tell she was genuinely in two minds and that while, on
the one hand she dearly wanted to be with her mother, on the other,
she recognised also that this was precisely the time she needed to
be near her work and availing of any opportunities that might arise
from it, which suited me as there was something in the prospect
of being alone in the house with Agnes while Mairead sickened in
a room at the end of the hall that seemed to me a breach of some
intimacy taboo, a complicity which made me a bit queasy, so that it
was easy to turn down her offer of help and

I rounded out the discussion by asking her if there was anything
else about the contamination I should know and she said

that rumour in the city was that there were upwards of three
to four hundred people in hospital wards with cramps and fever
and diarrhoea, sweating and shitting themselves into oblivion as
she vividly put it, suffering from cryptosporidiosis, a virus derived
from human waste which lodged in the digestive tract, so that, she
continued, it was now the case that the citizens were consuming
their own shit, the source of their own illness and there was something fatally concentric and self-generating about this, as if the virus
had circled back to its source to find its proper home where it settled
in for its evolutionary span, rising through degrees of refinement
every time it went round the U-bend, gradually gaining on some
perfection – hardiness and resistance and so on – with god-knows-
what results, probably reaching such a degree of refinement that it
would become totally resistant to every antidote and we would be
host to this new life form and, at this point I wondered

would she ever stop

mother of Jesus

stop

because

I could understand this sort of thing coming from Darragh, this kind of apocalyptic riffing was exactly the sort of stuff he thrived on, getting carried away on those visions of destruction which I've always believed were the special reserve of young men, all the aggravated amplitudes and graphic imagery they are prone to but which now, coming from Agnes, I found tiresome, the same kind of reasoned hysterics which, like Darragh, she half-believed and for the other half she was happy simply to pursue to its own fulfilment, a kind of ecstasy I tired of as

she now expanded her scenario to a city in crisis, her voice lathering on all the available images of civil collapse and destruction, her voice cast in the solemn tone of someone delivering an on-the-spot report from some urban disaster area and I let her go on a while longer as I had never heard her do this kind of thing before, never lose the run of herself, ravelling on like this, words and ideas spilling from her in a lurid rush and while standing there at the gable of the house I thought, for the first time in years

a smoke

Jesus, I'd love a smoke

out of nowhere that old hankering rising up in me, that draw in the back of my throat, the urge to go through the old ritual of taking out the packet of cigarettes and lighting one up, the need to do something with my hands and the old certainty that somehow the situation would be improved if I were to light up and feel that soothing bloom of smoke filling out my lungs, it all came back to me standing there under the shelter of the eaves, a habit I thought had waned away to nothing having given them up a couple of years back after Mairead had harped on at me for so long, pointing out that a history of heart disease on both sides of my family would make it the wise move especially when I turned forty-five and I could no longer afford to be so blithe about these things and it was about time I took responsibility and so on and so forth until

I did indeed make an effort, for whatever reason, quitting them several times, off and on, stuttering and stumbling but never managing to lower the habit below ten a day, never managing to cross that threshold into a smoke-free life, clothes and car always stinking and those mornings after a night on the beer, chain-smoking one after another, sitting on the side of the bed with that furry rasp in my lungs, passing it off to myself as phlegm, all those years when the kids were around, never able to quit but the minute

they'd grown up and left for college it was as if they drew the habit away with them because suddenly the old craving was gone, I'd had enough, something I could not explain and I just walked away from them New Year's night, smoked my last one at two o'clock in the morning, standing on the pavement outside one of the pubs in the village, four or five years ago with never a relapse or craving

until now

standing at the gable of the house, looking out over the fields towards the Westport road in the distance and the side of Croagh Patrick fading into the evening light, Agnes still speaking away on the other end of the line as a light shower of rain drifted over the house, thickening to a heavy mist which moved on to pile up in swathes against the slopes of Mweelrea, another wet evening as promised, nothing but solid rain from the beginning of March with no let up so you couldn't walk the land for fear of going up to your ankles in it and there was still another three weeks before the clocks would turn to summer time when darkness would not settle in till after seven o'clock and even if there was no assurance as yet that the weather would take up any time soon it was good to think of summer only a few weeks away with the sun higher in the sky and the first blackthorn around the house coming into flower while later on the woodbine, which Mairead had tended in the wild hedge, would scent up the whole back garden close to the house, this side of the sheds and the haggard beyond before

Agnes's voice tapered off, her apocalypse complete – the city's civil defence plans overwhelmed, riots in the streets, council chambers overrun and trashed by protestors – Agnes exhausted now, like the scenario itself, so she finished up telling me that she would let me know if she learned anything else and to give Mam her love before she

rung off, her voice suddenly gone as if it had snagged on the mist and was carried off into the failing light, leaving the phone dead in my hand, a warm sliver with the screen fading like some luminous shard from outer space which had travelled across stellar distances at great speed to arrive here in my hand where its glow was now losing its heat, gone, before I pocketed it and turned back into the house to check on Mairead and tell her that Agnes had just called but that I had told her not to come home as I figured she had other more pressing things to do – her work and everything – and Mairead nodded heavily, yes, that was the right thing to say, and it was good to have confirmed that I'd done the right thing so I could rest easy in myself for the rest of the evening, make something to eat and

later that night I sat alone in the sitting room, feeling the whole house strange around me with Mairead tossing in a fevered sleep among the soft toys, posters and CDs – all the detritus of Agnes's adolescence – Mairead now washed up there by the swell of her fever and drifting through the damp currents of her sleep as if she inhabited some separate medium in which everything was given over to a drift and fade, space and time warped so that those hours ahead of me appeared completely unmappable and unpredictable even if it was likely they would pass in the same inescapable boredom as the previous couple of days, a prospect which made me gloomy as there appeared no way out of it now – Mairead was too ill to sneak away from for a few pints – so that when the idea of Skyping Darragh came to me it took me a long moment to set it aside, because even if a chat with him was a pleasing prospect – I knew full well that any conversation now ran the risk of having to tell him of his mother's illness and, from what I could see, there was no good reason to mention it to him as it would probably do nothing but make him anxious about something that would run its course in a few days, something neither of us could do much about, so I forgot about it and got a beer from the fridge and settled down to scan through the TV channels, all thirty of them – sport, drama, docs, cartoons, the whole lot – only to inevitably lock onto Sky News where I learned that the actor Paul Scofield had passed away from leukaemia while the surge of troops into Iraq was ongoing and the weather for the following week would continue with more of the rain that had been blowing in from a cyclone in the mid-Atlantic for the past three weeks with no let-up till Thursday at the earliest which might bring a dry spell but with a sharp drop in temperature, at which point I got fed up and flicked on through the channels once more, films, comedy, sci-fi, more news, until I chanced upon a documentary which showed

a grown man lying on a floor covered with large sheets of paper, A2 sheets on which there were some very complex and detailed line drawings, page after page covered, and this narrow shouldered man in a white shirt stretched out in the middle of them, drawing away with pencil and rule, adding yet another detailed sheet to all those around him and I must have recognised the sort of drawings they were because I found myself sitting forward in the armchair, prodding the zapper in my hand to turn up the volume so that I could hear the voiceover tell me that this man – some French man whose name I can't remember – suffered from a sort of high-level autism that left him socially inept and completely without any sense of humour or irony but who was nevertheless designing out of thin air the most complete and complex urban plan history had ever known, a project which had come to light when a few of the drawings were used to illustrate a *Sunday Times Magazine* article on autism, which brought him to the attention of an urban planner at London City Council who marvelled at the precise beauty of its streets and thoroughfares but who was a lot more intrigued by the sprawling harmony hinted at beyond the margins of the cropped fragments and so took himself off to France to investigate this gifted planner whom no one in the urban design community had ever heard of, finding him eventually in a little village in the Vosges where he lived with his partner, a mathematician and herself autistic, and who, after he'd spent a couple of days there, convinced the planner that he had encountered a fully fledged genius – a visionary who had not only a coherent sense of the vast megalopolis which, after fifteen years, was still metastasising, day by day over pages and pages, an astonishing achievement in itself but more impressive from the point of view of a city planner was this man's ability to hold in his mind's eye a sense of the city as an enormous, dynamic organism which was continually morphing through the vast tides of those circadian rhythms that governed all its streets and infrastructure and which this seer outlined with sweeping gestures over the sheets of paper spread across the sitting-room floor, speaking in a toneless voice which swept through the city with a running commentary on how it was performing at any specific time of the day, how and where all its crowds and traffic were flowing and what routes they took to what points of convergence in the early morning rush hour, and what exactly the drain on utilities would be – how all its vertical and horizontal circuitry was functioning when water and electricity followed in the wake of crowds converging for work or entertainment in various parts and times of the city while disgorging a flow of sewage, hydrocarbons and CO_2 emissions from those same points, this savant holding in mind all the flows and shifts through the city's streets and conduit, vast rhythms he could gauge to any hour of the day, any day of the week or any holiday, a phenomenal feat which had the urban planner at a loss to find some comparative image or simile – he talked about a 3D chess game and a multi-tiered symphony of people and environment – all vivid and suggestive but each one falling some way short of the city's majestic, multi-harmonic sprawl – while all the time speaking to camera the seer himself was down on the floor behind him with his pencil and square, adding yet another precinct to the city's expanse – a working-class suburban enclave with housing grouped around schools and shopping facilities, parking and leisure amenities, the concrete substratum of a fully realised community – while the city now stood, after fifteen years' solid work but with no end yet in sight, as by far the biggest and most complex urban plan ever conceived by man or committee and which I could not help thinking, as I sipped my beer and watched, would, if he stuck at it and lived long enough, eclipse the whole fucking world, this map of a kingdom that existed nowhere on this earth but in his head, this masterpiece with its clueless overlord, a mad king who knew nothing of the real world but was nevertheless on such intimate terms with the infinite intricacies of his own mind that he needed nothing more than a rule and pencil to draw them forth and lay them on the paper, this city as a kind of neural maze, a cognitive map which would reach out, street by street, to cover the whole world and possibly for this reason or for some other I could not fathom, the programme filled me with a sour bloom of resentment the focus of which I could not clearly discern but which quickly had me feeling so foolish I was embarrassed to be alone with myself in the sitting room, feeling that someone invisible outside of myself was standing judge and jury over me, pointing a finger at me, saying

have you nothing better for doing at this time of night than getting pissed off at the television

seriously

so I tipped back the beer and ran a final check on Mairead who was turned on her side, eyes open, the whites like crescent chips in the dark light, her whole body throbbing sluggishly beneath the duvet, warm when I laid my hand on her forehead to sweep her hair back and make sure she had a glass of water on the bed-stand, these little considerations carried out in the light spilling through the open door from the hallway, moistened her face once more with a baby wipe and then kissed her on the forehead as she said

leave the hall light on and the door open a little

which I did, her lying there in the half-light as I made my way back to our bedroom where I fell into a deep sleep which was unwarped by any dreams, seven or eight good hours and

in the following days

I settled into the task of being Mairead's full-time carer but not before I had to ring in and take emergency sick leave from work, clearing it with my line manager, Fallon, who hemmed and hawed for a few moments before he came round eventually, as I knew he would, after reassuring him that we could reassign all those projects on my desk which were time-sensitive – a couple of site surveys, one map redraw and the terms of a safety cert which

I discussed directly over the phone with the main contractor, a man named Hanley from North Mayo, Pullathomas to be exact, a man who was politically well connected and a blunt fucker who bristled with frustration when I spoke to him that morning, his heavy bulk gasping down the line towards me, not happy to hear that he would have to put his project back a couple of days while I sorted things out at home, listening to him for a few minutes as

he began to moan and bitch about deadlines and budgets and tradesmen lined up outside the site waiting to start the next phase, grousing on like this for ten minutes before I cut across him and told him that the whole project was now coming under a total review because of new safety regulations which were being signed into law and which it now appeared might have a retroactive aspect to them so that all public contracts currently waiting to be signed off on would have to meet these new measures and it was all up in the air at the moment, all public works contracts anyway and

that quietened the fucker

as I knew it would because

there's nothing like the threat of new health and safety regulations to sicken a builder's hole, more paperwork and form-filling, new work practices to be negotiated and insurance clauses to be sorted out and sitting at

this kitchen table at nine o'clock in the morning

sitting here now

I had the satisfaction of hearing the bullish aggression leak out of him, sensing him slump at the other end of the line as he drew breath for a moment and considered whether or not he should go head-to-head with a county engineer who, for the moment at least, had him by the balls, something he obviously thought better of because the phone call ended a few moments later with a surly silence on his end after my own commitment to sort out the project immediately, give it my full attention when I got back from sick leave, that's all I can do, but as I put the phone down I thought to myself

you're only codding yourself

because I knew full well the first thing Hanley would do now would be to phone up one of his political connections and ask him about this bullshit safety legislation that was holding up a public project and jeopardising the work of twenty men with families, his way of letting the deputy know that he was

pissed off

the very words he would use

severely fucking pissed off because

if there's much more of this fuck-acting with regulations and conditions he would fuck off the site entirely with all his men and plant and put a lock on the gate and fight the whole fucking lot of them in court for breach of contract while the site thickened with weeds and rushes so that the whole thing would have to be retreated if work was to recommence while at the same time the price of labour and materials rising so that the original estimate on which the contract was priced would be shot to hell and the whole thing would now exceed budget and there would be a further delay in trying to source extra funding, trying to scrape money away from some other project and stepping on people's toes to do it and

did he really want this happening on his watch

this is what he'd ask the TD

did he

did he want this happening four miles away from his constituency office with people passing it day in, day out looking at this eyesore of a building-site overgrown with weeds, people going to mass on a Sunday morning looking at it – did he really want that happening in the heart of his own constituency with less than fifteen months before people went to the polls in a general election

did he

his very words, or

words to that effect because

Hanley's sullen rage lingered in the silence after the phone call and I knew full well that this was another of those arguments I was going to lose, one of those instances which illustrated clearly how the world is built by politicians and not engineers – the engineer's lament – a realisation I did not wonder at or lose sleep over any more, the day long gone when, as an engineer, I was worried at the certain prospect of being pressured from one side by politicians and the other by developers, both of them squeezing out all engineering and environmental considerations which was, I figured, likely to have happened when I returned to work after Mairead got better, how ever long that would take but during which

her strength ebbed on pulsing waves of heat and sweat with her throbbing at the centre of her own fevered halo while I brought water and cool towels as if I was summoned by the fever itself for the sole purpose of witnessing its calm ferocity and relentlessness while also beginning to marvel that something which had now begun to make headlines and editorial comment as

news

in the way I understood political phenomena to be news, had taken up residence under my roof

down the hall in the far bedroom, engineering and politics converging in the slight figure of my wife lying in bed, her body and soul now giving her an extension into the political arena in a way which, if she had been aware of, would have startled her, as Mairead was one of those people who saw voting and such chores of responsible citizenship as a necessary nuisance, walking into the polling booth with little or no interest in the outcome, one crowd as bad as the other, sometimes asking me beforehand in the car

who will I vote for or

is there any real choice here

with her belief that all elections, local or national, were essentially trivial tweakings of a calcified, monolithic system which was not amenable to proper reform, a kind of swamping and irreversible process while

in the following days I kept abreast of the virus story as it began to make headlines across all the national news outlets, gradually surfacing through newsprint and broadcast articles where it was cautiously spoken of as an environmental problem not a health problem, taking its place in a world vexed with those bigger and greater themes which were detailed across the five or six news bulletins I watched or listened to throughout the day, eyes and ears peeled for the slightest development in the story, realising

that I was one of those men who had always structured his

days around radio news bulletins right from the moment I got up in the morning and stood with my mug of tea in the kitchen listening to the sea area forecast with its sing-song litany of names from around the coast

Belmullet, East, five knots, fair, nine miles, 1018 millibars, steady

Roches Point Automatic, East-southeast, eleven knots, fair, ten miles, 1016 millibars, falling slowly

Valentia, East-southeast, eleven knots, cloudy, seven miles, 1020 millibars, falling slowly

falling slowly

followed by the time signal which led in the news, the sound of which always assured me that now the day was properly started, the world up and about its business with all its stories of conflict and upheaval at home and abroad cranking into gear, its tales of commercial and political fortune convulsing across borders and time-zones with currencies and governments rising and falling, the whole global comedy rounded out by the weather which invariably promised rain or a cold spell when

I would rinse out my cup and leave it on the draining board, then off to work where I'd do a couple of hours at my desk till eleven o'clock before reaching into the drawer and taking out my transistor radio with its silver antenna – I've always thought there was something plaintive about this small receiver trying to snag a signal within the heart of that concrete bunker – to listen to the headlines with a cup of coffee and a sandwich after which I'd return to work only to tune in again for the main news at one o'clock, the stiff midday fix with interviews and analysis that took me through to the six o'clock evening bulletin on the small television here in the kitchen by which time most of the day's national news stories will have come to a head and received their fullest analysis after which the nine o'clock news is generally a summary of the day's national events, unmissable for peace of mind at the end of the day but stale as regards new national issues which have at this hour, by and large, been put to bed for the night, so that now my attention broadens out to those global dramas which are in play across those jurisdictions that are still in daylight till finally, after midnight, by which time Mairead will have gone to bed, I'd spend a few last minutes standing here in the kitchen watching Sky News round up the day's major headlines before going to bed, all in all

dawn to dark

six or seven news bulletins needing my attention

all spaced out at regular intervals, the day structured like the monastic rule of some vigilant order synched to the world's rhythms and all its upheavals which, as history's vast unfolding, are part of my responsibility as a citizen to keep abreast of, attuning myself to their distant heaves because, even if such things are unlikely to touch me with the violent immediacy of bombs or bullets, who is to say that they would not lay their electric fingers on me in some other way which could push my life into some new alignment or along some other route so that

in this way news bulletins provided another rhythm to my day, a steady pulse across its length and it was only when I thought of it like this that I saw it as yet another thing

handed down from my father who was

a great listener to the news also, his own days set to the same tempo, sitting into his breakfast and dinner just as the time signal for news bulletins sounded, taking his cap off to hang it on the back of the chair as he lent an ear to the old valve radio which sat on the deep window sill, and

till those fevered days of Mairead's illness I had never seen my own news habit as anything other than that – a habit passed down from my father – but which now in the circumstances of Mairead's illness, it came with a sharpened sense of involvement in some broader process beyond myself which initially baffled me because while I might have some abstract recognition of myself as a citizen – a fully documented member of a democracy with a complete voting record in all elections since I had come of age – I never had any intimate sense of history's immediate forces affecting my day-to-day life, not even, I have to admit, during those work meetings where large public facilities and budgets were being decided upon, meet-ings in which I would sit with politicians and developers to argue this or that point or amendment or development while all the time knowing that the odds were stacked against me as an engineer and that in all likelihood I was going to lose an engineering decision to some political consideration, a verdict which would see some public facility shifted from its optimum site towards some other part of the county where it would best benefit the politician across the table who'd take pride of place at a ribbon-cutting ceremony and the attendant photo op, not even then did I have a full sense of myself as an engaged citizen within a political horizon, so heedless of it that, if the point were pressed to me, I would have been startled or even embarrassed by the notion which

began to weigh on me during those days when my wife lay sweating through two changes of sheets and pyjamas a day, her ordeal showing me that history and politics were now personal, no longer blithe abstractions or pallid concepts but physically present in the flesh and blood figure of Mairead whose plight inspired me to render the whole circumstance down to a manageable formula –

history was personal and politics was personal or

to put it another way

history and politics were now a severe intestinal disorder, spliced into the figure of my wife who sweated along the pale length of her body with the stylised, beatific glow of an allegorical figure in an altarpiece while

day by day, listening to the news bulletins, I developed a twitchy impatience towards those other global issues which commanded the main headlines as it became obvious that only when these grand themes had been treated and analysed would the news bulletins turn their attention to the environmental health hazard out west, a ragged postscript tagged onto the bottom of these bigger stories where it would be given a cursory review or status update, and this wait grated on my patience as I interpreted it as a sure sign that the story was failing to gain any proper hold in the nation's consciousness even as the crisis worsened and the city's hospital beds continued to fill up, the number of registered cases now tipping three hundred in the middle of the week so that

I began to feel this insult keenly, anger simmering within me as I craned forward in my chair to listen to the Western correspondent – an old man with a goatee who looked more like a professor of Classics than someone reporting on an environmental health issue – give the latest update with its gradual escalation and rising numbers, his account moving from these broad strokes to the logistical and engineering options being explored by the municipal authorities and

throughout all these accounts plus the attendant commentaries I found myself trying to hear something which fully recognised the reality of what it really meant to be someone like Mairead who was taking the brunt of it, all its sickness and wasting, but there was no such acknowledgement in those droning voices as councillors and engineers, one after another, came before mic and camera to speak in defensive assurances which leant heavily on the repetition of preprogrammed mantras that were carefully calibrated to contain nothing to which the speaker might be held accountable, spokesmen droning on as the days passed, pushing the story into some bloodless realm which left the individual human scale of the thing untouched, the human grit of the situation untold so that my anger mounted with each interview, something incredulous festering within me and well fermented by the time

the city's people organised the first major public protest meeting which took place in the grounds of the city offices, around two hundred people assembled in the garden and car park, some of them climbing onto the stone wall to speak to the crowd which had gathered in their coats and caps and umbrellas, standing in the rain which had fallen steadily since mid-morning, to voice at first their disbelief that this water crisis could happen in a coastal city with one of the highest mean annual rainfalls on the whole of the continent, a civic disaster which had reduced its people to the condition of third-world supplicants who were now forced to queue up for water at relief points throughout the suburbs, a shameful state of affairs which several speakers frankly admitted they were embarrassed about and

how long was this going to go on

they wanted to know, when would the contamination be traced so that the city might get back to its proper business

how long more

the question directed to a spokesman from City Hall who came out to address the crowd and assure them that the investigation of the city's water supply was ongoing with samples from several locations showing that the contamination was general throughout the supply lake so that it did not appear to be sourced from one particular spot and that in the next few days the air force would begin conducting overflights of the whole lake and those rivers which fed into it in the hope that a detailed aerial survey would reveal dump sites or sewage spillages in or around the lake itself or in the wider area, all this to be done before the new filtration system would be installed, the new system which was, at this very moment, in the process of being shipped from Canada and which would be installed in the city's purifying plant as soon as it arrived, within the next month or so, six weeks tops, a triple filtration system – barrier, chemical and ultra-violet light – which would exceed comfortably all EU health and safety standards so that the citizenry could be assured that once this present crisis was cleared up – as it would assuredly be – this city's water supply would exceed the highest standards of purity but until then the investigation was ongoing and that was all he could say at the moment so no, he could not put a timeframe on how long more the city could expect to have to boil its water, it would be irresponsible of him to say whether it would be days or weeks or months, he could not say, he would only be guessing if he did give a time, days or weeks or whatever, but a lot would depend on the visual survey of the following week, that was as much as he could say, except to thank the citizens for their patience and forbearance and for having shown such community spirit in the face of adversity, a compliment which provoked sullen murmuring from the crowd which had now spread across the car park and into the municipal gardens and green space beyond, some of whom had already taken up positions on the surrounding walls with placards and banners held aloft on this wet spring day with its sifted light which lent itself perfectly to the frustrated mood of the gathering which the spokesman seemed to interpret as something else because, apparently emboldened by the sound of his own voice carrying in such a broad, public space, he went on to assure them one final time that everything possible was being done – city engineers were working around the clock to get on top of the problem and that furthermore – here, he wanted to enter a personal note – as a native of this city himself

born and bred

seed, breed and generation, he

understood and felt keenly the distress this health hazard was causing its citizens, most especially those families with young children or elderly relatives in their care, he was especially mindful of these people's plight and he could assure them that no one wanted a swifter resolution to this crisis than he did and this was all being borne in mind by the authorities and this was a masterful touch, the quiet way with which this spokesman made such soulful play of a shared history and heritage, assuring them that he knew their pain and was with them in their anxiety and distress, his emollient words working their charm so smoothly and effectively that, for a moment, the entire crowd was disarmed and silent, shameful almost of their protest and at a loss as to what they might do next, possibly appalled also at their own willingness to be so easily placated but unable to do anything about it until, at the precise moment when the righteous anger of the crowd might have dissipated into thin air

a small woman raised her voice and drew attention with her observation that what angered the populace was not that this crisis was some technical or environmental failing or that it was yet another instance of incompetence or wilful disregard on the part of the authorities – no, this was not what angered her, nor indeed was it news to any of those gathered here – what angered her was that the covenant of care struck between the people and the city authorities was now broken and that a reservoir of public trust and goodwill had finally been squandered, leaving the electorate and taxpayers feeling foolish and implicated, since they themselves had placed these people in power and therefore shared some responsibility for the disaster and this woman herself – a middle-aged, well-turned-out lady who should, given the mild weather, more likely than not have been bedding in summer plants in her suburban garden – now told the story of how her seventeen-year-old son had missed so much school in the last ten days through constant bouts of vomiting and diarrhoea that if it went on much longer he was likely to be so far behind in his studies there would be no point in sitting his Leaving Cert and he would therefore, in all probability, have to repeat the entire academic year so, in a bold thrust, the lady asked rhetorically, would the city council be compensating him in some way for this wasted year which would leave him behind while he watched all his friends move on with their lives, a powerful story, overstated but deft in getting the crowd to focus its accusative energies around the image of this seventeen-year-old boy who no doubt was at home at this very hour, still in bed in the middle of the afternoon, sick or otherwise, but who would likely have been embarrassed to know how quickly his martyred circumstances had become the rallying point for such a public protest because, how ever faceless he may have been at that particular moment, it did not prevent his plight becoming the living example of how this civic hazard disrupted a person's life and whether this crisis was sourced in incompetence or, as some suspected, a culture of appeasement within City Hall which, for the longest time, had failed to police the conduct of those sectional interests – farmers and developers, principally – who might be directly responsible and which held such powerful electoral clout, whatever the cause of this breakdown it amounted to the same thing – an important clause in the contract between the citizen and the local authority had been broken and every person standing in the car park felt this, each with their own specific sense of betrayal not to mention that feeling of ridicule which seemed to exploit something gullible in their political faith, telling them that it was misplaced, that it was badly used or that it was inevitably bound to culminate in some fiasco like this, as much as to say

what did you expect

electing such clowns to public office

so that there was now a feeling among all those standing in the car park that, as the electorate, they were somehow complicit in this disaster whereby water, the very stuff of life itself, was now contaminated by way of whatever electoral foolishness they had wittingly or otherwise participated in, a consideration that had a sapping effect on the crowd which now stood bewildered by its own feelings and responsibilities, all its energy gone and vehemence drained, standing there in that rainy car park so that, after a few moments when it became obvious that no one had anything else to add, the crowd began to break up and drift away, but not before some photographs were taken which were used the following day to illustrate those front page articles which covered the event in all the city's papers, articles illustrated with pictures of

these people wrapped up in caps and coats beneath placards held in gloved hands, this civic drama which had at its core a bland aggregate of ordinary people who felt themselves anxious and embarrassed by their circumstances and the political choices they had made and

it was difficult watching all this on the television to feel any proper involvement in this drama, voices droning on while Mairead's illness pervaded the house like a malignant mist, a psychic fog that seeped into my own being and blurred the margins of my body so that I was glad to hear Darragh's voice that evening, Skyping me to ask

what's the story with the water contamination, things seem to have ratcheted up a bit over the last few days

it hasn't got any better, that's true and

transporting water to the suburbs in bulk carriers, people queueing up with plastic containers like it was a third-world country

it doesn't look good so

I gave him a swift account of what I knew, the ongoing investigation and the town hall politics and the military over-flights which so far had failed to identify the exact source of the contamination and the new filtration system which as yet was still on a drawing board in some engineering facility in Ottawa and the protests so

a city on the brink of civil insurrection, that's what you're saying – people marching in the streets calling for regime change, quarantine flags flying over City Hall, military over-flights and

not this shite with you as well Darragh, I said irritably, I've heard Agnes going on with this kind of nonsense and

Darragh held up his hand

woah, I agree, there's nothing as tiresome as the apocalypse but take it from me, there's something very worrying going on here there is

yes

and what's that

it's City Hall and how they're misunderstanding the people's fear – you mark my words, as long as City Hall continues to interpret this as a simple matter of service disruption they will never understand why the populace have reacted with such vehemence since

it's no big secret Darragh, people are fed up, this is another example of municipal incompetence and

it's more than that

is it

yes, there'll never be a shortage of administrative incompetence in that city and over the years the people have shown themselves to be more patient than most, but this is different, this is a disturbance of a different order entirely and

Darragh was leaning forward now, a close-up of his face filling the screen and even from the other side of the world I could feel the electric energy of his thinking, see it flaring in his eyes as he said

these people marching in the streets are protesting against what they see as a contamination of the very stuff of life itself – what angers them is that life itself has been fouled at source by some ontopolitical virus which is hosted by water so that

whoa – I have to stop you there, clean water in taps for tea and coffee and running gallons of it down the plughole when you're washing your teeth – that's what people understand and that's what the city authorities understand it as also

I know that

so you should know better than using a word like ontopolitical with an engineer – much less a politician, you could hardly expect to make much headway with it in any of the debates that'll decide how this pans out because as sure as anything

Darragh's face opened in a wide grin as he slumped back from the screen with a nod

yes, I got ahead of myself there for a moment – that thesis will have to be revisited if it is to have any traction in City Hall

yes, I would advise that

still though, it's interesting to see people on the march, a city full of students and artists, they're not often roused to protest like that, it'll be interesting to see where it leads

it will

so long as it doesn't turn out to be the smoking ban all over again

how do you mean

I remember the cigarette ban coming in and all the bitching and grousing people did about it – and you were louder than most – no one would tell you where to smoke because you came from a long line of men who smoked in the ancient way, the heroic way – standing at the bar with a pint in one hand and a fag in the other – the way your forefathers had done it, but the night the ban came in you and everyone else turned over like kittens and were out on the street smoking their fags in the rain so

you're saying this could be all bluster

I don't know, it would be great to think it's the real thing but we'll have to see, how's mam

mam's fine, she's lying down now

there's nothing wrong with her

no, of course not

I lied, without missing a beat, the decision to keep him in the dark apparently made within me without any conscious deliberation on my part because

it's just that I haven't heard from her in a while, it's not like her

she's very busy at the moment, mock exams and all that

give her my love, I'll Skype her sometime later this week

ok, take care of yourself – and do me a favour

yes

don't come online to her looking like that, shave and tidy yourself up or she'll have a conniption

it's a tough station dad, this Waltzing Matilda thing

so I see, look after yourself

will do – oh, one last thing

what

a joke

a joke

yeah, a great joke, you'll like it

it's two o'clock in the morning Darragh

this won't take a minute – four men, a lawyer, a doctor, an engineer and a politician are discussing which of their trades was the oldest, and the lawyer starts by saying that surely it was his because right back at the dawn of mankind Cain killed Abel – the first murder – and that was surely followed by some sort of judicial process which obviously called for lawyers and therefore lawyering had to be the oldest profession but, the doctor shook his head and said that before Cain and Abel, God created Eve from Adam's rib and this obviously involved some sort of surgery and post-operative care, all of which proved that medicine was the oldest trade but at this point the engineer stepped in and said you're both wrong because right back at the dawn of creation there was nothing but chaos until God brought heaven and earth out of the chaos and this monumental act of creation was the first piece of engineering and what more proof did they need to see that engineering was the oldest of all the professions to which the politician, who had been listening quietly all this time, turned to the engineer, he asked if he understood him correctly – heaven and earth engineered out of chaos – to which the engineer said yes and which the politician in turn replied to by saying

who do you think made the chaos

and Darragh grinned

I thought it was a good one, you'd like it

it is good, I'll try it out at work tomorrow, I'm going to say good night now, so take care

bye

bye

and the screen clouded to a fizzy interference before it blanked to darkness, the laptop closed on the desk with the room silent and my eyes with that scalded feel to them which would not be soothed away by anything but a couple of hours' sleep so I did a final check on Mairead before going to our own bedroom and lying under the covers with my eyes closed for a long time, drifting in that black sea behind my eyes which spread into the darkness around me, bounded around by walls floors and ceilings, the house itself, which like a child

I've always believed gets up to some foolishness during the night, whenever I fall asleep or turn my back on it, that's when the ghost house beneath the paint and fittings asserts itself, flickering like an X-ray with that neurological twitch and spasm which is imbedded in the concrete, in the vertical and horizontal run of all its plumbing and wiring, those systems which make the house a living thing with all its walls and the floors pulsing with oil and water and electricity, all the pressures and imbalances in these systems pushing and drawing their freight towards that equilibrium which stabilises the structure in a warm balance, this web of utilities a tiny part of that greater circum-terrestrial grid of services which draws the world into community, pinching it up into villages, towns and cities so that

whenever I close my eyes or let my attention drift I'm convinced that the whole house reverts to this kind of under-structure which supports the whole building, the roof over the exterior walls and loadbearing partitions, the weight distributed down into the foundation, the ghost neurology which upholds and haunts it, flickering just a scintilla away from pure abstraction or those originary lines lying on an architect's drawings, the pale sheets of engineering paper on which it was conceived so that when

drifting in that state between sleep and waking it is easy to believe I inhabit a monochrome x-ray world from which I might have evaporated, flesh and bone gone, eaten up, not by any physical rot or wasting but by some metaphysical virus which devours and leaves nothing of me behind but my own heartbeat suspended in mid-air, nothing but a fat systolic contraction of the light, waiting for the dawn and the sun to shine upon it so that I might coalesce around it once more, flesh and bone and

time and again

my world come round once more so that

it took a while after Agnes and Darragh went to college for Mairead and myself to experience the house's emptiness as a positive thing, as something other than that deserted space around us which so dismayed us in the immediate aftermath of their going away, those days in which the house hummed with such ringing vacancy we feared we might never throw off the sense of loss it brought with it, an absence which at first

Mairead felt more keenly than I, the loneliness of their empty bedrooms which were still crowded with all their teenage stuff – clothes and books and posters and CDs – things no longer needed in the new lives they had gone on to, all their bits and pieces, some of which went back to their childhood, all shelved and stacked, neat as never before but now frozen in place and there were many times in those first years after they left, when we would have welcomed again the chaos that comes with children in a house, the glad ruckus of a growing family around us, because

I know that Mairead would have welcomed a return of such chaos – the noise, their coming and going, music blaring behind bedroom doors, Darragh wandering through the house with bowls of cereal at all hours of the night – especially in the beginning when the house rang with absence, no stereos blaring, books and clothes neatly put away, a long period of adjustment needed before she eventually found herself happy in the house's ordered space, this four-bedroom dormer, the smallest of which we shared as an office together, where I did those bits and pieces of work I brought home with me some evenings and where

Mairead prepared her classes and did whatever corrections she needed to do, sitting with her feet up on the desk and letting page after page drift to the ground around her, never tidy, some-thing which irritated me because to walk into a room where she was working was to walk into a sort of blizzard that covered desks and floors with a clutter of paper and mugs and pens of various sorts, the floor treacherous with stray sheets of paper and those plastic sleeves that fade onto the varnished floor and are so difficult to see but which, more than once, have slid out from under my feet and nearly thrown me on the flat of my back, the whole mess grating on my nerves so that I just have to rein in my temper and tidy it all away onto the armchair and leave it there for her to sort through, make some space for myself before I can do any work and it was on one of these days, glancing up

I saw how Mairead was stalking her son's progress across the penal colony by way of a map on the wall behind the door, a political map of all the towns and cities on the east coast from Sydney up to Brisbane, with a series of coloured pins – reds, blues and yellows – marking out Darragh's straight-line progress as far as Brisbane where he took a hard left into the interior of Queensland, towns with names like Dalby and Toowoomba marked off – places which, for all I knew, might be nothing more than a sheep station in the middle of the desert – matter-a-dam, these were the places from where Mairead had received some sort of communication from her son so that was good enough reason for her to stab the map through the heart with one of her coloured pins, a conceit she had obviously borrowed from one of those late-night cop shows she liked to watch where world-weary detectives with broken marriages and drink problems tracked the progress of serial killers across a landscape with these same coloured pins marking out newly discovered corpses, some behavioural pattern encoded in their random distribution if only the cop stares at it long enough, a strange conceit neatly repurposed to her son's wanderings in the outback, from hostel to campfire, sleeping under the southern cross, his period in the wilderness as he put it, his dreamtime as Agnes called it and there

on the wall beside the door, one of Agnes's pieces, the tiny painting she gave me a couple of years ago, twenty-by-fifteen centimetres, oil on board, a little boy in short trousers and sweater standing beside a tar-barrel with a galvanised bucket on the ground beside him, the image sourced from one of my sister Eithne's old Polaroids, hundreds of which she had lying around in boxes since her childhood, the whole stash turned over to Agnes shortly after she went to art college, the photo dating from around the same time as the disassembled tractor in the hayshed, me looking straight into the lens with an urchin's curiosity, the image drawn up from the depths of the canvas by a flurry of brush strokes in blues and greys which centre not on the child's eyes but on the black head of hair helmeted over the almost blank face, so much vacant space in the background and around the tar-barrel itself that the whole effect is of a plaque of light prised out of the air, its edges squared but not framed, as close as dammit to an embodied memory, because I can never look at it without feeling the weight of the galvanised bucket in my hand or hearing that sound they made whenever they were set on the ground, that scraping crash of the bottom hitting the concrete, the handle settling onto the metal rim with that clanging rattle in

this spare bedroom where one of us would work while

the other would take up the kitchen table so that the house expanded room by room around the two of us and in this new emptiness we gradually, over a period of time, learned to expand and fill it once more, returning to our proper size after the years of childrearing, gaining a clearer view of each other also and pleased to find that the house, with all its denuded spaces, shelves and cupboards, was a companionable place where a lot less needed to be said now that our children's lives did not need to be reckoned with or organised so that we gradually arrived at a renewed closeness to each other, something of the light tenderness of our early years returning to us with a gladdening of both our spirits and

which spilled over in the kitchen a couple of times – often enough to be proud of – both of us overtaken by a passion which threw us across the room into a breathless heap, and after which we looked at each other in a blush of embarrassment, glad but uncertain at what we had just done, panting over the clothes that now lay strewn across the kitchen floor, my legs still trembling from the sudden, unaccustomed effort while Mairead laughed to find the pattern of the tablecloth imprinted on her belly, something in us revived beneath the light of the kitchen lamp but both of us wise enough to grasp the cliché of the moment and laugh at it, a moment of erotic comedy which marked what we saw in retrospect as the beginning of the second part of our marriage with its quiet renewal of our love for each other, a brightening of our new lives together which was

cut across by a long moan from the end of the hall, my cue to rush to her side just in time to hold her by the shoulders over the edge of the bed while she discharged a rush of bitter gall into the basin, her body buckling at the hips with the effort while I spoke some hopeless words of comfort

it's ok, it's ok, get it all up

while she purged herself, half out of the bed with her head

down over the basin till she was spent and spitting and then that delicate manoeuvre to straighten her back under the duvet where she would lie limp and pale, all puked out, drifting in a fervid realm beyond words, near lost to the world when, without turning, she would lay her hand on mine so that I was assured she was aware of me and recognised my efforts and in this way, through such small gestures we quickly built up a language of cues and responses through which we managed, and I found myself sharper to them than I would have thought, this new language or choreography which we were now assembling on the fly but

which already governed the entire mood of the house, drawing us together into an intimacy of heat and fever, so pervasive that it charged the air with a prickly ammonial smell that hung through the hall and rooms like a fog, the whole house now suffused with the smell of sickness, a sourness which snagged in my pores and dragged me through the house several times a day swinging a pink aerosol as if it were a censer, launching a feathery floral spray into the middle of each room, a kind of purifying ritual which bathed the house for a brief time in the cloying stench of roses or lily-of-the-valley before it was burned off by the smell of sickness which emanated from this slight woman who was now so disbelieving of her own condition that her voice threaded to a whisper of rage whenever she gathered herself to protest

I've never felt like this before, never

enraged that her body at this stage of her life could betray her in such a way, turning on her like this with such venom after so many years of sound service – this was what offended her most and gave her suffering such a grating edge of incredulity – having finally arrived at a time in her life which was exclusively her own and without the care of kids to compromise it – that it should be spoiled like this – this, more than the illness itself, was what angered her most and gave her that rancorous edge which carried with it a warning that I shouldn't meddle with her frustration, nor try to reconcile her to it in any way since

I was uncertain how to feel, as part of me was convinced that this illness was drawing us closer together in a way that was decisive, as if this new life with all its caring and cleaning, all its fetching and carrying, was some new kind of courtship dance we were doing towards each other, a dance through filth and fever which took me by surprise in so far as I had thought our lives together up to this had brought us as close as we were ever likely to be and that such new intimacy was, frankly, improbable at this age of our lives – too set in our ways, too long in the tooth – this closeness which breached so many delicate laws of personal privacy, something neither of us could have anticipated nor predicted how we would react to as

we were now carried towards each other on the tidal rhythm of her fever, rising and falling on those swells specific to the illness itself, every moment pushing our marriage beyond its usual, mannered intimacies and into a new knowing of each other which was beyond embarrassment and this was something which no news article or analysis could hope to capture, this flesh and filth intimacy was the very thing which leaked away in the telling of this news story as it came through the news bulletins and headlines to wash through

the house

this same house

in which I've lived the best part of three decades and put together all those habits and rituals which have made up my marriage and family life and where now, for some reason, this day has given me pause to dwell on these things

sitting here at the kitchen table with my sandwich and paper where

those memories of Mairead in her flushed and fevered wasting come as reverse echoes of

that time during her first pregnancy when she carried Agnes and I saw her come into the fullness of herself as her belly grew and her skin and hair took on that aura of radiant well-being which I found irresistible and was so drawn towards, those first months passing in a liquid surge of desire which drove me headlong into the new lushness of her body, an intimacy which may well have had a slight twist of something kinky to it as if being watched by the growing child inside her added some illicit tincture to what we got up to during that period when the weight and lushness of her pregnancy was so alluring it was as if the new being within her was lending her a sheen that went deeper than her skin or her hair and was in itself pure goodness and virtue shining forth, something truly radiant about it which for a while sparked our love life with a thrilling, elevating element, charging our lovemaking with a grittier sensitivity towards each other's touch, an awareness which, I began to interpret as an appeal that

I should meet it with an improved version of myself or at least work to make myself worthy of this new, pristine version of my young wife, a demand I took so seriously that I sat down and gave myself over to it with sober concentration, surveying my soul in the light of Mairead's pregnancy which showed on her as if she were illumined from within and which I read now as nothing less than a sacred injunction that I should look to my own soul and rid it of all those slurs and injuries which had accrued to it over my lifetime, all this in preparation for our child, Mairead so radiant that

something petty in me felt sorely jilted by her elevated condition which, day by day, appeared like a higher, more refined evolutionary stage and which inspired so little in me save this wish to turn inward and inventory my own soul, a self-defeating instinct, the end purpose of which was never clear to me except that it would definitely take precious time and energy and probably bring little more than a deeper sense of unworthiness, not merely in relation to Mairead, this numinous being with whom I now shared my life, but also in relation to the child growing inside her, already exercising such a governing influence on us so

while all this was easy to understand and make amends for in the abstract it was a much more vexing proposition in real life where it became clear to me that I was not so generous or flexible as I might have thought, finding it difficult to make that space within me which would have fully allowed that other being into our lives and, something even more difficult to acknowledge, the sorry fact that this lack of generosity on my part harkened back to

the beginning of our marriage when, it appears, I had some difficulty taking the whole thing seriously and grasped the very first opportunity to lapse so catastrophically, an event that brought with it a measure of bleak comedy which did nothing to soothe Mairead's pain and disbelief the day she stood here

in the middle of this kitchen floor, whispering to herself

bridge building, fucking bridge building with

her face fixed in that vacant expression the world recognises in stroke sufferers while I stood opposite her, completely undone by the evidence at her disposal – all of it circumstantial yes, but all of it adding up to a conviction beyond reasonable doubt or any plea of mitigating circumstances or diminished responsibility – the names and dates all correct, the witnesses accounts all corroborated, all the holes and contradictions in my own version wholly damming and, most telling of all – the part which had the clinching ring of truth to it – the complete absence of any clear motive on my account other than a soft opportunity from which I had neither the wit nor courage to back away and which now had me standing before her, knowing full well that any defence I might offer would be totally undermined by that sheepish expression to which I lapse in such moments as Mairead stood

here in this same kitchen

with her alone to decide whether our short marriage had already run its course or if it was still something she wanted to go on with and when she recovered something of her poise – that is to say, when her face unfroze to an expression of total shock – she realised that this was what she truly hated me for, for having levied this decision on her alone, whether or not to continue with the marriage, a decision which gave the initial appearance of offering a choice but which, after a moment's consideration, revealed itself to her to be no choice at all since Mairead now discovered

here on this kitchen floor

that – for all her intuitions and sprightly enthusiasms, all her books and her travel, her convent education and her languages – her upbringing as an only child of devout parents had made her conservative, with a deep inner conviction that would not allow her believe that her marriage was something that could be so easily set aside or walked away from, so that now she was effectively left with no choice at all and this was my deceitful manoeuvre – to have steered her into that narrow arena where her beliefs and instincts were set to war with each other, so that good and liberal as her feelings were at the time, and willing as they may have been to end the marriage, they could not override those age-old principles which were by now hardwired in her soul, leaving her completely stricken, standing there

on this kitchen floor

not four feet from this table

gathering herself to curse me from the bottom of her heart

fucking bridge building she repeated – in fucking Prague of all places and

with all the evidence which nailed me – names, dates and times – in her possession, Mairead standing there with that centre parting in her hair which always looked so severe to me, as if it threatened to pull the two sides of her head apart, so that when she left the house half an hour later, with her bags packed and her hair down around her shoulders, I too was stricken but with shock of a different sort, rooted to the kitchen floor with my back to the sink, appalled that my life had been so completely dismantled by the very person to whom it had been pledged not so long ago and that I was seeing it all swept aside because of a series of faltering stupidities, the sort any man might hope they are exempt from but which

in the seven weeks following her leaving me alone in the house I had plenty of time to acknowledge that, in all truth, these were exactly the kind of soft stupidities to which I was prone and that I was indeed the type of man who, for want of that wit which would have prophesied my marriage in ruins, found myself alone in this house after she took herself away in stony removal to her parents' home in North Mayo which I bombarded with all those phone calls and letters which exhausted every tone of pleading I was capable of, phone calls and letters which after a week, I sent off with as little hope of reply as if I had rolled up a length of paper and corked it into a bottle before flinging it overhand into the sea and watching it drift away on an outgoing tide – that was as much hope I had of a reply during that period, alone in this house so that

after seven weeks my nerve failed and I got into the car to drive north, up through Newport and Mulranny and up through the badlands of North Mayo, crossing the terra incognita of Ballycroy with its sweeping bogland which levels away to the horizon in an unbroken swathe beneath a sky of such gaping distance that Agnes would always claim the hazy blue washes out of which so many of her images surfaced was her ongoing memory of what she had seen from the back seat of the car during those summer journeys we took up to the grandparents' place, driving through this bog terrain with nothing around us but rolling waves of heather and hills lost in a haze of distance, Comanche country according to Darragh, who at that time was well into his cowboy phase, ploughing his way through those old paperbacks my father gave him

JT Edson, Louis L'Amour, Zane Grey while

deep in the bog, a chimney stack stood naked out of a concrete floor – all the stone walls carted away to some other project – a lonely sentinel now gazing into the distance across a sea of blue heather with stacks of turf along the road and the odd car lying on its side in a sheugh or up on a wall, these being the years before the breath-alyser put paid to drink-driving and made redundant a generation of panel-beaters, crashed cars and vans which Darragh, in the back seat saw as most likely the work of Comanche raiding parties which ranged across these plains, coming from as far south as the Mojave Desert on the Galway border and riding north-west up onto the Erris panhandle, savage war parties who rode great distances by moon-light across these boglands, ranging far from their southern lodges, into the homelands of the great northern tribes, the

Cheyenne, Sioux and Arapaho

or as they were know locally

Mitchells, Davitts and Stephenites

or so Darragh said from the back seat as

I drove north that day to win back my wife, turning up on her doorstep with a low sun at my back to be met by her father, a quiet man, newly retired from a long career in the bank and a Commissioner for Oaths who now stood before me wearing the same wounded air as his daughter, an expression of distaste on his face as if he could hardly believe anyone would bring such cheap melodrama to his home, with all its attendant crudity and antics, this man who was now looking out over my shoulder, up and down the road as if I alone, standing there in front of him, were hardly sufficient in myself to have knocked on his door and drawn him from the depths of the house to where he now stood blinking in the midday light and breathing heavily from the emphysema that would kill him three years down the road, wheezing as if he had come a long distance over hazardous terrain and not, as was really the case, the full twenty yards from the back of the house to where he now stood listening to my plea with that expression of sorrowful fatigue loosening his features, an expression he had no doubt practised over the years dealing with various petitioners and supplicants who had come before him for loans or overdrafts or mortgages for one thing or another, this practised expression of regret on which there was now etched a sorrowful inevitability while I, seven weeks into our separation and still feeling my way in the role of the abandoned husband stood before this reluctant inquisitor, bleary-eyed and unshaven, anxious to show I was making a poor job of my new circumstances, stood there pleading my case, a hopeless task in that I was completely in the wrong and we both knew it, this man who had been so well disposed to me during the years I had courted his daughter, now stood on his doorstep with this sorrowful expression on his face, telling me in that practised way that I had no friends here and that I would be as well to turn around and go back the way I had come and that I needed to give her time – this was the expression he used

give her time

as if it were mine to give, as if somehow I had set aside a reservoir of time for just this purpose and could now draw on it before handing it over to her to do with as she pleased, something which would alleviate her pain, something which would salve her shame, something, anything which would bring her back to me, this time that her father seemed to think was mine to give even as Mairead herself was coming towards her due-date which was three months distant, taking on the curves and lines of a pod and that paleness of complexion which was near luminous and how I glimpsed her over her father's shoulder that day, glowing behind him in the shadows of the hallway, her face adrift in the gloom, the whites of her eyes like two jittery moons of some minor constellation as I heard myself calling to her

Mairead, for god's sake

as her father shifted his body into the centre of the door and I saw reflected in his face my own terror that I would plough through him, this man in his late sixties, and leave him sprawling on the floor as the shadows behind him lurched to a choked sob and she was gone so I stood back, to her father's relief and my own, both of us heaving with fright till he raised his hand once more and said

give her time

before closing the door in my face, as gentle a rejection as you could have wished for, comfortable almost, so that for the next few minutes I stood there, fixed on looking at the door-knocker which was suspended at eye level before me and knowing that I could have stayed there comfortably, dried out with rejection, for as long as it took me to turn to stone or longer before I eventually managed to uproot myself from the spot and move off, got into the car and

drove back the sixty miles or so to this house here, one of those pale car journeys of which I have no memory whatsoever, a journey that took me through several small towns and villages, over narrow roads cutting through wide bogland areas and windy roads that clung to a shelved pass around a sea inlet and only that I eventually found myself standing in this kitchen two hours later I could easily have believed that I had dematerialised on Mairead's doorstep and rematerialised here, sixty miles away in the kitchen of my own house without the trouble of physically travelling the intervening distance, since only such a complete dissolve of the self could account for the total absence of detailed memory of that complex journey, it being something of a miracle to have arrived here safe and sound at all but yet, knowing that this

was not the first time this had happened to me, driving halfway across the county to arrive safely at my destination, every mile sucked away in a vortex of absent-mindedness, a complete vacancy of spirit overcoming me so often that I would not care to number the times I have been recalled to startled attention behind the wheel of the car with no immediate knowledge of where I am before that shocked realisation that I have driven ten or fifteen miles of a busy road, into oncoming traffic, negotiated all sorts of bends and hazards, put towns and villages behind me but, somehow the whole thing having occurred in some adjacent dreamtime with my mind elsewhere while my hands and feet went through that empty sequences of moves and adjustments which kept the car on the road and pointed in the right direction

gears, brakes, accelerator and indicator left or right and

without stutter or stammer, sixty miles or more driven by some un-minded ghost of myself, a shadow-man

who now stood in this kitchen which

in Mairead's absence, had succumbed to the dirt and disarray of the single man's existence, that type of filth and dishevelment which gathers to shame and self-abandonment, the sort of grime that coats everything with a veil of grease and which draws books and papers across the floor to pile up in corners and on seats or under cushions, that gathering disorder where everything in the room begins to lie at an angle and a distance from their proper place, that slight degree of imprecision which gives the impression that the whole place is beginning to uproot itself, piece by piece and move away from me altogether, papers and cups and knives and forks moving along the shelves and worktops while the pictures themselves drifted also, leaving their angled smoke shadows on the wall, everything migrating across the room towards some vanishing point into which everything would disappear, such gathering filth and chaos that the place had begun to resemble the lair of some creature who eats and sleeps in close proximity to itself, a place littered with fur and gnawed bones amid a scum of deepening filth so that I stood at the sink hardly able to believe I was capable of such desolation, willing to ascribe it to someone else, not me, because surely this was the work of some malignant household spirit who went about its malicious work in the dead of night, and it says something about my state of mind that I stood here

in this kitchen

elaborating and embellishing this fantasy for some time instead of taking responsibility for what was happening around me because in truth what really tormented me was that all this filth and disorder offended my engineer's sense of structure, everything out of place and proper alignment, everything gathering towards some point of chaos beyond which it would be impossible to restore the place to its proper order and yet I stood looking at it, locked into a silent battle with the house itself and all the things which were slowly vacating their proper place, furniture and dishes and cutlery all over the place, curtains hanging awry and chairs and tables strewn about while books and papers slid across the floor, everything slowly shifting through the house as if they had a meeting to keep somewhere else, possibly in some higher realm where all this chaos would resolve into a refined harmony which had no need of my hand or intervention so

I stood back and let the place run to wrack and ruin around me for another two weeks before

Mairead eventually brought the stand-off to an end the day I turned from the sink to find her standing in the middle of the floor, twitchy and etiolated, like one of those apparitions who materialise at times of crisis, standing there with her bags beside her on the floor as if the past nine weeks had never happened and we were now at that juncture in our lives where we had to find those options which would enable us to fix whatever it was that led us to this point where we now stood eyeing each other across the kitchen floor with an abyss between us, fully recognising that our next words would define how we would manage the rest of our days together and as we stood there it became obvious that, with the autumn light closing in around us, we were now becalmed in a marriage which had lost direction but which we could not turn our backs on as the child she was carrying now complicated the situation with something more serious – these were the thoughts running through me as I stepped towards her with my right hand raised, swearing

never again, as God is my judge and

those weeks of separation had given Mairead a resolve which she did not have to put words to so that

her silence said everything she had to say and

eighteen months later, when our family was rounded out by Darragh's arrival we drew on the strength of the oath sworn over her belly that day and even if I could not explain its exact terms or conditions, which remained vague but stringent, it served to draw the focus of our lives away from ourselves and towards our children, so that even if it was not the ideal way to begin family life together, it is safe to say that a lot of good marriages have been built on a lot less as we settled into a love of each other for the sake of our two kids, securing them within the embrace of a loving family life, adamant they would not want for anything and that if, in any way, they sensed the desperation which sometimes swelled up between Mairead and myself they would have experienced it as nothing but a kind of distant grating on the margins of their lives, hardly anything at all, just the slightest dissonance, nothing to worry themselves about or keep them awake at night, listening in the dark to our strangled voices and stifled recriminations, so that in this way

they may have suffered our love for them as a desperate load, especially Agnes, an attentive child who was acutely sensitive to the slightest vibe between her parents and who, when very young, quickly developed a protective aura of airy distance around her which sometimes baffled and hurt both myself and Mairead at the time, but which we also suspected she used as a ploy to find her way out from under that love she was so relentlessly subject to, bearing down upon her so heavily, and beneath which she might have found herself so full of childish anxiety that, young and all as she was, she could not settle in the world and was wholly intolerant of its shortcomings, things never perfect, always needing correction or amendment of some sort or another – the sleeves of her coat too long, her food too hot or too cold or too lumpy – forever working herself up into a ball of frustration whenever she found herself unable to accommodate that smidgen of mess or chaos which is necessary to keep the world turning and human so that sometimes, as a toddler, she was overtaken with one of those pale, blue-lipped rages which threatened to strangle her and which she took off to her room where she would smoulder and grind face-down in her pillow, those tantrums before she perfected the fits of breath holding which she would draw down with her eyes closed and her throat locked, all raging concentration as her face turned puce and then blue before she would faint to the floor in a crumpled heap, Mairead in panicked sobs over her prone body, certain those first few times that she had lost her and slow to believe the GP who assured her that you cannot hold your breath unto death and that it was nothing, it was something which she would grow out of, which she did, a couple of years passing after which she eventually came through a thorny growth phase that was

very different to Darragh's way in the world which, as a child, was to give us as wide a berth as possible, as if he had come into the world with a clear sense of how things stood between Mairead and myself and had decided from the beginning that he wanted to go his own way and have very little to do with us so that if he ever felt our genuine love he did nothing to acknowledge it, laying it aside as gently as he could, as if it had never been offered, becoming another distant child, eternally preoccupied with various building projects spread throughout the house, constructs which seemed carefully conceived to involve no one but himself, the boy-builder who even at that young age had an independence of spirit about him that was easy to admire, something stubborn in his childish insistence on going his own way, labouring with bricks and construction kits in shadowed corners of the house where he raised so many besieged castles and cities and forts, harassed settlements and stockades, small parables of beleaguerment everywhere we turned, room after room, the whole house expanding to some fragmented vision of adversity which seemed to consume his whole childhood, making him an overly solemn kid for such long periods that we were resigned to seeing him being eternally preoccupied and slightly old before his time, that was till sometime in his early teens when he confused us further by rousing himself and coming towards us with open arms, a ready smile and a smart-assed turn of phrase like someone who had been gone on a long journey but who was now greeting us on his return with a relaxed willingness to participate in family life, becoming suddenly the more sociable of our two children since Agnes had by now almost withdrawn herself completely to her bedroom which she had turned into an artist's studio of sorts, the whole place cluttered with jars and brushes and rolls of paper along the work bench I had installed for her against one wall, this room in which Mairead worried she might poison herself with all its vapours of oils and turpentine, a dizzying haze swelling through the house whenever her bedroom door opened but which Agnes assured us had no effect whatsoever on her, and which she often eulogised in poetic terms whenever we voiced our concern about it, telling us not to worry, the windows were open, the room was well aired and besides, paint was now her element and if she drifted away on a cloud of its vapours then that was fine by her, she would be one with her medium and that would be the fulfilment of her deepest wish, one of those speeches that Darragh would later refer to as

the ecstasy of Agnes

Agnes the Unhinged

those several names he called her in that way of prodding and poking which became their way of relating to each other during their teen years when Agnes took up the studied role of the scholar-artist while Darragh set aside his sharper mind to caper around and tease her, not exactly trying to highjack her efforts but driven daft in himself by his own abilities which were real and glittering but were cut through with a fatal measure of laziness which to this day has short-circuited so many of those projects he has started – the PhD he registered for but which, to the best of my knowledge, he never wrote a line of, or the year he intended working in Africa with some NGO, digging aquifers on the edge of the Sahara, two full months going around getting vetted by the guards, medical clearances, jabs and shots, getting visas sorted out, papers and application forms piling up around him and then

nothing

not a thing

the whole project evaporating into thin air and all the forms and documents on the desk drowning in a rising swell of more paper, this time his notes on the 1981 Republican hunger strike as a strategy video game, an idea he was going to pitch to one of those game development companies that had set up in Galway with the hope of tapping into a steady stream of IT graduates, all his nights spent poring over accounts of the hunger strike till he had amassed a broad and detailed comprehension of the background material and the complex political context in which the strike occurred with all its ebbs and flows, all its moves and countermoves till, for whatever reason, this idea too just seemed to fade away into oblivion as

he gradually stopped talking about it and did not care to be questioned or reminded about it so we just marked it down as another of his enterprises which had come to nothing, neither Mairead nor myself really surprised now – worried yes, but not surprised – because this seemed to be that time in his life when he could suck the life out of any project no matter how promising it appeared, all Darragh had to do was lay his hand on it and somehow it wilted and died, the good gone from it before it was ever fully conceived, things half started before being fully abandoned, aborted projects building up all around him, his life a breakers yard of such things, till the day

he pulled the round-the-world ticket out of his jacket and stood here on this kitchen floor gazing at it as if it had materialised from on high with no effort on his part whatsoever, a ticket with an itinerary which would circumnavigate the globe by way of Thailand, Sydney, Perth, Hawaii, Boston and back home to Dublin, this permit that would take him to the ends of the earth where he would spend a season wandering in the wilderness trying to find whatever it was he had lost, but with Mairead looking at him from where I'm sitting now, in two minds about the whole thing, glad to see him doing something, anything, but sorry that this something was taking him away from her, putting the whole world between him and

do you have money for this trip – the question blurted from me before I realised

yes, I do

how

I've been working

what sort of work

making medical components

he looked up from the ticket in his hand, the bemused expression still on his face medical components, I thought you were studying

I am – I was – it's complicated

I'll bet, so what were you doing with these medical components

this company – AbMed – they needed extra hands to fulfil an emergency contract for the American army, the coalition forces in Iraq

there was an emergency so they sent for you

yes Dad, others recognise my worth even if my family do not, anyway, I spent three months sweeping stents and catheters with UV light for flaws, I got well paid for it, that's where the money came from and

did you know about this, I said to Mairead

I think it's great, she waved the question aside, he has a ticket to the world and his own money and

Christ

I weary of my son sometimes

even from the other side of the world he has this psychic ability to reach across latitudes and time zones and lay his twitchy hand on my heart and squeeze it which sets me to worrying about him all over again, the thought of him enough to dampen any mood and

a change in the light now

all radiance washed from it as if it is worn out, residual of light which has passed on to elsewhere and

how strange this day is

something about it which, sitting here and looking out on the back garden, gives the impression that it has already turned through the best part of itself, nothing left that is not pallid or faded beneath a sun too bright for this time of year, stalled over the world at too high a declension, bleaching the proper tones from everything while

sitting here at this table

waiting for my wife and kids to return to this kitchen with this anxious feeling that everything around me has settled into places and patterns unknown to me, things no different or mysterious in themselves but everything off a degree or two, this slight imprecision all around me as if things have shifted out of position just enough to make my hand hover over them for an instant before picking them up or moving them back to where they should be, some things wholly out of place, like this tablecloth in front of me, a white tablecloth which, if memory serves, is normally never used except at Christmas but which now, on the second of November, is spread out before me like a snow field with all the vast extension of a tundra, white and unblemished and rolling onto its own frozen horizons, my hands outspread over it as if I were extending some sort of blessing upon it from on high, or trying to steady it against some instability in the table beneath or the house itself, panicked by the idea that

everything in this room might suddenly rise up through the ceiling to some proper place in the sky above, chairs and tables and cupboards and worktops, everything rising up into the air, while drawing with them all those connections which have now made me so hyper-aware and awash with a giddy fit of enraged irrationality, sitting here, grinding with frustration, something peevish in me upset at having my expectations confused by this tablecloth or the chair at the other end of the table for Christ's sake, standing with its back to the wall when normally it should be pushed into the table, that type of thing twisting me up into such sudden rage that makes me want to rise from the table

seeing myself rise

and take it by the two legs to smash it against the wall, the desire so strong I can feel its collapsing impact, the give in its legs and frame as it disintegrates, the shock of it through my arms as it splinters apart with every nerve and sinew of my body on edge, this anxiety cutting through me like referred pain or interference, the source of which is elsewhere, possibly outside myself at arm's length but still close enough to be inside my circumference, something which will not allow me to rest in the here-and-now on

this day

this fucking day

that has done nothing but drive me deeper into a grating dread which seems so determined to conceal its proper cause and which is all the more worrying since there is no doubt whatsoever of its reality or that it is underwritten in some imminent catastrophe

for me

or upon me

or through me

this fear which is

the whole mood of my vigil at this table for however long it's been since the Angelus bell struck so that even

while sitting here with my milk and sandwich, gusted to the core of my bones with the conviction that my wife and children will never come this way again, never return, this dread singing through me from the headlines of the foreign news page of the newspaper – all news feels foreign today – telling me that an outbreak of cholera in West Africa has endangered thousands of lives and threatens to cover a large section of the western part of the sub-Saharan continent, reaching into Chad and Cameroon, while somewhere in South Korea an outbreak of avian flu has crossed the species barrier, diagnosed in a twenty-two-year-old medical student who is currently in quarantine, God's creatures bound together in a common suffering, our aches and pains one and the same as those of the duck and the turkey and the chicken and

stop

mother of Jesus stop

this is how the mind unravels in nonsense and rubbish

if given its head

the mind in repose, unspooling to infinity, slackening to these ridiculous musings which are too easily passed off as thought, these glib associations, mental echoes which reverb with our anxiety to stay wake and wise to the world or at least attentive to as much of its circumstances as we can grasp while

come to think of it

thinking of it now

now being thought

it must have been this same sort of unspooling coupled with the same fatal aptness for fantasy that consumed my father and unravelled his mind in that last year of his life, especially during those last months when he lost his grip on the world completely and withdrew to the old house where there was only himself and the dog to keep each other company in those days after Onnie's death, the long winter nights when the full weight of her absence must have come upon him with so much fear and loneliness that his grief was eclipsed completely in disbelief at the fact that his wife of over forty years could ever leave him for any reason whatsoever – death included – leave him all alone now, a fate he had never envisioned nor prepared himself for so that when it did come the raw shock of it scrambled his sense of the world so thoroughly it was as if something essential to the proper balance of the universe itself had been casually set aside and replaced with some new but shoddier circumstance which so keenly insulted something delicate within him that

in no time at all his strength and resolve was undone, he slackened and lost interest in the world before withdrawing completely to the house with the dog where, in the half-light of those narrow rooms, behind drawn curtains, his confusion and grief deepened to that fatal awkwardness with which there is no talking to so that very suddenly he grew angry and rancorous and fell out with myself and Eithne, took against us with such sudden vehemence in those weeks after Onnie's funeral that we had no time to fathom its proper cause but were nevertheless left in no doubt by his rage that some shameful blame had accrued to both of us for some reason or other because when we went to see him he dismissed us from behind the closed front door, telling us to leave and not come back and calling us a

a shower of cunts and nothing but

his curse upon us that day with both of us standing there looking at each other in disbelief, not knowing what to do and when I took a walk around the house I saw that he had the curtains drawn in every window and the back door locked with no way in so there was nothing for it but to leave, we'd come back and try again in a couple of days but then

he sold off all his livestock and hens leaving just himself and Rex alone in the house now with the two gates coming into the yard barred also, secured with two balks of timber tied from pillar to pillar so that the postman had to climb up over the sod fence and walk down the path to shove the letters and mass cards under the door which was bolted also and

all this happened before Onnie's month's mind mass

by which time also he had begun to show the first signs of letting himself go, growing a beard that bristled out from his jaws in a way that threatened to engulf his whole head – a genuinely shocking sight on a man who had been clean-shaven his whole life but who now would not hear a word against it saying that his father had had a beard and his father before him had had one and so too had our Lord – a better man than either of them – and if a beard was good enough for those men then it was good enough for him also and that was an end to it just as it most certainly

marked the point at which he really began to neglect himself, not eating right and no wash or shave either, with the same clothes on him day in, day out while he grew thinner and thinner inside them, the shirt slack over his narrow chest and the trousers barely hanging on his hips – but the hair and beard still growing, thickening like a furze bush around his head – and no fire or heat on in the house anymore so that it got damp and filthy with black mould growing down the walls and nothing but the smell of piss meeting me at the door those few times he let me in to see him with a few bits and pieces to find him sitting there in the dark, all alone in the glare of the television screen looking at *Bosco* or some other kid's programme and a can of fly spray on the table when

one evening he fell asleep in front of the open fire, sods burning and coals falling onto the hearth and he woke up to find his wellingtons soldered to his feet, melted in the heat around his ankles and he would have been in serious trouble only he had good wool socks on under them and he managed to hobble to the kitchen table where he got out the bread knife to cut them away, socks and trousers and wellingtons lying in a heap in the middle of the floor, the smell of burnt rubber thick in the air as

I stood appalled in the murk of that room and said
you can't live like this
like what
like this, the state of the place
and you'd know how I should live
I know that there has to be something better than this and
a look came over his face which stopped me
I saw her last night he said

you saw who

Onnie, I saw Onnie

Jesus Christ, Dad, Mam's been dead for three months and

I woke up last night and she was standing at the end of the bed looking at me – she had two bags of shopping with her and do you know what she said

she's dead, Dad, I know it's hard

she said, go over and see the state of the grave I'm lying in and

I've told you before, we've been through this – you can't put a headstone on the grave yet, you have to give the ground time to settle – eleven months to a year, that's the usual waiting time with

his eyes brimming as if his broken heart had opened some spring which flowed up through him and him standing there alone in the half-light of the kitchen, the dog out eating the grass along the margins of the road and

sometimes, if you were passing you might see him at the gable of the house, leaning on the stick and smoking, watching the cars going to town in the evening but, if you stopped to talk to him over the fence he'd take off like a frightened hen and you'd hear him pulling the bolts on the door from the road and you could imagine him sitting there alone in the waning light of the kitchen, watching the television, wasting away in confusion and neglect while winter closed in around him and the television stayed on but the bulbs started to go out in one room after another as doors were closed for the last time on these same rooms with bottles and unread newspapers piled up on the chairs and the dresser and the sofa under the window, while all around him the house gradually came apart with paint peeling and curtains fraying and doors swelled in their frames from the dampness

till the day

I stood outside the barred gate pleading with him to sign a grant application form so that he could get the house renovated, the whole thing sealed and insulated, windows and doors and the whole lot painted, all he had to do was put his name to the bottom of the application form, that's all he had to do, I'd look after the rest, organise the paperwork and contract the job out to a registered builder, all he had to do was sign his name, but would he sign would he fuck sign

I will in my fuck sign, he said, from inside the gate,

I'll sign fuck-all or put an X on anything either, he roared, coming here with your forms looking for signatures – by Jesus, you must think I'm fierce innocent if you expect me to fall for that one – but I'll tell you one thing now and not two things – I know well what your game is – I'll sign that form and the next thing I'll find myself in the county home and this house will be sold out from under me and yourself and your sister dividing it up between ye, isn't that what you're up to, isn't that what you're after

it's not what I'm up to and it's not what I'm after and

like fuck it's not – take your application form and your grant and your contracts and fuck off back to where you came from and

that's the thanks I got

standing outside the gate waving the form at him, begging him to see reason and telling him that it was only for his own good and that this was the right thing to do and all I wanted was that he'd have a roof over his head and warmth – a small bit of comfort living on his own and, my hand to god, I had no intention of putting him in the county home or any other home for that matter because this was his home, I knew that, no one wanted to put him away and

my heart clenched in my chest with a desperate love for this man who had been the hero of my life but who now was so confused he was incapable of seeing who or what was good for him, and this above all else cut me to the bone, how a man who had walked so sure-footedly through the world could now misread it so completely that he could see no good in anything anymore, not even in his own son, me standing outside the gate with my temper gone and my patience gone but still pleading with him and for myself that he should

sign the fucking form, for the love of Jesus

talking to the back of his head now because he was hobbling away down the path to the house and I watched him go inside and pull the door behind him, and even at that distance I could hear the bolts ramming home, the sound echoing through my head as I stood there a few minutes longer, hardly able to move from heartbreak and despair before I eventually pushed myself off the gate and drove back home to phone Eithne that evening and tell her what had happened, beginning a long argument with her and losing my temper, trying to convince her that I had done all I could do to help him, begged and pleaded with him, pushed the forms under his nose but it was no good, nothing was any good, there was no talking to him and

what the hell did she want me to do

what more could I do

wrestle him to the ground and force him to sign, was that what she wanted because if she thought she could do a better job she was welcome to try, I was at my wits' end with the whole fucking thing and and

it's all grief, all that anger is grief, Eithne said at the other end

what do you mean grief, falling out with everyone, abusing people, that's the funniest grief I've ever come across

anger is a well-known stage of the grieving process so

I could feel a geyser of frustration coming to a head within me

Jesus, Eithne, don't go giving me that pop psychology shite – I'm his son and if he can't

if this is the way you spoke to him I'm not surprised that

I slammed down the phone, or she slammed down the phone or both of us slammed down the phone together, either way the call ended with a bang and I sat there in a rage before going to the cupboard and opening a bottle of Jameson to sit drinking in this kitchen till the early hours of the morning and that was the last word I spoke to Eithne and

it was around this time also, and for whatever reason, that he upped and

bought a new tractor

I swear to Jesus

a span new John Deere, a small 5E, about 60 hp, and with no cab on it, reminding me of the old Massey Ferguson 35 he had long ago – standing in the yard, gleaming in its green paint and god knows what it cost, I was afraid to ask him because he began talking straight away of his plans to hire out to agricultural contractors for silage-making and turf-cutting and so on, with him driving of course – this man who could hardly walk without the aid of a stick, the power in his legs gone, him near crippled with dampness in his bones – and he housed the tractor in the old shed at the end of the yard and put a fine galvanised roof over it, but that's as much as he ever did with it because if he started it five or six times after that that was about the height of it, he never did any work with it, none that I ever knew of anyway – who was going to hire a man who could hardly walk, tractor or no tractor, he could hardly pull himself up on it – so it stayed there in the shed with the same fill of diesel it had arrived in the yard with and whenever he wasn't gazing at it from the kitchen window he was out with a cloth wiping the windscreen or buffing the headlamps, polishing it like it was his special toy, which of course it was because this was his second childhood and all this care and attention for a fucking tractor when his own house was going to wrack and ruin about him with dampness running down the walls of every room and a scraw of black mould now growing in the bathroom but

he hardly had the tractor in the yard a month when he sat into it and turned it on and it stalled stone dead on him, no stir out of it, lights and gauges coming on all right but no spark or turn on the ignition, not a gig out of it and when, by chance, I went over to him that evening he was looking into the engine with all its mass of wiring and electronics, all confused and clueless and I had a look at it myself but couldn't get her started so I put in a call to the garage where he'd bought it and got a man on the other end who remem-bered the sale and was surprised to hear the complaint and who asked the usual questions

no, the battery had a full charge

no, all the wiring was connected as far as I could see and

yes, the lights were coming up

after which he stalled for a moment before saying

leave it with me a minute, I'll get back to you

which he did, fair play, and I took the call at the far end of the yard watching my father standing beside the dead tractor, looking upset and bewildered as I called to him you won't believe this

believe what

seemingly your tractor's ignition has been disabled by satellite

what

yes, by satellite, an anti-theft device

they're saying I'm a thief

no one's saying you're a thief

I'm not a thief

there's been some delay in your payment registering, so their system has no record yet of a transaction, as far as the system is concerned the tractor is stolen and

so it is saying I'm a thief

it's not saying that, it's a security device fitted to a lot of plant and farm machinery, it'll be switched on in an hour and

with nothing else to be done we turned to look up at the sky as if we might spot that enabling pulse or spark from on high, neither of us with any clue what we were waiting for, whether or not the satellite was in some sort of stationary orbit over us or whether we had to wait for it to rise above the horizon before it would reach out across the heavens and turn the ignition on our tractor and

it was easy to feel foolish standing there on the wet concrete looking up at the grey sky, neither of us with anything to say as the moment deepened to that feeling of helpless stupidity when there is nothing you can do before he threw up his hands and turned for the house without a word, the wild head on him and the hobbling walk

where are you going

but no word out of him as he pulled the door behind him and it might be hindsight putting this shade on the whole thing but I've always believed that was the moment he parted company with the world, both of them with nothing to say turning their backs on each other because

a couple of weeks later he was found lying on the concrete walk outside the house by a neighbour over the village, Mattie Moran, who was on his way into town to collect his dole when he spotted him from the road and pulled over to hop in across the wall and go down on his knee beside him, putting his ear on his chest to hear if he was breathing before picking him up and laying him into the back seat of the car, stick and all, telling me afterwards that

it was like lifting a bundle of sticks – there was more meat on a sparrow's ankle and he

drove him to the hospital where he stayed for the next three weeks and they washed and fed him while they ran all those tests which finally revealed the pancreatic cancer that would kill him within a couple of weeks, by which time there was less than six stone of him in the bed and only that he still had the wild head of hair on him you could hardly see his face in the middle of the pillow, but I combed it and did my best to tidy it and then I put him in his grandchild's confirmation suit because he was now so shrunken none of his own would fit him and we lowered his coffin into the grave beside Onnie on the twenty-seventh of November and I stood there with Mairead and Agnes and Darragh beside me, the four of us huddled together in the chilly sunshine reciting a decade of the Rosary, the First Glorious Mystery, the Resurrection, our murmured prayers carried away on the breeze and while standing there, on the lip of his grave I thought that this was surely a day for the big questions

life, the universe, the whole fucking thing

nothing less seemed adequate to the moment and I did indeed find myself sifting through the sorrow of his last year and wondering to myself whose idea of justice was satisfied in his final confusion and humiliation and to what end or purpose had he been allowed to waste away in such confused, ragged ignominy, these questions sifting through my mind beneath the murmured responses to the Rosary but

I must have been wrong

it was neither the time nor the place for such questions, for I stood there under a November sky that had turned the colour of concrete and watched the gravediggers shovel the soil over his coffin when a man came up to me and said

I'm sorry for your loss, but he wouldn't swap places with us now, he's with Onnie and that was all he cared about and

he was hardly three months buried when I went into Coffey's

and ordered a plain granite headstone and border with black and white quartz gravel to be put up before the month was out, which drew another call from Eithne, giving out to me that she hadn't been consulted and that it was too soon to put up a headstone plus a whole slew of other things and I told her that she shouldn't feel left out, that I would split the bill with her, she shouldn't worry about that and

you know well that's not what I mean she said

do I, well I'll tell you this – it won't be your bed he'll come sitting on the end of when he comes back to haunt

for Christ's sake Marcus, she said

so I banged the phone down once more and it would be a full six months before I talked to her again, when she called to the house and put out the hand-of-peace with tears and hugs, her anger well behind her, mine also burned away, and telling me that she had been to the graveyard and that she appreciated the job I'd done, a really nice job and that it suited them both, not flashy in any way and thanks for writing

Erected by the Family

that was nice, she appreciated it and sure enough she pulled out her pen and wrote me a cheque for half the cost of the whole thing and there wasn't another word said about it as we sat there realising for the first time that we were without a father or mother and

does that make us orphans now, Eithne wondered, sniffling into a hankie, do you think

we might be a bit old for that, two middle-aged adults with families, I think those things rule us out but

I'm not so sure, I didn't know there was an age limit on it, besides, I feel orphaned and

her face softened into grief, both parents gone in little over a year, that's hard, that's very hard and

it is and it was

twelve months which pushed us into a brother-sister intimacy new to both of us, with a desire to reach out with phone calls and texts passing between us just to make sure we were all right, even if that was precisely the question we never asked as we kept our messages to a deadpan of information exchange and gossip, jokes and quips,

these bland words hiding and nurturing this new and baffling need
for each other which grew from our shared loss, nothing odd in it,
the fate of half the world, but none the less desolate for it, which
even as we sat there in the sitting room that day was not anything
we could foresee, me and the sister reaching out to each other and

    still

    still something twitchy and indistinct about this day

    now into the early afternoon, twenty to one by the clock on the
wall and

    that buzz in the radio sounds as if the signal is coming through
a blizzard of interference, some sort of grainy impedance breaking
up the songs no matter what station it's tuned to, national or local,
every voice and melody reduced to a grainy burr of static, nothing
coming through at all but the certainty of being wholly displaced
here in this house, my own house and the uncanny feeling of dragging my own after-image with me like an intermittent being, strobing
and flickering even while

    sitting here with my hands placed flat on the table in front of
me or

    going through the rooms, up and down the hall, one moment
to the next, fading and pulsing, overwhelmed in light one moment,
shadow the next, visible as a flame in sunlight so that anyone who looks
upon me would have to angle their gaze to see me clearly because

    within days

    I developed a sharp eye for every change in Mairead's condition
and what each signified, all the peaks and troughs of her moods
speaking clearly to me so that whenever she lay back in the pillow
with her mouth open I knew her to be momentarily becalmed in one
of those shallow respites that punctuated the long periods of cramp
twisting through her stomach, lying there luminous in the aftermath
of such spasms, drawing febrile breath into the shallow depths of her
lungs with her arms by her side as if she were laid out to be waked
among a watching congregation of Agnes's dolls and soft toys before
she would eventually move and swing her shins out over the side of
the bed to sit for another moment, bracing herself with both hands
planted down beside her before propelling herself out the door and

down the hall in a desperate lunge to the shower in which I had placed one of the plastic chairs from the garden so that she could sit with her head bowed, soaping her crotch and underarms beneath the warm cascade for ten minutes or so, the water pounding down on her as she sat there like a ruined princess before she would stand up, swaying in the steaming heat with her towel gathering around her so that I could carry her back to the bedroom to dry her and put her into fresh pyjamas, then angling her back under the sheets where she would lie breathless, every pulse trip-hammering through her body till it levelled out to where she could drift off to sleep once more, all this happening without any word passing between us, a job done in silence and not clouded with speech because I knew these lucid moments were so precious to her that she would not want to waste them in talk, and when I had her in bed I would lie in beside her, resting my hand on her, feeling her hip-bone poking through the flesh as she linked her arm in mine, the two of us lying there, arm in arm in the shaded room and drifting in this heated intimacy, I with nothing to give save the assurance that I was there beside her, nothing but my warm bulk and that silence which we gradually filled out together so that

fuck me

Mother of Jesus

a picture looking up at me

this picture in the local paper showing four men in suits standing in front of a new national school, all smiling at the camera and holding a length of ribbon between them, the one in the middle preparing to cut it with a shiny new scissors, their faces open to the camera in a broad expression of civic satisfaction, the man with the scissors looking especially pleased, standing with his chin up-tilted and his chest out

Deputy John Francis Moylette

or The Legislator as Halloran refers to him

his presence so vivid now that the sight of him in this picture closes the walls around me, same as

hearing his voice on the phone did that day in the office, the breathless rasp of a man under pressure, wheezing and puffing as I sat back in the chair and checked the time on my watch – ten past twelve – and braced myself because it's never a good thing when an engineer gets a call from a politician in the middle of the day, you know well that two different world views are likely to clash and how ever it starts off there is only ever going to be one result and I knew straight off from his tone that this was going to be the case today also and that his patience was gone before he started, the way he launched straight into it with no hello or goodbye or any greeting whatsoever, just a torrent of words, beginning with

Marcus, do you read the papers

yes John, I read the *Irish Times* every day

I'm not talking about the *Irish Times*, I'm talking about *The Mayo News* and the *Western People*, do you read them

not always, not every week

I thought as much, so I'm going to spell it out for you, paint you a picture so to speak – a picture should be a lot clearer to an engineer, clearer than words anyway since

Moylette was cut from the same cloth as Halloran, the same ready way with populist appeal and gesture – the photo of him putting his hawk and trowel into the boot of his car when he drove to Dublin to take up his seat in Leinster House is often reproduced – but more belligerent and long winded, his phone calls to council offices especially dreaded because – bulked out as they always were with anecdotal pleading and exceptional cases – they could go on for anything up to an hour leaving the hearer worn down and likely to make all sorts of concessions just to be shut of him so that when the phone was hung up you were sometimes confused about what you may or may not have agreed to and

are you with me Marcus

I'm still here

good, now, you may or may not have noticed but I've spent the last three years trying to build an electoral base in the south-west corner of this county, the largest and most far-flung constituency in the whole country – leaflets, clinics, church gate collections – the whole lot, anything to harvest a quota of first preferences in an area with no major urban centre, just a few scattered villages, an area which is, by and large covered with some of the widest bogs and the highest mountains in the whole province, an area populated in the main by black-faced sheep, none of whom, to the best of my knowledge has the vote, because if they did I would be sitting on a nice fat surplus, all those hoggets and rams and ewes voting for me, but that day isn't today or tomorrow so till then I have to take to the highways and the byways of this county for funerals and festivals and football matches and god knows what else to get my name and face in the paper as often as possible so that I can be seen to be doing the type of work that benefits the community and is remembered by the electorate whenever the next election is called, so that when the good people of this constituency are standing alone in the privacy of the polling booth and they see the name of John Francis Moylette on their ballot paper they will hopefully remember that I'm the man whose face they saw in the paper at some launch or some opening or some social event or other, John Francis Moylette, the man who was there at those crucial moments and they'll remember that and be moved to put a tick after my name so that I can be re-elected and continue to do good work for the people of this county and are you with me so far Marcus

I'm still here John

I said weakly, slumped at my desk, this torrent of words washing through me and knowing full well from his relentless tone what was coming and he knew that I knew because this was an old dance we were doing now, we both knew the moves and we both knew that he was just winding himself up to the full measure of his temper because what had passed up to now was only the preamble, the introduction to his major theme which he now took up, saying

good, I'm glad I have your attention because this is where it gets a small bit awkward – I got a call from a mutual friend yesterday, Shamie Curran the building contractor, I gather you know him

I know Shamie

good, well Shamie expressed a large degree of dissatisfaction with you on account of what he claims is your unwarranted reluctance as an engineer to sign off on a public works project to which he is the sole contractor – namely the new national school in Derragarramh – is he right or is he pulling my leg and

I sighed and tried to keep my voice level because even though I had been waiting for this phone call for the last couple of weeks nothing apparently, in all that waiting, had prepared me for the wash of fatigue it was now bringing with it, that warm surge of hope-lessness which now coursed through my whole being as I leaned back in my chair and said

you know well he's right John – I refused to sign off on the foun-dation for sound engineering reasons, there's a report outlining those same reasons which I'm pretty sure has made its way to your desk by now

that may be so but I don't have time to read every report that piles up on this desk – I wouldn't see the outside of this office if I did – but the long and the short of it is that I gather you have some worries about the foundation

no, not strictly the foundation but the concrete going into the foundation

it's concrete, what's the problem with it – it's not strong enough or what

no, there's nothing wrong with the concrete

it's strong enough

it's not that but

now I saw he was trying to get me to say something which would undermine my position, namely admit that the concrete was defec-tive and he continued with a honed edge to his voice

I'm confused Marcus, either the concrete is strong enough or it's not strong enough, what else can be wrong with it, I can't see the difficulty

the difficulty, as I've outlined in my report, is that the foun-dation is made up of three separate but interlocking rafts which exert all sorts of pressures on each other so as such they should all be poured from the same batch of concrete but, and this is where the problem lies, the on-site slump tests show that this was not the case – what we have in this case is three separate rafts from three separate pours of concrete, different aggregates, different compo-sition ratios and

what the hell does it matter so long as it sets and it's strong enough – I've a bad feeling I'm wasting my time here Marcus, that I could be doing something a lot wiser and

by now I had the school plans spread out on the desk in front of me so I could see from the drawings the size and orientation of the whole school building relative to the site and the main road which ran outside its front gate and also, within its pencilled walls, the classrooms and bathrooms opening onto a main corridor which ran inside the front door connecting the full length of the building to the staff room at its furthest end and the emergency exits at the other so that looking down at it from my god's eye perspective with the roof peeled back, it was easy to see how desks and classes would be orientated in such a way as to have afternoon sunlight streaming in from the side windows on the bowed heads of the pupils as they worked at their sums or spellings till the bell went at two o'clock when they would pack up their bags before streaming out into the hallway, three classrooms opening out into the hallway, so that from this height, with a top-down view over them, it was easy to imagine their little heads bobbing around like a mass of footballs in a river current, all streaming into the hall, through the front door and out onto the forecourt beyond where the buses were safely parked in the recessed area outside the front gate and all things considered it truly was something to marvel at – how this schematic on white paper could translate so easily from an architect's and engineer's mind into a smoothly functioning public facility – this small rural national school which

would draw together the children of four townlands and which, as it stood now on this sheet of A2, was by any measure, a credit to everyone involved in it, the planners and architects and whoever had handed down the guidelines from the Department of Education and even Moylette himself who had, no doubt, worked hard trying to convince all sides that this new school was in everyone's best interest and that to relinquish their attachment to their own smaller but older and less efficient schools would enable their children to come together in that wider spirit of modern community which this school signified and then

I remembered the concrete foundation beneath the whole

structure and without conscious prompting on my part the engineer in me was already speaking to say that

the problem comes from the fact that there are three different foundation slabs locked into each other, three different pours of concrete and the danger comes in the next hot or cold spell when they have to expand and contract which, because of their different compositions, they will do so at different speeds and different pressures, that's where the difficulty lies so

for the love of Jesus, Marcus, Moylette broke in, you're a conscientious man and it does you credit but this is a national school we're talking about here, not a fucking nuclear reactor, what's the worst that can happen – the foundation expands and contracts and a few doors go askew on their hinges, cracks in the plaster and that's about it – you should remember that Curran has bricklayers and plumbers and electricians lined up outside the gate to work on this so

my voice cut across him, streaking ahead of my own wish to keep my tone reasonable and moderate, telling him bluntly that

when that foundation begins to crack – as it surely will – doors hanging off their hinges will be the least of your problems because any building raised on those slabs will tear itself apart in three different directions whenever the temperature goes through a sudden change and as far as bricklayers and plasterers are concerned I have to say that I am out of sympathy with them as

a long, sudden silence stretched out between us during which the phone warmed in my hand, becoming slick with sweat till the moment was broken from the other end, Moylette picking up the conversation once more in a tone hardly tempered with any consideration of what I had just outlined, saying

I'll tell you a story Marcus and after you've listened to it you can then weigh your conscience as an engineer against what I have to try and do to please people of this community, what I'm up against – are you with me

I'm not against you John

you have a funny way of showing it – this story begins two years ago when I lost a very public battle with the Department of Education to keep three small national schools open in the heart of my constituency, an issue which affected a significant section of my core vote, men and women I had to stand in front of and tell that their schools were to be closed down, their boards of management dissolved and that from now on those of them with kids would have to drive four or five miles to school each morning – that was the story I needed them to forget so that they could focus on the fact that they now had a shiny new school at the centre of the parish with three new teachers, recreation rooms, basketball courts, cloakrooms, the whole lot – this was the promise I sold them in exchange for them having lost their little schools, getting them to sit down with various mediation services so that I could get the members of the disbanded boards of management to agree to the new school with a new amalgamated governing body and finally, when I have all this in place – months and months of work, meetings and presentations and calling in favours from all over the place and the whole thing ready to go, what happens – I get a call from Curran telling me that two months on he is still waiting for a clearance cert for the completed foundation, that he has block-layers and plasterers lined up outside the gate ready to work and

I ran those slump tests myself and

who the hell runs on-site slump tests, Moylette roared, his patience finally exhausted as

any engineer who sees two concrete trucks with different markings coming onto a site, that's who runs slump tests so

don't talk to me about concrete

Moylette cut in

I served my time with concrete, you know that well and just so you have no doubts, I still have my hawk and trowel and spirit level in the boot of the car in case the day comes when the returning officer gets up on the podium and announces to the world that the people of this constituency have rejected me – when that day comes I won't have to walk far to pick up my tools and start again so don't talk to me about concrete or mortar and

John, it's easy to come on the phone here and

that's where you're wrong Marcus, it's not easy, it's not a bit easy, I have better things for doing with my time than pestering you or anyone else with this sort of thing but if it has to be done I'll do it and while I have you I'm going to paint another picture, something that will be clear to an engineer like you, this is how I see it – about eighteen months from now I see myself wearing my best suit and my sunniest smile and I'm standing between a few other local dignitaries holding a big shiny scissors to cut the ribbon which opens the lovely new school behind me, I'm there with a big smile on my face for the camera, shaking hands with everyone around me and speaking to mothers and fathers so that in future, every time they come to pick up little Chloe or Keelin they'll pause for a moment and remember me, thinking to themselves

fair play to Moylette, he sorted it out, he was as good as his word because

mark my words, that is the only way this whole thing is going to pan out and the sooner you set aside your engineer's scruples and put your name to the clearance cert the sooner we can get on with it and

no engineer can sign off on

fuck engineers, Moylette roared, his temper now routed

engineers don't make the world, you should know that more than anyone, politics and politicians make the world and I'm telling you now I do not give one fuck whose name appears on that cert but

that's the difference between you and me John

what difference

the difference between a politician and an engineer, your decisions have only to hold up for four or five years – one electoral cycle and you are acclaimed a hero – but my decisions need a longer lifespan than that or my reputation is in shreds so

my temper was burning away now and I was afraid I was going to lose the head and start fucking him down the phone so I just closed my eyes and sat back in the chair, reining in my horses a bit and lowering my voice to thank him for calling and telling him that his concerns were noted, goodbye and we'll talk again, before

I put the phone down with a bad, sour feeling simmering in the bottom of my belly because I knew full well what was happening, I could physically feel it, the clamping pressure with that thickening of the air which always comes as

    the squeeze

    the fucking squeeze

    with everything tightening around me, the air and light contracting between the walls, except this time there was something choking about the way it stiffened around me in that fucking bunker of an office, a place I could never stick for more than a couple of hours at a stretch before it drove me out into the bright corridor which runs the length of the building, as it did when I left the phone down that day, surged from my desk, driven by a fit of temper and this swelling pressure closing around me, out into the corridor and down the stairs where I pushed through the revolving doors into the grey light of a March afternoon to stand on the sidewalk with a few other office workers who were having an afternoon smoke, their backs to the wall when I joined them, glad of the fresh air and the cold way it went down into my chest with that wet smell in the air after a day's rain, trying to calm down and put some order on my thoughts, this

    happening shortly before Mairead got sick, an incident I spoke to her about because the whole thing began preying on my mind so I gave her a general outline of the situation which both myself and Moylette found ourselves in, specifically how my name on a clearance cert would release both of us from our bind, except I too had a clear vision of how this whole thing would pan out in four or five years' time if I did, when

    the building had fully settled into itself, by which time it would have come through a handful of summers and winters and been subject to the first radical temperature changes which would have expanded and contracted the foundation raft underneath it, creating those shearing pressures along its length which would draw it apart to three different points of the compass, the cracks starting in the floor and moving up the walls millimetre by millimetre, day by day, shifting the corners and the lintels over the doors, cross ties and floor joists rupturing the under-floor heating so that when it is closed down after the first leaks start coming up through the floor and the insurance company sends in their assessors he will only have to take one look at the cracks starting up from ground level and then peel back the floorboards to uncover those joints clearly marking those divisions where three separate pours of concrete were laid, he will see immediately what's happened and will stand there wondering

who the fuck signed off on this

whoever it was, he should be shot with a ball of his own shit and

that's how I explained it to Mairead while

we sat at this table

a couple of days after Moylette's phone call, by which time the whole thing had clarified for me a little so that even if for the moment I could not see any way out of the impasse – the tension between politics and engineering – I was grateful to her for the patient way she listened, grateful also for the clarity of her confusion when she said

I don't understand, I can see how both of you are being pressured on this but I can't understand what leverage he has to make you sign – you're not directly accountable to him, there is no direct chain of authority in all this as far as I can see

that's true but when it comes down to it politics will trump engineering in a case like this – electoral pressure will ensure that this gets built sooner or later with or without my name on it

how does that work out – if your name is not on it whose name will be signed to it

the whole thing will get smudged, the cert could go missing or the county manager will probably take it out of my hands and the whole thing will go through on a nod and a wink

so that's how it's done

I'm not saying that's how it will be done but Moylette won't let it sit on my desk forever and sooner or later it will have to move elsewhere and I'm just telling you one way it might be solved so

I understood it was the Department of Education who has responsibility for schools, not county councils

it usually is but sometimes there are joint ventures when there are issues with roads and utilities and

politics

exactly

so now you need a plan

yes

and do you have one

I don't have one, I'm going to sit on it until a written demand that I put my name on it lands on my desk, when it does I'll have to give it more thought – that's the best I can come up with at the moment and all of which

was taken out of my hands a few days later when Mairead became ill and I had to take sick leave so the project was still on my desk when I left that Friday evening and I thought no more about it during the time I spent nursing her, my mind completely taken up with other things so that it was only towards the end, when she started getting that bit stronger and I drove to town to get that tonic for her that I passed by the site on the Westport road which was now closed up behind sheets of blue plywood and Curran Construction signs nailed up so

tell me what happened the day they put in the foundation

Mairead asked as

she set two mugs of tea on the table and cut a large slice of cake, using the old, ash-handled bread knife that someone had gifted us as a wedding present over twenty years ago, a beautiful knife which down the years had become an old friend and was by now invested with a totemic significance – for me especially when, a couple of years into our marriage, Mairead held it up one day to examine it, turning it in the light to show me how it had become rounded and worn with the bevelled edges of the ash handle faintly bleached from continual washing and the blade itself showing signs of all the times it had been sharpened against the steel, those fine lines angled back from the edge as she held it up by the blade, the moment gleaming in the sort of light that offered a clear view of the knife's descent from its first consideration in the murk of prehistory as a blunt river cobble or a shard of flint, through all its brittle bronze and ferric variants, step by step down the causal line of descent till it arrived safely in her hand, honed and fully evolved through balanced alloys, all its clumsiness pared away but carrying the marks of frequent use which prompted her to say

I love that we're living the kind of life where things are wearing down around us

her blessing on our lives together and all the stuff which had gathered to it, knives, furniture, appliances and utensils, all the things which crossed the grain of our days, losing some of their gloss and sheen in their contact with us but their rounded edges and corners now fitting our hands more easily, leaning to their purpose with greater ease and balance and if I loved all that – which I did – I was even more grateful to be sharing a life with someone who could draw attention to such things and think them worthy of comment and at that moment the prospect of a life with Mairead stretched out ahead of me with

you're daydreaming

what

I said tell me about the day the foundation went in

yes, I was, my mind elsewhere

same as it was the morning I pulled into the construction site, just as it was coming up to nine o'clock so I sat in the car listening to the news on the radio before I got out into one of those dry March mornings which, even at that early hour, with a cold blue sky overhead, promised to be perfect for pouring concrete and there

were five or six men already on-site, a couple of them in high-visibility vests, one of them sitting in the back of the van pulling on his boots, two others already inside the timbered shuttering, walking carefully over the steel mesh underfoot, checking the wire ties beneath, hunkering down over it for a closer look, men killing time for a few minutes because as yet there was no sign of the concrete trucks so I pulled on the high-vis jacket as Curran himself, the contractor, came towards me, folding his phone away into the jacket and calling to me in a loud voice as if I were a lot further away than the ten feet separating us, yelling

two minutes, they're just out the road

and we shook hands and walked over to the timbered frame and I saw straight away that the steel mesh over the radon barrier was a tidy piece of work, all the excess wire on the ties neatly snipped away and fastened at every intersection so there was no

danger of it moving when the concrete was poured or when it hard-
ened and it was clear that there were good tradesmen at work here
and as ever it was a pleasure to stand and admire neat work and
notice all those small finishing details which reveal just how much
a man respects his own trade even if his work, like these neatly
clipped ties, would ultimately be buried under concrete for the
rest of eternity, it was still easy to admire such care and attention
and Curran must have seen my approval because he added that

the two Crayns are putting up the blocks

Walter and Frank

Walter and Frank, they'll be here in a couple of weeks and
you could see he was pleased to have contracted the two brothers
who were generally acknowledged to be the best block-layers in the
area, block-layers whom roofers and plasterers loved following after
because they knew that the walls would be smooth and swept and
their own work would look tidy also, roofers especially appreciated
them, they knew that the walls would not need any building up or
levelling, the whole thing would be neat and tidy or, as one carpenter
said about following their work

you just lay your roof down on the walls like you were putting
on your cap as

the first of the concrete trucks turned in at the site entrance,
the driver gearing down and braking to a halt at the entrance to hail
Curran, leaning out to take directions onto the site before slowly
rolling on again, the lorry making its way down the path and the
driver steering with one hand and leaning out the side window to
get a sense of how solid the temporary surface was because there
was a slight give under the wheels as he kept her going steady with
the ground compacting under the great weight, rolling on slowly
until it pulled up beside the concrete pump which rose from the
back of its truck and angled up over the site like a praying mantis
and by now the two men had stepped outside the shuttering and
were standing by with shovels and floats ready as the driver jumped
down from the cab to have a few words with Curran as he set about
coupling the pump to the truck and

every man scanned the sky and there was general agreement

that the day would keep fine, there might be a few showers all right later on but there would be no harm in it as long as this cold spell held, the driver saying thoughtfully

a great day for cooling soup or pouring a foundation, whichever job was in front of you before

the concrete sluiced from the pressurised hose over the middle of the shuttering, pouring out in a thick slurry over the radon barrier, pooling and then spreading under its own weight before eventually rising over the steel mesh when the men moved in with floats to spread it out evenly to the corners, by which time I had performed the first slump test, upending a cone of concrete on the spot-board and measuring the slump after the cone had been removed from around it, to find that the fall was well within tolerance so that was ok, and I swept the concrete off the board and stood back to watch the men level out the screed, one of them stepping through it with the vibrator under his arm, pokering it into the concrete which immediately lost all its resistance and liquefied to settle into its natural level between the shuttered sides so that the two men coming behind him could smooth it over with a screeding board, drawing it over the wet surface to leave it glossed and smooth behind them and even though

I've seen it done umpteen times before, there is still something to wonder at in the pouring of a concrete foundation, the way it draws so many skills and strengths together, the timing and cooperation needed and the way the rising and spreading tide of concrete itself demarks, as no other stage in the building process can, the actual from the theoretical, makes the whole thing real in a way that site-clearing or the digging out of the foundation itself can never do, all these are definite staging posts in any structure's transition from the abstract but none of them separate so clearly the ideal realm of plans and paperwork from the physical world than the pouring of concrete, the building at last beginning its rise out of the ground and seeing it for so many years on so many public buildings – libraries, water-purifying plants and so on – twenty years of this still had not taken the excitement out of it for me, that uncanny sense of a building beginning to take on mass and shape in the blue light of the world where so many things can go wrong between this first pour and that ceremonial occasion when

the building is finally dedicated to its civic purpose with some official event to mark its opening which will of course be attended by all the local bigwigs – the local priest, members of the GAA, the parish council – all those local organisations which organise the life of any small town or village in this part of the world and since

I have attended so many of these ribbon-cutting ceremonies, stood out of shot with my hands folded across my chest, I sometimes allow myself the belief that I have given my life to something which has been on the side of human betterment, an idea which takes hold of me with such insistence that the part of me which needs to have faith in things starts seeing it as a religious vocation with its own rituals and articles of faith not to mention a reckoning in some vaulted and girdered hereafter where engineer's souls are weighed and evaluated after a lifetime's wear and tear in the friction of this world, standing before some tribunal where you point to your works and say

these are the things I have signed my name to, these are the things to which I have given my best energies and inspiration

these hospitals and libraries

these water treatment plants

these sewage works

these public lighting schemes

these primary and secondary roads

these public water schemes

these supply reservoirs

these miles of walk and cycle paths

these bridges

these private dwellings scattered the length and breadth of the county

the work of a civil engineer

amen

and the work of one man's quarter century, all I've done since I signed up to this job in my mid-twenties and which, year by year, I have lent my name to, projects which if taken all together, would amount to a fully serviced metropolis with adequate housing for a hundred-thousand souls, give or take, plus facilities for health and education and recreation with complete infrastructure, a sizeable city, the scale of the whole thing startling when it is drawn together like that since year after year I have never given much thought to what it might all amount to, just turning up in the office day after day where my desk and computer and drawing instruments wait for me or arriving on a site to make sure that things are running to plan and that there are not too many differences between what is on paper and what is coming into being as timber and concrete and stone because

this is my work

this is what I have believed in

something Darragh has harped on since hearing of my time in the seminary, chiding me that I have traded one faith for another

have I

so it appears, he said, turned your back on the cross to take up the theodolite

Jesus

it's well known that engineers picked up where God left off

that passed me by

He worked six days flat out, separating heaven from earth, light from darkness, on the seventh He took a step back and handed over His square and dividers to you and your kind, you'll manage from here lads He said, or words to that effect

so that's where we take our authority from

yes, the ancient of days, down on one knee on the edge of heaven, setting His square and dividers to the void, hair and beard streaming in the cosmic wind, the Creator, not to be confused or equated with the enfeebled version who snookered Himself down the road and had to take out a contract on His own son

I thought they were one and the same

you'd be surprised how many believe that

and this was at a time when he was deep in his bedroom boffin phase, living his life by the light of a computer monitor, wholly immersed in a strategic world building game called *Civilization* in which he had built up a heavily garrisoned city from a tiny river valley settlement in the space of two months, a citadel which, when he had it secured and provisioned became the seat of a despot who gradually began deploying armies farther and farther from the city walls to lay waste to outlying homesteads and settlements, expansionist ambitions which Darragh seemed keen to nurture – a strong leader, that's what he told me – so when he explained the mechanics of the game to me I sat down in his darkened bedroom to try my hand at it with the clear lines of a neoclassical city already unfurling across my imagination, a place of sunlit plazas and public fountains, libraries, municipal baths and childcare facilities alongside public thoroughfares which achieved that happy ratio of retail and residential space, balancing the competing demands of business and residential communities in an urban space, all this embracing a broad central park which would throng in the summer months with picnicking families and tourists listening to free concerts and outdoor theatrical events – a vision of urban planning in the service of its happy citizenry and

all of which was a massive evolutionary leap up from the primaeval forests and marshy barrens I found myself in when the game opened and my avatar – a querulous, muscled bloke in animal skins and horned helmet who looked like he would have been handy rustling and pillaging but who did not inspire confidence as the founder of city states – stood looking around him on a marshy plain with no steed or implement to hand but whom, in a simple point and click game, I could not cajole into digging a well or erecting a crude bush shelter, leaving him exposed to the cruel night temperatures which did for him in my first couple of attempts and which proved a more prolonged agony than the pack of dogs which tore him apart also or the marshy depths which swallowed him under a clear sky with no one to hear his cries for help, all the ways in which my civilisations failed to take hold and faltered, the game freezing as my avatar drowned, froze or got torn apart, the screen closing to black with the definitive annulment

Game Over

coming up black on white, like the end of the world itself

Game Over

and Darragh behind me, bursting his hole laughing, crowing typical engineer, too proud to bend the back while

I protested that

I'd bend it if there was something to work with

Darragh chuckling away to himself, enjoying me making a hames of things

it's a good job we weren't depending on you to found the first settlement, we'd still be knapping flints on the margins of history – I suppose that's why there's no record of Adam being an engineer and

you've fallen asleep again

what

you were telling me what happened when the second load of concrete was poured – Christ, are you always drifting off like this

sorry, I was thinking about something else there

same as when that second concrete truck pulled onto the site and I saw straight away that there was something odd about this one truck because the first had come from Corcoran's – the yellow and purple markings on the side – but this was blue, from Ward's and that was strange – two separate suppliers of concrete to the same site but as yet it didn't matter so long as the compositional makeup of both batches were the same, which of course

they weren't

were they fuck

and I had only to look at the results of the slump tests to see how different they were, different aggregates, different mix ratios, plain to see there on the spot board, the two cones of concrete with their different slumps and disintegration before I put up my hand and shouted at Curran

hold on a minute, I yelled over the noise of the truck, hold on and

he came towards me with no expression on his big face but knowing full well what was going to happen, I could see it in his fucking gait, the shoulders pulled up around the ears, the jaw already clenched

what, he says, what

you know damn well what, you can't pour that concrete into that foundation what do you mean, that concrete

you can't pour this concrete because it's a different batch and it will set differently against what's already poured – you're long enough at this game to know, you shouldn't have to be told

so what do you want me to do with it

I don't care what you do with it but you can't pour it here so

Curran raised his arm towards the truck

there's nine cubic metres of concrete there and if you think I'm turning it around and sending it back to the yard you can think again and

he was looking at me now fit to kill, the two feet planted apart like he was going to draw out on me and it was very exposed standing there in the cold facing him and the five men who stood behind him with shovels and screeding boards, men wanting to get on with their work but who now saw me as nothing but an obstacle, a fucking paper-pusher with some technical objection or piece of red tape, citing some new piece of EU legislation, typical civil service shite which holds up real work so

you tell me so what the fuck I'm going to pour into that shuttering, Curran shouted as

I can't tell you what to pour into it but I can tell you that if you pour that load of concrete I won't sign off on it and it will be a long day before you lay a block on that foundation raft – I can guarantee you that and

Curran stiffened as if he had run up against a glass wall and now I was truly frightened because this was the end of our argument, there was no other place for either of us to go, short and all as it was we had run each other out of options and now we stood locked in position with no ready escape on either side, eyeballing each other across ten feet of hard-core, both of us too angry and frightened to back down in front of the other men, as the moment lengthened to breaking point before Curran finally had the inspiration to reach into his anorak and take out his mobile which he starts prodding with his thumb and eyeing me, saying

I'll put an end to this fuck-acting as

he lowered his head onto the mobile to start shouting

hello, hello

while I stood there listening because even though I should have taken the chance to fuck off the site while he was talking I was anxious to hear what would happen so I stood looking at his broad back but couldn't hear anything over the sound of the truck, while his mouth was buried in the mobile and he had everyone's attention now, the men standing around looking at him, nervous at this new turn of events and the driver beside the pump with his hand on the pressure lever, ready to drop it at a second's notice but still watching the big man in the anorak who was pacing back and forth in the grey light, looking down at the ground where the tops of his rigger boots kicked along the hard-core surface before he turned around and his voice carried towards me

sound, that'll do so

as he snapped the phone shut and waved his arm up into the grey light

pour it out to fuck, he roared, pour it out and

he strode towards the cement truck before he pulled up, remembering that I was still standing there so he turns back to me, still roaring

you can stand there all you like, but that concrete is going to be poured today and there's fuck all you can do about it and I don't know what the fuck a county engineer is doing on my site anyway so

it's county jurisdiction Curran, our responsibility, that's what I'm doing here and

with that, the driver's hand fell on the lever and the engine-pitch rose as the concrete poured out the hose and onto the steel mesh, the three men standing over it with shovels waiting for it to rise up under their boots and that was the last thing I saw before I walked out to the road and got into the car and drove off so

you're saying that whoever was on the end of that phone call with Curran had some sort of influence

I'm saying that generally it's easy to tell when the political pressure is being put on you, you develop an antenna for it, you learn to hear the voice behind whoever it is you're dealing with – you learn that x will front for y but not for z and so on, it's a kind of coded referral and after a while there is no mistaking it

Christ, it sounds like it's a freemasonry, all nod and wink and

the vast majority of decisions are above board and go through without a hitch, but now and again, there are considerations which have nothing to do with engineering and that's when you feel your arm being twisted so that

why would two different yards supply concrete to the same job

that's the question, my belief is that the contract was split between two suppliers because that school is the last public works project of this size slated for the next two years, it's an open secret in the building trade there's no more money in the public purse for anything like this in the foreseeable future so they sat down and came in at the same price so there was political pressure to split the contract and

that sounds like collusion

that's exactly what it is – there's only a handful of cement works in this county – four or five and they are all going after the same number of dwindling public contracts so they probably sat down and talked it out among themselves, possibly three of them said something like they have enough work for the next eighteen months or so and two of them said that they have all their orders filled so they need the work and once they have that decided the two who are looking for the contract decide on the price they will go in at so that the others will overbid them or not bid at all

but you still have two bidders coming in at the same price, you could toss a coin and award it to one of them

you could but before the contract goes through the full tendering process you enlist your local public representative and drop hints about the thirty or forty jobs which depend on winning this contract, the thirty or forty households which will be badly affected coming up to election time

a friend at court

something like that, the two councillors now sit down and see that it is in both their interest to have the contract split between the two yards in their parts of the county

but it's only a couple of loads of concrete

it's a lot more than that – there's all the block-work, all the aggregate and maintenance, lintels, kerbing, hardcore and surfacing – this contract will keep these two yards tipping over for another twelve months – who knows what might have happened by then and

Mairead shook her head in wonderment, a smile opening out all her features and I was glad of this lightness in her response, it lifted something from me and did me good so that

her face before me now

Mairead across the table from me as

clearly as if she really was in front of me, her face as it was in the days before she took ill, its winter paleness fading with those fresh spring days, her spirits brightened from bedding in the first plants in her flowerbeds at the front of the house, a task she always said never failed to quicken something in her soul and which I had come to see as the sign that marked the true passing of winter no matter what the calendar might say so that when I came around the corner of the house that day

she was sitting in the garden

wearing her quilted jacket and tracksuit bottoms with both hands clasped around a mug of coffee – appearing exactly as the woman she was – an attractive middle-aged school teacher who was taking time out after a few hours gardening and who, even in these relaxed, unguarded moments was never far from that school-marmish neatness which she carried from her classroom and which, in the early years of our marriage, we made good use of when she would play the role of the prim schoolteacher taking it from the rough-hewn but sensitive laggard at the back of the class, bent over the table, in the hallway, wherever – neither of us claiming there was anything original about the fantasy but both of us stepping into our roles with such gusto that our energies carried us into a place where we found ourselves overtaken with a greedy appetite for each other, sometimes so intense that Mairead said she thought there was something cosmic about it and that she felt capable of fucking the world into redemption

her own words

fucking our way past the pettiness and desperation which some-times overcame us in our day-to-day lives, so that twisted together in the act of love we found our way towards that one molten moment in which only that which was true and unsullied in us would survive, everything else burned away, leaving us truly naked with all our senses open to giving the best of ourselves to each other and to the world we had created around us, something which thankfully, happened often enough back then to allow us now, in middle age

to sit across the table from each other and reflect that we'd had our proper share of such passion, we had not short-changed that part of ourselves while

all this comes to me now in such an unbroken torrent

sitting here at this table

faces and words and all sorts of fragments falling through me in staggered, interleaved depths with nothing behind them except some dark oblivion which threatens to suck me down into it, some black gravity which pulls at me, dragging at the tips of my fingers so that to dwell on it any longer might cause me to slip from myself completely for the want of something solid to focus on like

the spring bloom which visited Mairead's cheeks in those days before she became ill

this blush which I have always seen as another sign of winter's passing, bringing with it the glad news that our world had turned into a warmer and differently lighted place where we could stand easier in our flesh and bones without the winter cold to bind us and indeed Mairead, as always after the first of March, had already moved the garden furniture from the shed into the back garden so it was no surprise to see her sitting there when I came around by the gable that day, sitting in her quilted jacket with a mug of coffee and a book, the day nowhere near warm enough with its stone-coloured sky overhead but Mairead as always holding to her belief that the sun had to be coaxed up into the sky and that it was her job to show it the way by sitting at the garden table in the middle of a grey March afternoon with cold-roses in her cheeks

mistress of her own domain

which was of course was the very feature that tipped Mairead in favour of this particular house when she first saw it so many years ago, the house itself ordinary enough but the unusually big garden held out the promise of trapped sunlight so that during those summer weeks when we were scouting for a place to buy she visited this particular one on three separate occasions, each time returning an hour later to stand in the middle of the garden with her face turned upwards like a pale sunflower till the third evening, around nine o'clock at night with the shadow of the house itself halfway to the sod fence which marked the site's mearing, she lowered her face and said

yes, this is what we're looking for

and it was only then it dawned on me that she had been checking out the angle of the sun at high summer and was happy to find that the greater part of the garden did not pass into shadow till after half nine at night so that

when I saw her that spring afternoon, with the sun slanting into it at a low angle and honed with a chill edge, she was sitting at the table in the middle of the lawn, all tucked up in a padded jacket and a mug of coffee in her hand, wired up to her iPod and reading away, and the

strangest thing

so strange

coming upon her unawares like that, my wife of twenty-five years sitting in profile with her hair swept to her shoulder and her crooked way of holding her head whenever she was listening intently or concentrating, I saw that

a whole person and their life

cohered clearly around these few details and how, if ever this woman had to be remade, the world could start with the light and line of this pose which was so characteristic of her whole being, drawing down out of the ether her configuration, her structure and alignment, all the lines and contours which make her up as the woman she was on that day, with her health and spirit intact and content, this moment in which she was lost to herself in books and music, heedless to the whole world in a way that allowed something true and unguarded of herself to present so clearly that I found myself standing at the corner of the house, gazing at her from a distance, hardly able to believe that I had shared a quarter of a century with this woman who, in a few days would have her health taken from her by

a viral event which would not only spread to a citywide scale but would also prove attentive enough to fasten into the narrow crevice of this woman's ordinary life where its filth and virulence would prove so difficult to remove while all the time

Agnes's despatches from the disaster area

continued to keep me abreast of things, her calls coming every evening around seven o'clock when I was sitting at the kitchen table looking out over the garden to the mountains in the distance which rose up into the grey dusk of spring, her voice on the other end telling me in a tone of cautious excitement that word had got out in the city about her installation and that it was drawing a steady flow of foot traffic through the gallery,

people who appeared to genuinely engage with the work over and above the usual well-wishers with the invigilators and the gallery owner showing her the visitor's book which was steadily filling up with enthusiastic comments and observations which, by and large, read the exhibition as a welcome artistic engagement with some of the more difficult social issues that for too long had been ignored by a visual arts culture which seemed only too willing to withdraw into a private rhetoric at a time when it might be expected to engage with its wider social environment, plus the fact that there had also been one favourable print review in a Sunday broadsheet – an unusual enough happening Agnes assured me – which had picked up on her theme of the body as a rhetorical field, a fitting conjunction for a time when the city itself was in the national news for reasons to do with the sovereignty and integrity of the body within a democracy, a positive review she said which stressed the relevance of the piece beyond the narrow precinct of this city, such a thoughtful essay that Agnes was hopeful the two-page spread with its colour illustration might draw the attention of some curator from one of the more adventurous galleries in Dublin – there was a chance it might happen but she wasn't holding her breath, she knew how difficult it was to break out of the provincial art scene but, for the moment

she was enjoying that glow of well-being which comes after a prolonged bout of concentrated work, very tired now and getting lots of sleep but feeling good and in fact it was only today that she had been back to her studio for the first time since the installation went up, spending the morning sorting through all her stuff, all the notes and newspaper clippings along with the sketches and templates she had worked from and there was a lot more tidying to be done than she had thought so it would probably need another day at least before the job would be complete, but never mind, it was a good feeling to have old work cleared from the studio and to have created that open space ahead of her now in which new experiments were possible, she was looking forward to that exploration and no, she wasn't sure what she would do next but she had a feeling she might

return to oils, she felt them drawing her once more and she missed their slow application, the way they cured to their proper resolution over weeks before finally fixing themselves, she missed the way time measured itself to a slower beat whenever she worked with them, it would be relaxing to be back among the smell and feel of it, oils mixed with linseed, a welcome change at least from the intimate relationship she had struck lately with her own blood – speaking of which

something odd

she was now getting used to being drawn up in the streets by those fringe members of the visual arts community who were eager to make known their admiration for the brave – their word – work she had completed, artists her own age with tattoos and piercings and too much mascara and

it's weird Dad, she said, I've been showing oil on canvas all this time and was able to pass unmolested on the street but the moment I leave down my brush and take up a syringe, people are anxious to see me as some sort of Jeanne d'Arc or someone like that, someone bent on self-sacrifice, the exemplary sufferer who's supposed to stand against I don't know what and

I was happy to listen to Agnes going on in this mode for a while because it was assuring to know that one of us at least was out there having a good time, engaging with the world in a way that did not sicken or frighten her and as a father it was good to hear in her voice the sound of someone coming into their own, my daughter taking a decisive step towards herself, a curious feeling which had me in two minds, as if I were welcoming and saying goodbye to her in the same moment, all the anxious feelings a father has for a daughter as

she recounted these things, lending proper weight to all the detail but careful not to linger too much and have her story bogged down while at the same time trying to rein in her enthusiasm because the tremor of excitement in her voice was obvious as was the strain it put on her trying to dampen it down, a young woman not yet so far gone in adulthood that she could not be gusted away on a sudden burst of excitement, and for the first time – out of nowhere – I found myself wondering why she never seemed to have a boyfriend or suitor of any sort, had no one ever breached that standoffishness which was her front to the world or was that just a polished shell behind which there was a lonely and uncertain young woman in her prime and despite my troubles, sitting there at the table, there was space enough within me for a wave of anxiety to course through my entire body at the very idea that my daughter might be lonely in some way unknown to herself, that so early in her life she might have mistaken her own aloneness as a type of serenity, a destiny of her own choosing which she had successfully passed off to herself as an heroic isolation while of course there was

about her also the awareness that all this stuff about her exhibition was merely background noise, a preamble to our main theme which was of course the current status of the crypto outbreak, the latest news, which in spite of my fatherly solicitude was what I really wanted to know and this was where I gave my full attention because even if her reports changed little with the passing days my own need-to-know required daily updates which confirmed that

with its engineers still unable to identify the source of the contamination, the boil-water notice would hold throughout the city for the foreseeable future so instead, much was being made by City Hall of the new treatment facility which was under construction, an ultra-modern installation adjacent to the existing plant comprised of an infrared filtration system which would supplement the existing barrier-membrane in zapping those biological particles and organic matter which managed to pass through it and all of which would ensure that the city's water supply would far exceed existing standards of purity for years into the future, but when pressed the spokesman admitted that the commissioning and construction of such a facility presented very real engineering difficulties and the projected completion date lay at least some months into the future, a snag which took much of the gloss off the news and caused the citizenry to throw up their hands in dismay, shaking their heads in disbelief and exercising once more a wholly expanded lexicon of frustration, while the tourist and hospitality sector ground its teeth and prophesied untold damage to the city's economy, not to mention lasting damage to the city's global reputation as a cultural destination and

there appears to be no end to the incompetence of the city authorities

Agnes affirmed with a tired sarcasm which was new to her and not pleasant to hear in someone who till so recently had never voiced any political opinion whatsoever as far as I could remember, her having viewed with indifference every news programme that happened to be on television or radio as if the wider upheavals of the world had nothing to do with her whatsoever, which in truth they may not have because she was of that generation born to a world of plenty, never knowing what it was to do without or what it was to be frugal and thereby never having developed the coping skills to deal with any reversal, economic or political or civic like this one which must have baffled her, come as some shock to her, this dramatic instance of civil incompetence which had caused the illness of so many people and listening to her it was difficult not to feel glad on the one hand that she had finally woken up to the world in one of its less capable moods while, on the other, upset that she should be put upon in any way whatsoever – a father's rush to protect his child from everything, even her own innocence with the

long and the short of the whole thing being

that the boil-water notice would hold for another month at least or for as long as the number of cases needing hospital admission continued to rise, not rising so steeply now but still touching four hundred, a sickening populace evenly drawn from all areas of the city, the older working-class estates north of the river across to the newer, middle-class enclaves in the south ward, which stretches along the coast road, the virus favouring no particular demographic or area, everyone familiar now with the sight of bulk water carriers pulling into housing estates and cul-de-sacs with mothers and kids queueing up to fill plastic containers, this image now an established shorthand for the whole crisis across print and broadcast media and

that was it, those were the facts as far as the crisis itself was concerned, Agnes telling them quickly but with a child's eagerness to be as comprehensive as possible, as if a complete recital with all the trimmings might be conclusive and exhaustive, a sort of vanquishing spell set against it which would drain it of some essential vigour and displace it into some adjacent world where it would be rendered harmless, turning on itself and chewing itself into oblivion and

as I listened something in me leaked towards her and, in that awkward, faltering way of middle-aged men with mature daughters I found myself trying to assure her that everything would turn out all right, this was merely one of those things which the passing of time would make harmless and someday soon Mairead would be up and about her work with a smile on her face and a song on her lips, telling her in as soothing a tone as I could manage that

your mother is fine Agnes, don't worry, yes she's definitely improving, and she's not as fevered as yesterday – she drank a small cup of soup today – the first thing she's managed to hold down in three days so that's a good sign and her sleep is not so broken any more, none of that awful thrashing around under the sheets which she suffered during the first days so all in all she has every sign of getting better and stronger, but of course there is no use me telling you that she'll be back to anything like her real strength for a little while and

my sense of these words dropping into a void as they came out of my mouth filled me with despair, something so feeble about them it was hardly credible that they could be of any comfort to anyone since they would do little whatsoever but embarrass both of us, this awkward attempt at soothing my daughter which drove our conversation into a pregnant lull from which she eventually took sudden inspiration to put us both out of our misery with a bright account of what she had planned for the weekend, yet another of those awkward trips or jaunts she always seemed to be taking on her own to some small town or village in the middle of the country, jaunts which involved bus connections and waiting alone at rain-swept country stations, field work she sometimes described them as but none of which, now that I thought of it, ever sounded hopeful or fun as these excursions were always enveloped in some aura of penitence, something of the pilgrimage about them which was dismaying to hear in a way that was difficult to grasp but which lodged like smoke in my soul, nagging and anxious-making but nevertheless I told her to have a great time and I could hear her subside with relief that the call was finally at an end and that she had once more successfully done her job, fulfilled the role of the dutiful daughter so that now she would sign off with

oh, I nearly forgot

yes,

two things, first, I've told Darragh about Mam, I let it slip last night when I was talking to him – I know you wanted to keep it from him but

there was no point in getting him worried

I know and he's not worried, he's angry, he's very upset, you'll hear this when you talk to him, I'm sorry but it was my big mouth and

don't worry about it, he had to find out sometime and better you than me – you said there was something else

yes, there's a big demonstration planned for next week, the artistic community is getting together to protest the whole contamination thing and I've been asked to participate in some sort of street pageant

why you

I don't know, it must have something to do with my new celebrity

what sort of pageant

I don't know yet, dressing up and stuff I'd imagine, but I'm looking forward to it so that's it, I'll let you know how it goes

ok, look after yourself

I will, love to yourself and Mam

ok

bye

bye

which brought the call to an end, killing the phone in my hand in such a delicate way – light draining from the screen – that I placed it gently on the table for fear any sudden movements might disturb some lingering element of Agnes's love and farewell, the phone on the table hopelessly inert in

the raw silence which always washed through me after these calls, always leaving me feeling lightened, not in the sense of being unburdened but more in the way of one who has undergone some trial and come through it not wholly unscathed, bruised in a way which left me tentative and anxious in some way beyond what the call itself was responsible for so that I spent the rest of the evening going through the house with the hoover and cleaning the bathroom just to take my mind off whatever it was now grating with such an anxious itch, something which made me wary of Darragh's call later that night, his face

looming out of the screen towards me with his hair longer and his anger still stoked from what Agnes had told him, the distant sense of Mairead's suffering clearly aggravating his hopeless frustration at being unable to do anything other than ranting and heaping curses on the heads of those engineers and politicians he now lit upon, a scalding tirade that I listened to for a few minutes, a venomous cascade of fucks which confirmed for me that there had always been this sudden rage lurking beneath all his crowing and cackling and I was glad Mairead was not witnessing this anger on her account because while it was easy to predict that Darragh would feel deeply on her behalf and would need little prompting to cast himself in the role of her defender I was not so sure that she would have admired the mixture of snarling rage and frustration which spilled from him now, his face receding into the dark shadows of his cheeks and his hair wild around his head in that mad way which sure enough brought to mind his grandfather in the last bewildered months of his life, a memory which frightened me and caused me to cut across him, barking

I have better things for doing Darragh than listening to this guff at this time of the night you could have told me

and what could you have done

I should have known

your mother and I made the decision to keep quiet about it because we didn't want to be putting worry on you

yah

and because we knew that this was how you'd react

and how is that

this brainless ranting

how am I supposed to react

with a bit more cop-on than this effing and blinding you're going on with, if you think this kind of thing is going to make her any better you'd better think again

so what am I supposed to do

nothing Darragh, because there is nothing to be done, your mother is over the worst of it, the doctor was in at her and she's weak but that's all that's wrong with her and she'll be back on her feet soon – words to douse his anger and put his mind at rest which they seemed to do after

he blew off steam for another few minutes, heaping more curses on the heads of engineers and politicians alike before he turned to another theme, his anger lending a caustic edge to his usual clowning tone when he said

I believe Agnes is gathering her own coven about her – any day soon she'll be minting her own religion

English Darragh, for God's sake

I'm talking about Agnes Dei, she tells me that she's become a totemic figure for a sensitive emo crowd

you're speaking in tongues again Darragh – that went over my head, emo what

it would have been called goth in your day, Dad – emo is a more virulent strain of that old disorder, it's that worldview in which black is the new white and life is the new death

you can't put it any plainer than that

no

and what has this to do with Agnes

she tells me that she's being stopped in the street by these emo girls who want to touch the hem of her garment, it's all about her work of course, they recognise a kindred sufferer, and in fairness it's easy to see how that installation could become a sacred spot for a small church of self-harmers, a little congregation of cutters and anorexics and dysmorphs, all with their own stigmata of tats and piercings

you're losing me again Darragh

these are the last days Dad, the signs are everywhere, the writing's on the wall and the people on the march, pestilence washing through the city – mark my words any day now they're going to raise a yellow flag over the town hall and place the whole metropolitan area under quarantine and behind razor wire – that's the kind of shambles in which a secular saint like Agnes would flourish

this sort of guff wears me out, Darragh

oh don't worry Dad, you'll have your own part to play in all this fairly soon, any day now the four of us will all be sitting around in a circle, the holy family, each of us in turn raising a vein so that the New Testament can be written afresh there's good reason why this sort of thing is called the cutting edge

and you believe we have some responsibility for all of this

in fairness you have only yourself to blame Dad, yourself and Mam – what were you thinking when you named her Agnes, didn't you know that name is destiny, you should look it up some time and see what was laid out for her

this is all very tiring, Darragh

you're a tough audience Dad, I have to say

I'm tired, that's all

well I suppose we won't solve it all tonight

hardly

ok, keep checking your email, I'll let you know when I'm likely to be online, and give all my love to Mam, let me know when she is ready to take a call from me

I will, ok

bye

bye

after which he seemed to reach towards me with his palm

outstretched, fingers filling the screen for a darkening moment before it switched off and the line which connected us across the globe dissolved to a black portal, leaving me adrift for a moment, my mind still locked into the conversation we'd just had before I closed down the laptop, the sound of which drew the sitting room with its walls and pictures in around me in the darkness with

Mairead down the hall in Agnes's room, among the teddies and soft toys, sleeping easier now with her face turned onto the pillow, her breath levelled out and drawing gently, her body now almost purged of the virus, the wracking days of vomiting and sweating behind her just as

the contamination finally rose to the top of the news agenda, climbing over the headlines of all those other stories, surmounting those larger brooding issues which were stacking up on the political horizon like some catastrophic high-pressure weather system, darkening the sky to promise of all sorts of devastation – stories of wage agreements, unemployment crises and so on, all of them inhabiting the most abstract realm of figures and geopolitics, none of them as yet achieving that immediate heft of bodily and civic catastrophe which gave the contamination story its gathering allure, as it still showed no sign of going away, if anything its persistence in the boil-water notice and the still escalating number of patients marked it out as a story with genuine resilience, an obstinacy one could easily associate with a viral event that would give it endurance, with a note of irony which ran through every report, the reminder that

this was the wettest city in Ireland, a coastal city with a mean annual rainfall twenty percent above the national average and

listening to all this on the nine o'clock news it seemed to me wholly beyond belief now that after all this time no one or no cause had been identified as the source of the crisis, no one to point to and say

this person and their actions

are the reason my wife is in bed with her strength leaking from every pore of her body, sour dreams of revenge coming to torment me which seemed reasonable and justified but, with no proper focus for my wrath, I proved to be a poor hand at revenge fantasies so my resentment turned towards

sitting at this table and

thinking these thoughts or

being thought by them

that sense of

myself filling out the space of their being, being taken up with the idea or

being the idea that

my entire existence is these same thoughts, that each rolling idea, as it occurs now is wholly responsible for my

being here

like

something lost, a revenant who has returned to his house at some grey hour to find the place boarded up and abandoned, becalmed in a sea of weeds and dandelion clocks, a line of grey crows along the ridge-tile, a child's construct around which time itself has taken a detour leaving it to weather and deteriorate in some way other than it should so that now, drifting through it while

sitting at this table

conscious of something stagnant in the house itself, as if all its pulses and rhythms have been swept from it so that time itself is legless here with all things, myself included, suspended in a kind of stalled duration, an infinitely extended moment spinning like an unmeshed gear, a stillness within which no knife will blunt, no mirror will tarnish, no paint will peel, no hunger will grasp my belly nor will I ever have to shave as

time itself could decay here, lapse completely in such a way as to leave this place like some stagnant inverse realm, the countervailing force of the whole world

the source of all opposites

where all things are stood on their head, some realm in which bread is poured and water is cut and our shadows have tired of us and got to their feet before walking away with their stick-men comrades, striding away over fields and commonage, barbed wire fences and dry stone walls, falling into step with each other as they pick up that steady stride which enables them to leave this world altogether and head off towards some other jurisdiction beyond the horizon where they and their kind thrive and god knows who they answer to so

stop

for the love of Jesus

stop talking

getting carried away like this on

tidal waves of nonsense, swept so far away from myself that it's easy to forget, the aching towards my own end which draws me on while alive to this moment, sitting here at this table, so improbably here, the

cosmic odds so hopelessly stacked against me

being here as

this electric interval held within its circumference of flesh and bone, the full sense of myself to myself as a kind of bounded harmonic, a bouquet of rhythms meshing into one over-emergent melody which homes me within the wider rhythms of the world, the horizonal melody of the cosmos, the celestial harmonic which inscribes me against the biggest magnitudes, the furthest edge of the universe and

stop

Jesus

because

one two buckle my shoe

three four knock at the door

five six pick-up sticks

seven eight

seven eight

seven

as the crisis stretched on, the number of patients rose above four hundred and began putting a serious strain on the city's health services, a number that cloaked what many observers believed to be a massive under-swell of sufferers who were not recorded in hospital wards but who did have an inverse presence in the rising tide of public and private sector absenteeism across all industries, the hospitality industry and the civil service in particular, a degree of absenteeism whose real numbers tallied towards three thousand, the figures supported by anecdotal evidence which the city's authorities refused to acknowledge, or did so only to disparage as gross exaggeration and when pressed merely pointed to the number of hospital beds taken up with registered sufferers as the only true and reliable measure of the outbreak as no amount of anecdotal testimony could be considered accurate evidence of the crisis and while

the caginess of their response might have been understandable in terms of giving assurance to the outside world that the outbreak was indeed being carefully managed and contained, it also angered the populace deeper whose sardonic scepticism of the early days had given way to a kind of heedlessness which had them turning a deaf ear and a blind eye to all those newsletters and advisories which still continued to appear in public places like doctors' surgeries or on supermarket notice boards, so heedless to it now that

a cloud of weariness enveloped the whole story as it played out over the national airwaves, all coverage coloured with a note of schadenfreude that a city which had made such a lucrative reputation as a cultural mecca with its twelve month calendar of festivals and celebrations should now be struck down with a biblical pestilence – not the wages of sin exactly but surely just recompense for a kind of fecklessness which seemed to afflict a place which had given itself so wholeheartedly to carnevale, no sympathy to spare for

a story that appeared to linger on so that the city itself now seemed becalmed in its own unmoving filth, stagnant as the algae cloud which thickened in the rising temperatures of those days, a toxic bloom under the sun which swarmed through the city's nervous system and the digestive tracts of its inhabitants, shifting responsibility for the crisis onto the city itself, or more accurately onto

the rapid expansion of the city over the past decade with its large housing developments along the coast road which had radically increased the draw on the city's supply lake, lowering its levels so that its purity was further compromised by the increased amount of slurry fertiliser that had washed into the lake during those spring weeks of steady rainfall, the flow going through the pipe overwhelming the filtration system and admitting the Cryptosporidium into the water pipes, which then spread through those same wards of a city that had grown at such an uninhibited rate throughout the preceding decade so that when

the civic authorities sought to locate the exact origin of the disaster it found that it could not be pinpointed to one specific cause, human or environmental, but that its primary source was in the convergence of adverse circumstances – decrepit technology and torrential rains, overdevelopment and agricultural slurry – which smudged and spread responsibility for the crisis in such a way as to make the whole idea of accountability a murky realm in which there was little willingness on the part of the authorities to point the finger at farmers or engineers or those planners and developers who had allowed the city to grow beyond its ability to keep itself supplied with potable water so that with

no blame or responsibility gathering anywhere

the story hung through the city's ambience as a kind of rolling fog which, with each passing day, thickened to a whitewash over the whole crisis in which it became clear that no one would be blamed nor held responsible, the city now so enwrapped in a murk that

it began to inhabit a kind of dreamtime when its past and future unfolded simultaneously, a whole city dreaming itself with all its buildings, young and old, all its tarred and cobbled streets, all its clocks and steeples, all its signs and monuments and statuary, all its horizontal services, water and electricity, every part of it twitched between its real existence and its own dream-life where it morphed through all the changes of itself, its history unfolding in one ongoing delirium, culminating on the night

this city of pageants and festivals

its patience gone and its voice hoarse

politically at its wits' end

raided its wardrobe and fancy-dress box to gather up its masks and face-paint so that it might deck itself out in its most ghastly colours and come staggering through the cobbled streets as

a company of zombies, moving with more purpose than you would imagine while trailing their winding cloths through the narrow

lanes of the Latin quarter where they met up with a stilted Bo Peep –
ten feet tall and with six days' growth of beard under a platinum fright
wig – shepherding a small flock of sheep away from flying spiders that
menaced them from overhead, their pitiful bleating causing them
to herd in a circle, bumping and tripping over each other just as a
company of golden samba queens spilled out of a nearby pub and
two by two, to the tune of 'The Girl from Ipanema' they herded the
sheep up the main pedestrian street, all plumed and gilded and gathering to their beat buskers and jugglers and a couple of fire-eaters
who were naked to the waist and smelling of kerosene, all falling
into step beside the zombies who had made common cause with the
spiders, taking the lash of Bo Peep's scourge along the pedestrian
area with their own reflections in the large shop windows moving
step by step with them to draw a family of clowns from a side street,
mammy and daddy and two kids with wide red grins which threatened to engulf their heads and Elvis and Charlie Chaplin, both with
their hands in their pockets and deep in conversation, both fell into
step with no apparent heed of where they were headed, drawn on by
some horizontal gravity which pulled from another side street the full
complement of the medieval music society in full raiment, friars and
pardoners, merchants and mendicants, maidens and widows fronted
by a knight in knitted chain-mail and a wooden sword, all with their
lutes and recorders and tambourines, doing what they could to rejig
a madrigal to the samba beat, the procession moving on till it came to
the top of the street where the park opened up beneath the banners
of the city's founding fathers which now flew over this congregation
which appeared to have been drawn from some realm where the
living and the dead stood shoulder to shoulder sharing a joke and a
fag as a hen party of mermaids appeared with devil's horns and an
L-plate stitched to the girl's chest who passed around a naggin of
vodka and insisted on sharing it with a family of Fir Bolgs, swaying
bulbous giants whose useless arms and height made the job impossible and threatened to spoil the girl's fun for a moment before she
disappeared into the maw of a multi-coloured dragon who appeared
from around the corner of the public toilets, lowering his mouth
over her to pick her up bodily amid much squawking laughter, her

tanned legs kicking from the dragon's mouth who now turned and made off with her into the centre of the park where the figure of a fifty-foot Lemuel Gulliver was the natural focal point for all those other characters now streaming out of the night, two children in corpse-paint holding Morticia's hand, the child with a square head and a bolt through his neck, paler children with capes and fangs – some cowled, with their own scythes and hourglasses – plus all the little girls in Irish dancing costumes who had their hair done up in fluorescent curlers on top of their heads like small Medusas beside those kids in cowboy suits and Indian feathers – kids out way past their bedtime on a school night but happy to recognise old friends – Snow White and her seven butties, Dopey and Sneezy and the whole gang, all tooled up with picks and shovels and marching to the beat

hey ho, hey ho

it's off to work we go

whistling their little tune and drawn on by the rhythm of the samba beat they shouldered their picks and headed off across the grass towards the corner of the square where they fell in behind a small flatbed truck which was mounted by a trio of charred demons playing lead and rhythm guitars and drums, churning out a bass rhythm which hits the centre of the chest as it drew on the cortege with Gulliver leading the rest of the assembled night creatures as they funnelled into the narrow street with their whistles and tambourines, making space to skip and dance, ghouls and trolls and zombies picking up a kind of jigging two-step which took them past the Magdalene monument and across the intersection where traffic had to come to a halt, up the hill by the bus station and student hostel by which time everyone had taken up their proper place in the procession, the demon car leading the way with its bludgeoning rhythms and Snow White's dwarves setting the military tone of the procession, marching along beneath the towering figure who was kept upright by so many outriders with ropes and stays, then manoeuvred carefully into the car park and up the path towards the city offices as if he were about to knock on its tiny door and request admittance at this late hour though, as he approached, the whole facade

disappeared on cue behind a massive white sheet which

cascaded from the roof of the building, falling under its own weight from the top of the fifth story, unfolding in a soft billowing which carried it gently the last couple of feet to the ground before the dead gaze of the giant Gulliver who was now faced with a blank wall of pale fabric rippling across with those shadows cast by the lights from the parking lot behind the gathered congregation of ghouls and ghosts and mummers who now thronged the open area as far back as the car park, some standing on top of the wall which fronted onto the road, every hollow eye fixed on the civic building whose whole front had disappeared behind a white curtain so that the front presented nothing but the blank face of a mausoleum, the building readily lending itself to the illusion, five stories rising square-faced in a blank precipice as if it had been waiting there since its inau-guration for its own effacement, blinded by this sheet which was now overcast by a projection of blue, childish waves within which all sorts of marine creatures happily cavorted, the whole building submerged and over the top of which

Agnes now stood

stepping out to the edge of the lake precipice and this time she was indeed naked, shockingly so with her white body catching the light from the car park, shadowing her breasts across so that she appeared as if half of her was cut away into darkness, her body now precisely the sort that would stand as an heraldic pillar, a cary-atid and

all this

in my mind's eye the following morning when I read the account in the national paper, the

naked girl standing on the edge of the sunken mausoleum as if she were a statue carved to that purpose with the glare from beneath lighting up the juncture between her hips, as she stepped forward in full possession of the moment, upheld in the gaze of the assembled ghouls, everyone teetering on the edge of some climactic gesture that would clinch the whole spectacle into a coherent act of political protest, something which, if not equal to the city's confusion would be at least dramatic and striking enough to illustrate how it had the collective wit to gather itself for this moment in which she would either fall or take flight, the only options when you have walked this close to the edge with

the picture on the front page showing her with her arms outspread and tipping forward off the edge of the building, the image catching her at the precise moment her feet leave the edge of the building and gravity takes hold of her as she begins to plunge through the night air, the expressions on the faces of the onlookers still calm as their reactions lag a full second behind she who is already in mid-flight with

my own heart skipping a beat to see her stalled for a split second in mid-air before plunging through the blackened light onto the hidden air cushion beneath which swelled out of the ground, appearing to engulf her as she landed in its centre so that it rose up around her, swallowing her in a soft tumorous growth in front of the building, the gasp from the crowd simultaneous with the curved folds of the cushion rising up around her, as if the crowd's shock gave it the substance to billow up towards my blue-skinned daughter before it gradually subsided and she was raised up on a small plinth within the dying bloom to emerge as a kind of Venus on the half-shell from beneath the blue projected waves of the lake that rippled across her body and

the whole thing was clunky, hempen homespun in its execution but the point of it all clear enough – City Hall and all who sailed in her, politicians and engineers, dead and drowned beneath the waves of this political protest and

did you see what our daughter got up to last night, Mairead wanted to know the following day, shaming us in front of the nation, not a stitch on her

yes, I saw

and were you shocked this time

I'm not so easily shocked any more

good, she replied, and sunk back in the pillow with a tired smile drawing her face open so

I'm a bit confused though, I said, the water thing is easy to understand but the jumping off the roof bit, what was that all about

I was a bit lost myself with that – I hope she calls today, she might explain it, maybe they hope it will be the sort of inspiring image or event that will rouse the city to more urgent protest

is that what they want

maybe it is, getting people to rise up and start a political and social renewal, startle the people out of their torpor and

you sound like Darragh

well, he didn't lick it off the stones you know and

it's coming back to me now, the stones and

driving to town that day

the trip to town with

Mairead sitting up in the bed, her first day on the turn, her first day getting better and

the pain of it all

this fucking pain when

I drove to town to pick up that prescription for her, some sort of a tonic prescribed by Dr Cosgrave to build her up towards the end of her illness, by which time she was seriously thin and enfeebled, her lowest ebb but the very point at which she began to rally, the illness draining from her like a neap tide, leaving her sitting up in bed against a pile of pillows, pale and breathless with her body labouring to keep her upright, the worst of it definitely over but weak as water so that Dr Cosgrave prescribed her this tonic after she examined her for the last time, pronouncing herself happy that she was indeed on the mend and that all the signs were good, her appetite gradually returning to cups of soup and toast after so long taking nothing but glasses of tepid water to wash the virus from her body, every puke and purge drawing with it some of her own colouring so that she was now almost translucent from all the weight she had lost but

that's nothing to panic about

Dr Cosgrave assured us, smiling around at both of us in the dimly lit room

she's lost weight but she has the summer months ahead of her to get stronger and build herself up and this will help her

she said, as she tore the script from her book and handed it to me and I understood that it was some sort of a tonic in capsule form,

something to be taken three times a day after meals and that I would
have to skip into Westport and get it for her as

she frowned up at me, her voice rasping

a tonic – it sounds so old fashioned, do people still take that
sort of thing

I guess so, at least that's what this prescription calls for

it sounds like something from an age of poultices and leeches

I think you've had enough of leeches and bugs, will you be ok
for an hour or two while I get this

yes, I'll be fine

do you need anything else

bring back apple juice

ok

and will you take my car, it hasn't been started in a while, it
could probably do with a quick spin

ok, it's half eleven now, I'll be back around one o'clock, is that ok

yes, I'll be fine

she smiled at me, her thin face opening along sharper lines
than I was used to but still unmistakably hers

it'll do you good to get away for a few hours

you're trying to get rid of me

yes, I'm waiting for my fancy man to come and see me the minute
you're out the door

well I won't get in his way, there's water here and a towel and

that's all I need, go on before I change my mind and one last thing

yes

you did a good job

what job

looking after me, you did a good job looking after me, thank you

yes

and I grabbed her keys from the bowl on the hall-stand, pulled
the door behind me and went out to the car, her old Corolla, which
stood at the gable in shadow and stillness with leaves and twigs caught
in the wipers and a scurf of dust on the windscreen, all the markers
of time passing converging on it, the wind and rain already going
about the patient work of wearing it down, this car which had lain

dormant for so long that I stood to look at it a moment, to marvel before I opened the door and sat into her, wondering to myself

will she start

I'll bet the battery's dead in her

as I pushed the seat back to give myself some legroom so that my knees were not up under the steering wheel and adjusted the seat-angle as I could never sit comfortably into a car after Mairead, whose legs are a lot shorter than mine and who always likes to sit forward in the seat, whereas I like to lean back from the steering wheel, settling myself in but still wondering

will she start

is the battery dead

as I turned the key in the ignition to bring up all the lights in the dash before a couple of sluggish, laboured turns of the engine finally caught and the causal chain from ignition spark to engine turn was completed smoothly and held as the car surged to life with a healthy growl which carried through the floor panels and up through the seat so that I could feel it vibrate in the bottom of my spine as I pumped the accelerator a few times, warming her up, the noise of the engine rising and falling against the gable of the house, and in that roaring moment all neglect and idleness was set aside as the engine sung out in some mysterious way which thrilled me but embarrassed me by bringing tears to my eyes, sitting there and pumping the accelerator while all the gauges in the dash rose to their proper levels

temp, oil, revs and petrol

of which there was over half a tank, more than enough for the journey ahead so I sat there a few moments longer revving her, feeling extraordinarily happy and impressed that this car had started so easily after lying idle so long in rain and cold, this fifteen-year-old car which had a full circuit of the clock behind it, most of it racked up during the kids' teenage years with all its trips to

discos, cinemas, summer camps, football matches

all the childhood and adolescent occasions to which, I have to admit, Mairead more often than I ferried the kids and their friends, so much so that she was especially attached to it, a sentimental link to that special part of our family's life, a repository of all our times together which would be gone forever if it were scrapped, even if for the time being there was no pressing reason why it should be, as year after year it passed the NCT, flying through the test with none of those major engineering flaws that would consign it to the breakers yard, each year returning a snag list of small fails

mirrors, number plates, shocks, lights, tracking and steering but

never any major parts needing replacement, nor mechanical failure after fifteen years bouncing across the roads of West Mayo, till it had gradually become clear that this car might keep going forever like some pristine machine that had been engineered in some frictionless realm, knowing nothing of deterioration or obsolescence as long as the body hung together, which, in fairness, might not be too many years longer as corrosion had begun to eat along the bottom of the door and the edges of the bonnet, which was to be expected, but so long as the floor-panels held out and the road did not start showing under our arses, I didn't have to weld steel plates onto the chassis, and

I sat there a while longer enjoying the sound of the engine humming away as if it were a melody from a better world where things ran to their proper purpose – a world where things worked as they should – before I fired some water up on the windscreen and was momentarily blinded as the dirt thickened under the wipers, driven across the screen in a heavy scurf for a few moments before it gradually cleared a broad sweep through which I could see clearly by which time the sound of the engine had sunk into my own flesh and bones, synching with my own shorter rhythms in such a sweet way that when I

put her into first to

turn out onto the main road and moved her up through the gears I experienced a shameless, rising joy in my heart as if finally, for the first time in a long while I was hearing something good, something which was not of this world's raucous tumult but which spoke of that harmonic order which underlay everyone and everything, the gentle vibrations running through my spine and up my arms so that after a few miles I was relaxed in a way I had not been in weeks, settled back with the radio on and, it was a beautiful day

with the sun high in the sky as the road ahead ploughed through the blue air, disappearing into the day's depth along the lower slopes of Croagh Patrick on my right and the green sea to my left, such a vivid wash of light off the mountains that I recognised it immediately as one of those startling days when the beauty of this whole area is new again, the harmony and coherence of all its shades and colours washing down to the sea which was laid out like a mirror all the way across the bay to Achill Island and Mulranny, one of those days which makes you wonder how we could ever be forgetful of it because that is what happens, driving this coast road so often from Louisburgh to Westport, my morning route to work with its mountains falling through a chroma of blues and greens into the shallow, glaciated inlet of Clew Bay, a road ingrained on the very contours of my mind and so much a part of me that sometimes I have to make a conscious effort to really see it at all which was what I attempted to do that day, concentrate in such a way as to take in all those details that have passed by me unheeded on so many of my journeys along this route but

I had no sooner resolved to do this and cleared my mind of all distractions in order to soak up everything than I completely forgot about it, let the resolution slip away so cleanly that the next thing I knew I had arrived in the middle of Westport and was pulling the car into the kerb along the mall at the bottom of the main street – ten miles driven in the blink of an eye but no memory of any of it – one of my favourite places as there is something lovely on a sunny day in getting out of the car under those elm trees and stopping in their shade for a moment to listen to the slow moving river which runs through the town – so slow you can hardly hear it at all – and after I locked up the car I headed off, thinking to myself I was lucky to get such a good spot in the middle of the day because there was a good crowd in town, a steady stream of cars passing over the bridge into Main Street with a run of sunlight glinting off the windscreens and a flow of pedestrians making their way along the pavements, this unexpectedly bright day bringing people out in good numbers to turn their pale faces to the sun as

I crossed the street to the chemist where I handed the prescription to a young uniformed woman behind the counter who glanced at me and told me with a smile that it would take five minutes so I said

fine, no rush

which was the truth but which now left me standing around feeling a bit self-conscious with nothing around me but stacks and shelves of women's potions and perfumes, twisting and turning, conscious of being well out of place and not knowing where to look so I was a bit relieved to spot the section with the male toiletries nearby, shelves of the stuff, aftershave and body sprays and hair gels and so on

Farenheit and One and Hugo Boss and Diesel and Beckham and

each one of them with testers so I took one up and turned it over, sprayed it and smelled it and then another and before I knew it I was enveloped in a sickly mist of conflicting scents with my sense of smell hopelessly confused, feeling slightly dizzy and I almost bolted for the door in embarrassment but I saw also that there was a stand with sunglasses on it and I thought I might hide there for a few moments longer, working my way through them one by one, round ones and square ones and plastic frame and metal frame, checking my appearance on the narrow vertical mirror running up the side of the stand, thinking that if the weather kept sunny like this I might get a pair, possibly wire-framed ones with that scholarly touch, but none of them seemed to do anything for me, or rather each made me look foolish in one way or another, too comic or too odd or too obviously chasing something I no longer possessed, each of them altering my face slightly but so radically that I did not recognise the man who looked back at me out of the narrow mirror, a silly experience which vexed me and left me feeling embarrassed so that I sighed with relief when the girl behind the counter returned eventually, smiling and holding up a little package which I took, purchasing also a small tube of heartburn lozenges which were on display beside the till because I'd had this burning sensation in my chest ever since I woke up that morning, took my change and made my way out of the shop onto the busy pavement where I stood for a moment to stow the package in the pocket of my jacket, glad to have that job done, before crossing the street to get the paper in the shop on the corner where I bought two – the national paper and the local one – plus a carton of apple juice and took them three doors further up to a small coffee shop which had a clear view of the main street as far as the clock at the top and which was just beginning to fill up now as it was after twelve and obviously some people like myself had it in mind to get in ahead of the lunchtime rush for a bite to eat – a few suited office workers, men and women from the banks probably and a few solicitors whom I recognised and nodded to along with the usual scattering of tourists in boots and Gore-Tex – where I managed to get a table at the very back which gave me a clear view of the whole place and out onto the street, so I set the papers down and ordered a cup of coffee with a club sandwich from the young waitress and while it had been my intention to scan through the papers and catch up with the world I now found myself wholly engrossed in the people who were filling up this small coffee shop which hardly had more than eight or nine tables in all, the nearest of which was taken up by a young woman sitting alone, dressed in a pinstripe suit and reading the sports pages of a tabloid which carried the story of a premiership footballer thought to be on the verge of a move from Arsenal back to Barcelona, the club which had nurtured his talent as a child and this story appeared to be holding her complete attention as she was sitting with her head bowed over the tabloid which caused her hair to fall down the side of her face as she held her soup spoon over the paper and it was interesting to see a woman so obviously lost in the soap-opera politics of English football, this woman who had about her that lush, affluent attractiveness which was so different to Mairead's and which sometimes I found myself lusting after, a feeling which always convinced me I was betraying Mairead who was physically so different to this woman who was now turning the pages of her newspaper with no idea whatsoever that a complete stranger was having these thoughts about her while

at the table inside the window, a tourist couple with their big all-weather jackets draped on the chairs behind them were tending to a little girl sitting in a high chair, being spoon-fed from a jar by the father who was all kitted out in the regulation gear for unpredictable weather – boots, cargo pants and fleece – while his wife beside him sorted through her wallet – a woman in her mid-forties with the airy look of a hillwalker or a marathon runner, one of those disciplines that had burned away the same body fat which was so obvious in the round, comfortable girl in the high chair, so clearly relishing her food, chewing happily but with half of it smeared all over her chin and with a ready way of thumping the little table in front of her if she was not being fed fast enough, a habit which, judging by the expression of open delight on her father's face, had great ability to charm him, and would probably do so into her adult years as I saw also that this man had about him that same, slightly dazed expression I have noticed sometimes on Mairead whenever she dealt with Darragh, that faint slippage of the critical faculties on this man too, as if he was seeing the child for the first time and not, as was likely the case, witnessing her little charm-show for the umpteenth, with all those mannerisms already gathering, which would set and refine her to the woman she would become while he in turn would gradually have a sense of himself slackening and coming apart at the same time, as

his wife returned from paying at the counter to begin gathering up their coats and bags, bringing a quiet surge of purpose to the scene, organising and shepherding them through the narrow spaces towards the door while

over to my left a smaller, more intimate drama was unfolding between a woman in her thirties and an older man in an open-neck shirt with cufflinks, the woman leaning into him, trying to gain his attention while his whole focus was on tending to his pipe, scraping out the bowl with a little penknife and tapping it onto the side of his saucer, glancing up from his scraping and tapping to look the young woman in the eye by way of assuring her that he was indeed listening to her, giving her his full attention, or as much of that attention left over from tending to his pipe, she leaning across the table with her jaw set as if it would underline whatever it was she was saying or trying to convince him of, the whole scene so physically intimate that I wondered what their relationship was as there was obviously some close connection – professional or romantic – but it was hard to say because while the woman's anxiety was very real, palpable to any onlooker, it could have fitted either scenario as there was not only the pleading of romantic breakdown, but also an urgent need to persuade this older man in a way which inclined me to believe that this might be a professional matter and that some workplace drama had occurred which still needed clarifying or smoothing over in some way or other because there was no mistaking the look on the woman's face as anything other than a visible fear she was being misunderstood, the fear that some gain or position has been jeopardised, or that some reputation, hard won but fragile, had been sullied in some way or other but, whether this was the case or not, one thing was obvious and it was that the man would rather not have had to hear about it on his lunch break because there was something aggrieved about him now in the way he was bent over his pipe, scraping out the bowl and sighting through the stem, the whole rigmarole and ceremony of it reminding me that it had been a very long time since I had seen anyone smoke a pipe in public – or in private for that matter – and it was strange, a scene from another world, a memory from a recent historical epoch when a small room like this would have been blue with smoke, food or no food, clothes and hair impregnated with it and having to be washed out the same evening as

these thoughts were interrupted when the waitress arrived with my order, leaving it down neatly on the table – coffee and a club sandwich with the cutlery wrapped in a napkin – the whole thing so neatly assembled and expert looking that I sat for a moment to admire the whole ensemble, the coffee with its brassy smell sunk beneath a creamy head which I was reluctant to disturb and the tidy way the sandwich was laid on the plate beside a small green salad – angled towards me like a hip-roof and skewered at both ends by two cocktail sticks – the whole thing so complete in itself that it seemed only right to admire it before I dismantled and ate it which is what I did after letting it sit for as long as it took me to put milk into the coffee and stir it around, after which it was a further pleasure to discover that the sandwich tasted as good as it looked and that there was no disparity or margin between its appearance and its taste which was moist with crisp lettuce, tomatoes and chicken between slices of warm toast and even before biting into it

this moment here

this crowded room with its clutter of chairs and tables

these people, with their separate thoughts and lives

I was overwhelmed with a sense of what a strange privilege it was to be able to sit in this coffee shop among other people who did not wish me any harm and who would, more likely than not, be happy for me if they were to know that I was having a good day – that my wife was on the mend and that my car had started and that this was a tasty sandwich and that the sun was shining outside – none of these people would begrudge me any of this and all would appreciate the expert way this sandwich was put together and how everything about it revealed a degree of attentiveness which went beyond mere expertise and spoke something of a care and commitment which was gently humbling, so unexpected and baffling also to come across something so banal which filled me with a sense of how improbable life was and how this unlikely construct – a sandwich for Christ's sake – could communicate such intimate grace that

I was now completely overtaken with a foolish excess of gratitude for this half hour in this coffee shop, a quiet spell among decent people, good food and the careful work of those who ran it so that for one moment in which time and space seemed to plummet through me in terraced depths which had me reaching out to grip the edge of the table, I had a rushing sense of the cosmic odds stacked against this here-and-now, how unlikely and how contingent it was on so many other things taking their proper place in the wider circumstance of the universe and exerting their right degree of pressure on the contextual circumstances so that for one moment, sitting there with a cup of coffee in my hand and the chair bracing my back I had a clear view down through the vortex of my whole being, down through all the linked circumstances that had combined to place me here at this specific moment in time and this wave of gratitude and terror swept through me with such violent force that I feared I would mortify myself by breaking down in tears, an ecstasy of joy and terror for the world and everything in it, an unbidden feeling which was so overpowering that it was as much as I could do to hold myself together for as long as it took me to get up and make my way between tables to pay the bill at the cash register where, in a voice ridiculously choked, I replied to the girl's kind query as she totted up the bill that

yes, everything was fine, thank you very much

which drew a sweet smile as she took the ten euro note and returned the change to my hand before I headed back through the maze of tables and chairs to the door and out onto the pavement to find that a watery sun now lit the day, flaring off the passing cars, splintering off windscreens and the glass fronts on the opposite side of the street, light echoing beyond its real capacity to illumine the day, the whole world over-lit in some way or other as I stood there squinting and shading my eyes, regretting that I had not bought one of those pairs of sunglasses no matter how daft they looked on me but the chemist was now on the other side of the street and I thought it would be better to get into the car and drive home as by this time I had been away from Mairead for nearly an hour and a half which is nothing in itself but which had me feeling a bit antsy even if in all likelihood she was probably only too glad to be rid of me for a while, free of my anxious fluttering around her, that role into which I had fallen all too easily and fitted so comfortably almost before I had bethought myself, fussing over her, forever checking to see that she was all right

was there not something I could get her

did she want anything to eat

I could put something on for her

an omelette or a bowl of soup

tea

anything

this ceaseless clucking around her till it became obvious, even to myself that her welfare was not the point of it at all but that it was all symptomatic of my own need to reassure myself that I was doing a good job, proving myself to be a good husband and carer, a man who was not so stale or far gone in his most calcified habits that he could not find something new within himself, namely these caring skills and soothing gestures which were, till this, undreamt of and unlikely less than a month ago but now flowering to such light and soothing touches that I had begun to move through the house like a ghost myself, all misted light and billowing gauze, leached of so much colour and muscle I could barely leave the impress of a finger on my wife, but not

it would seem

exempt from physical pain myself as the heartburn in my chest flared up there on the sunlit pavement and I had to take another of those lozenges to ease the sour pain when

this is all coming back to me with

this tightness drawing together bone and sinew across my chest – that cup of coffee, which was no doubt good but strong, just the sort to give you the jitters I had now, twitchy like some sort of gritty interference running across my nerves which propelled me down the street and across the intersection at the bottom where I'd left the car, sat into her and threw the newspapers into the back seat and drawing the seatbelt across my chest I felt the bulk of the prescription package in my jacket pocket so I pulled it out and left it onto the passenger seat before starting her up and pulling out into the street and straight away

I forgot myself

forgot myself completely in a

long stretch of pure absent-mindedness which lasted as long as it took to drive from one side of the town to the other, all the time manoeuvring carefully in slow traffic, stopping to let pedestrians cross and other cars move out into the street, moving up and down through the gears, so many complex and thoughtless manoeuvres but somehow arriving safely on the other side of town with no memory whatsoever of having passed slowly through the streets, another of those long, vacant intervals during which the soul goes walkabout, comes unmoored and drifts away on its own when

I came to and remembered myself

on the other side of the town to find that I had decided to turn right at the top of the hill and take the Rosbeg road for home, that stretch of road called the golden mile which turns around by the coast with the sea on the right hand side and where, at high tide it comes in from a long way out over sand into the shallow quays, the tide full in at this hour while the burning in my chest had not been eased one bit by those lozenges I'd taken because if anything it seemed to have got worse, tightened in such a way as to draw all my energy towards it and

Mother of Jesus

I drove around the coast road, passing those large mansions on the left side of the road which belonged to lawyers and doctors and business folk, those houses with oversized windows which look out over the sea and reflect the rhythms of the light and the glare of the sun back onto the road so that it seems as if the sea is on both sides of the road and that you are journeying through some place privileged with an overabundance of light before the road turned a corner and the trees on both sides closed in over the car and the light pushed back to admit just that proper degree of darkness in which things are seen in their true colour and shadow – stone walls looming over the road on both sides and the trees arching overhead with the sun winking down through the leaves, a mile, two miles before it turned out into the fullness of the sun once more for another mile or so, leading into an open bend where I slowed down to take the right hand turn at the T-junction, where the road broadens out to a wide corner with

the Imperial Hotel standing there on the left behind its high, blistered walls, filthy and eyeless in its broken grounds, derelict for two decades now inside those scrolled iron gates, a sorry sight, the more so because no one knows properly how or why it came to such dilapidation at the precise moment when its tennis courts and swimming pool made it the most glamorous spot in the whole region, my mother remembering especially the ballroom with its maple floor and how she had danced there so many times, recalling that

you could just float across it and we did, your father and I, several times when we were courting and the crowds that used come there in those days, they'd come from all over and

that was before the place was suddenly closed back in the eighties, all the staff let go and the electricity cut after Easter eighty-three or eighty-four, the blinds closed, the curtains pulled, and the scroll gates padlocked, the whole place shut down with no one knowing the reason why or no one getting any explanation which of course led to lots of speculation and stories – there were debts, the numbers were not coming anymore, there was a waster of a son in London who had made off with the title deeds and so on and so on, either way the owners were never seen again so the hotel just sat there and settled

    block by block

    room by room

    into its own gathering dilapidation with paint peeling and dust gathering throughout its rooms and weeds breaking up through the hard surface of the tennis courts, and the tarmac in the car park also coming up in blistering slabs as the timber fence at the back began to disintegrate which gave access to all the kids from around who came to explore its rooms and corridors and take the opportunity to peg stones up at the small windows, knocking them out one by one as the cattle from the neighbouring fields began to drift through the gaps in the fence where the slats had rotted away completely to wander through the grounds, black and red Angus cows with their calves in tow, loping quietly through the gardens and along by the swimming pool on summer's evenings, lying down on the tiled patio beside plaster balustrades which were now green with the moss of neglect until the owner of the herd – a man by the name of Fallon – whose grazing land ran from the shoreline to the back of the hotel – raised up the sloping floor of the swimming pool with a couple of tons of hard-core and gravel and put in a metal barrier at the deep end from where, when winter set in, he would feed the cattle each evening, hay and silage tipped in over the edge, this herd of cattle feeding at one end of a tiled swimming pool, after which they would move on with their heads dipped till they found their way to the broken emergency exit with its door swung open which allowed them enter the ballroom to the left side of the stage, this herd of cattle coming through in single file to find themselves in the open expanse of the maple dance floor, between walls hung with satin drapes now black with rot and the mirror ball on its chain over the centre of the floor, the finest dance hall in West Mayo full of Angus cattle, and there they would lie down and close their eyes, chewing the cud until they were turned out in the morning and this had been going on for so long now that Fallon had acquired some sort of squatter's rights to the place and was now the principal in the ongoing court-case that had yet to decide the fate of the hotel which on days like this, with the sun slanting through its broken windows and across its balustrades, always

appeared to me like the sacked palace of some tyrant, some ruthless overlord of a Caribbean island kingdom which was favoured with a temperate climate and substantial mineral wealth but which was nonetheless dogged by civil incompetence and corruption, by spiralling inflation rates and a despicable human rights record, the whole place evocative of some extraordinary dispensation which must have reigned in these parts without us ever recognising it or seeing it for what it really was before the broader drama of the world's distant circumstances swept it aside for something else so that now it stood

eyeless and decrepit, all its arches and colonnades peeling away to reveal the grey concrete underneath, the place rotting and crumbling away to some patient schedule of its own, all its rooms and recesses, all its stairs and corridors quietly swarming with every type of rot and decay and dilapidation, every possible variant on the wider creep of collapse which was now drawing it apart block by block, lath by lath, tile by tile, the whole place having gathered to itself the attentiveness of very possible ruin, that which is native to concrete and that which is native to timber and that which is native to metal, each of them in their own way and at their own pace gradually levelling the whole structure to the ground even as it

got smaller and smaller in my rear-view mirror, disappearing completely as

I rounded the bend for home at Belclare, following the sea road once more along the coast, slowing down a little, no hurry now that I was nearly there so that my gaze settled on those bright pockets of glare which winked and shifted in a dappled morph on the water's surface, a mosaic of light and texture from the tide mark all the way across what at this point is the narrowest span of Clew Bay with all its islands crowded so close to the shoreline, the sight of which always brought to mind one of those facts I still remember from my Inter Cert Geography all those years ago – that detail about how

this whole area is a glaciated valley dating back to the pre-Cambrian era, that time in the world's youth when the light was clearer and this whole region lay under a glacier six miles deep which scoured the land east to west, depositing drumlins of sand and gravel along the length of this bay, these little egg-shaped island humps in the water which taper off in whatever direction the glacier was moving, a piece of knowledge from my early teens still lodged in my head thirty-five years later when no doubt other, more valuable things, have long been forgotten and

I slowed down because

I needed to pull into the side of the road for a minute, into that layby near the Deerpark which the council have used for years to dump gravel and hard-core for road surfacing because

now I remember

I remember this pain

fucking Jesus

this pain in my chest spreading through my arms and down the backs of my legs, causing me to brace both hands on the steering wheel and close my eyes for a moment, as if either of these reactions would drive it away, pulling into the lay-by and parking between two mounds of gravel, knocking her out of gear but leaving the engine running because this pain, which was now clawing its way through me, would surely pass in a minute and then I would be on my way home to Mairead who by now would be starting to worry about me as

the pain worsened

clamping across my chest so

I wound down the window to let a gust of fresh air in and opened my shirt, pulled open the collar, a few buttons, to get some cold air on my chest, that might do the trick, ease the pain a little because it was seriously fucking bad now, rooted like a black sun in my chest from where it flowed out to the furthest parts of me, down the hands and feet and into the small of my back, like some electric foliage firing its way through me, wrapping itself around my whole nervous system and choking me right up to the top of my skull with steel claws, my breath rising in jagged heaves from my chest with my body rigid in the seat as

I caught sight of the clock in the dash and saw that it was coming up to one o'clock

the one o'clock news, so I

reached out and turned on the radio and sure enough the last ads were leading into the time signal for the bulletin – the pips – and something frantic in me scrambled to focus on them as though they were solid things to which I might hang onto with both hands and steady myself, a hopeless idea even as I formed it but in desperation seemed to be my only option – setting the time-signal pips against this savage pain in my chest and

Jesus, this fucking pain

this world of pain as

my body burned, head to toe with a molten current which flared in the smallest molecule of my being, pain like nothing I had ever felt before, chest and arms engulfed and my vision warped in blue depths of electrical waves as the light darkened and

I remember thinking in panicked despair that

I'll just hang on to the pips and then the news headlines will come on so I'll listen to them for a few minutes, that's all I have to do, just listen to the newsreader tell me what's happening in the wider world which lies outside this pain in my chest, tell me the world is filled with strikes and pay disputes … that economic indicators continue to fall all over the place … that there are road deaths and stabbings … that there are car bombings in Baghdad and stalled offensives in Helmand … that a child is missing or that a body has been found … that accident and emergency wards are inundated and that patients are lying on trolleys in hospital corridors … that the polls indicate … that the courts have recognised and warrants have been issued … that there are disputed election results but that someone has already declared themselves president for life … that legislation has finally been passed or has been referred to the supreme court … that the whole warp and weft of the world is ongoing, circumstances rising up and falling down

rising up and falling down because

if I knew that these things were still happening, still ongoing, how ever awful or distant they may be, then I would be happy to know that the world was about its proper business and that I, as a citizen and engineer was still part of it all, and that no matter how far away these things may be I would still have some stake in them simply by dint of drawing breath and raising a pulse and hearing about it on this car radio, I would have an involvement in these affairs no matter how tenuous or tangential because that was part of my circumstance as a man who took these things seriously

pain or no pain

fucking Jesus

so that it was essential now that I pay attention, pay attention to kill this fire in my chest and give myself over to whatever I was now going to hear when sure enough, thank Christ

I heard the pips

pip, pip, pip

the time signal for the one o'clock news pulsing across the air-waves, calling the whole nation to attention, the time signal followed by the fanfare theme music just as the pain embedded itself deeper through my chest, burning across every rhythm which upheld my body, searing through every pulse which measured me, smudging them under a scalding red tide which scorched within me to drive my shoe deep into the foot-well, slamming hard on the accelerator so that the engine screamed out over the radio and I strained to hear the newscaster greet the nation with

good afternoon, this is Friday, March the 21st, here are the headlines, as

I was thrust up out of myself on a wash of pain, a spar breaking in my chest, crying out as my head was thrown back against the seat, mouth agape and my spine rigid to slam my shoe down into the foot-well once more, ramming the accelerator to the floor again and now the car was screaming over a hundred thousand revs, a throaty roar with a metallic whine at its centre, so loud it would surely draw some-one's attention, some man or woman out walking the road would hear it and come to the car where they would see me with my head thrown back and my mouth open, my hand reaching across towards

Mairead's prescription in the passenger seat, clawing towards that package which seemed to lie at such an infinite distance from me with pain lacing through my chest as if some essential structural component, some load-bearing lintel, had come asunder in my chest and I was engulfed in pain to hear again

Friday, March 21st

the day on which my wife was widowed and my two children lost their father, the day my name was unhinged from the man who owned it, such a clear and detailed memory of my own death at the precise moment I said to myself through blinding pain

I'll just listen to these news headlines when

at that precise moment

the vast harmonic of my whole being was undone and I came apart in sheets and waves, torrential and ever falling, my grip on all those markers which gathered and held me to this world completely gone as the light around me blackened and for a split moment I saw the world in negative as all its colours bled to a narrow palette of black and grey with a complex melding of all shapes and outlines into each other, the mountains and sea converging onto the wind-screen in front of me and

somewhere above the earth the sun failed

burned out from within, exhausted now and nothing but a massive cinder drifting through the chasm of space, collapsing in on its own warm core before that too collapsed on itself so that all light was now residual, ashen and dragging its own darkness down the void as all around me every colour waned to its specific darkness, all things slackening and run down while

time itself began to contract so tightly

it would surely freeze at any moment and

any moment now, there will be no now and

there may be these things but

none of these things

will be now

to see myself

lying in that car, stretched out behind the steering wheel with my body locked in its final throes, my left arm thrown across the passenger seat, clutching Mairead's prescription in my hand, my whole upper body twisted towards it with

my foot rammed on the accelerator and the engine gunned to the last, the car screaming at a hundred thousand revs, screaming

this is how an engineer loses himself

no accuracy anymore, all my angles tilted to infinity

finally unbound from myself into

a vast oblivion and

what was needed at this moment was not prayer or song but one final moment of desperate strength-gathering so that I might utter some bawling, annihilating curse, some anathema drawn up from the depths of the world's being where all inverse prayers are rooted in the first gasp of the world's existence, the first twitch of the void, something I could draw from these depths and lay on the world only because

man and boy, father and son, husband and engineer

I have known it to be a sacred and beautiful place, hallowed by human endeavour and energies, crossed with love and the continual weave of human circumstance, and since

this is my wit's end

my post mortem aria

my engineer's lament

with my mind vacant of everything good and affirmative, it is the place from where I will give vent to some terrible curse, rolling it from my black mouth across the vast acreage of space, rolling it to its furthest horizons and further again so that it chisels a new edge to the universe, working itself out to the staggered depths of the void where in this moment God might hear me and come looking for me, recognising a fellow engineer, my howling curse the sound of a decent man gone to his grave too soon, a man who went about his work and raised a family, everything about him marked by that degree of moderation which he could now set against the darkness out of which he would come looking for me, as I did for him, ever hopeful of finding our way to each other in this blackness which is our way and guide, down into the thickening night where prayer and curse are conjoined at the one root in the inaugural moment of being, down into those depths where only true believers can find their way, those with the light drained from their eyes so that they can have full night vision and access to the complete absence of themselves where, hand on my heart, I can say

I died in that lay-by

died surrounded by tons of sand and gravel and hard-core with my mouth open in a black howl to take leave of myself as, without missing a beat

my body had already picked up the rhythms of decay which had begun to work immediately in my soft flesh, that momentary heat spike which gave way to the falling temperature of rot with my blood passing from oxygenated red to black as the universal cellular explosions which bring on that spillage of filth within my organs which will eventually purge from every orifice of my body even as I

found my way home

home again

to sit at this table

and drift through these rooms

room by room, agitated beyond all comfort, as if the giddiness of this day had got into my body and is now setting up again that grating current inside me which brushes my nerve ends and has me so jittery there is nothing for it but to keep moving, drifting from room to room like one of those sea creatures who cannot stay still for fear they may sink and drown, everything solid in me draining away towards the floor, going from

room to room

killing these couple of hours before my wife and kids return, trying to shrug off this sense that all things around me are unstable and barely rooted in the here-and-now and that the slightest pressure will cause everything to tip away from me as if it were all cardboard scenery or, like this house, that the slightest push will send the whole thing skyward into the grey light leaving me

am

alone here in the open space of the world with no walls or roofs or floors around me, the sole inhabitant of a vast, white space which is swept clear of fences and homesteads and plants and trees, all gone, the world as complete erasure since even the sun itself is drawn from the sky leaving me wholly alone, fading in whatever way it is we fade from the world

animal, mineral, vegetable

father, husband, citizen

my body drawing its soul in its wake or vice versa until that total withdrawal into the vast whiteness is visible only as a brimming absence so that finally there is nothing left, body and soul all gone, and these residual pulses and rhythms which for these waning moments, abide in their own recurrent measure, nothing more than a vague strobing of the air before they too are obliterated in that self-engulfing light which closes over everything to be

cast out beyond darkness into that vast unbroken commonage of space and time, into that vast oblivion in which there are no markings or contours to steer by nor any songs to sing me home and where there is nothing else for it but to keep going, one foot in front of the other

the head down and keep going

keep going

keep going to fuck